Gone Cold

ALSO BY DOUGLAS CORLEONE

Simon Fisk Novels

Payoff

Good as Gone

Kevin Corvelli Mysteries

Last Lawyer Standing

Night on Fire

One Man's Paradise

Gone Cold

DOUGLAS CORLEONE

 Minotaur Books ☠ New York

This is a work of fiction. All of the characters, organizations, and events portrayed in this novel are either products of the author's imagination or are used fictitiously.

www.minotaurbooks.com

The Library of Congress Cataloging-in-Publication Data is available upon request.

ISBN 978-1-250-06578-0 (hardcover)
ISBN 978-1-4668-7278-3 (e-book)

First Edition: August 2015

10 9 8 7 6 5 4 3 2 1

FOR JILL

One mustn't look at the abyss, because there is at the bottom an inexpressible charm that attracts us.

—GUSTAVE FLAUBERT

Gone Cold

Prologue

Have you ever thought maybe your daughter could still be alive?"

I felt my lower lip tremble.

"I lost hope that she was alive long ago, and I'd never want that hope back. Not in a million years. Not for one second. But I will forever be looking. In every shop, every café, every open home window in every city or town in every country on every continent. I can't help myself. I want to know what happened to her and why. And I want to know who took her."

I shook my head and swallowed hard as I thought about Ostermann knocking Dietrich Braun and Karl Finster out cold in the alley behind SO36 back in Kreuzberg.

"The violence I would do to that man, Ana, it can't be put into words."

Part One

THE GHOSTS
OF DUBLIN

Chapter 1

Usual, Simon?"

"Sure."

As Casey turned to the espresso machine I gazed out the familiar window with the peeling green and gold letters reading TERRY'S PUB—EST. 1992. Snowflakes continued falling hard as rain on the opposite side of the glass. It was another cold one, eight to ten inches expected here in Washington, D.C., a full foot in the suburbs, at least.

"Case," I said, "mind making that an Irish coffee instead?"

"No problem, Simon."

I'd been coming to Terry's for over twenty years. The original owner, Terrance Davies, was a fellow Londoner who had given me my first real job. During my four years at American University, I'd worked my way up from barback to bartender to night manager. And though I'd never really taken to drinking, I found myself returning to Terry's long after graduation. It was a quiet pub, a place where I could show up an hour or so before closing and nurse a pint or two of Harp while Terry relished me with stories of the home city. London. The "motherland" as he often referred to it.

I watched Casey pour the two ounces of Bushmills, toss in a teaspoon of brown sugar, then combine the steaming coffee before stirring and floating the heavy cream.

He turned, set the mug down in front of me. Casey O'Connell possessed what you'd generously call a beer belly, which stretched the faded black fabric of his Baltimore Ravens T-shirt to its limit in the vicinity of his navel. With his shaggy red hair and matching beard, he looked a bit like Zach Galifianakis of *Hangover* fame, following one of the Wolf Pack's notorious nights in Las Vegas.

Casey had been working here for the better part of a decade, took over the bartending duties a few years after Terry sold the pub to Nigel Cummings and returned to the UK.

"Any luck?" Casey said.

"Nothing," I told him.

Casey was one of the few people who knew how I'd spent the previous eleven months. Knew that I'd transformed my studio apartment on Dumbarton Street here in D.C. into a war room.

Currently mounted on my studio's four walls was every shred of evidence collected by the FBI and D.C. Police in connection with my daughter Hailey's disappearance twelve years ago. Included were photographs of the house in Georgetown from which Hailey was taken. Witness statements, mug shots, lab reports, news articles, and maps of every major city in the United States and Canada, and a few cities in Mexico, Central and South America, Europe, and Asia as well. Last February I'd made a promise to myself; I would finally discover who took my six-year-old daughter and why, or I would die trying.

Why now? That was what Casey had asked when I first told him last March. The answer was simple: This was the first time in eleven years that I didn't have to work for a living. After Hailey was taken, I resigned from the U.S. Marshals but quickly began work as a private investigator, specializing in cases involving parental abductions. All too often, an estranged spouse will tear up the court's custody order and flee with their child to a country that doesn't recognize U.S. custody decisions. There were a surprising number of such countries. Russia, India, and Japan, just to name a few.

Roughly two years ago, I was heading to Charles de Gaulle when my taxi was pulled over by the French National Police. A cop named Lieutenant Davignon escorted me to a two-story cottage in a quiet, rural village roughly forty kilometers north of Paris, where he made me an offer: help locate a missing young American girl stolen from her parents' room at the Hotel d'Étonner in Champs-Élysées and he wouldn't arrest me for kidnapping the young boy I'd just liberated from his abusive mother in Bordeaux. Ultimately, it was an offer I couldn't refuse.

Taking the case effectively ended my policy of not getting involved in "stranger abductions," cases in which the kidnapper was unknown and most likely unrelated to the victim.

Less than a year later I found myself at the multimillion-dollar estate of a movie mogul named Edgar Trenton. Edgar's teenage daughter had been taken during a violent home invasion in Los Angeles while Edgar was attending a film festival in Berlin. At the time, I'd felt I owed Edgar Trenton. Years before, he'd agreed to nix a movie adaptation of the book about my own daughter's kidnapping. He'd paid well for the rights, yet turned them over to me for free when I asked. I'd have taken on his case for free too but he'd insisted on paying me and paying me well. Later, when I was able to recover the $8.5 million ransom from a *mara* in Panama City, he'd given me a significant bonus. Enough to sustain me for at least a few years and to fund my search for Hailey, wherever and however long it took me.

I took a sip of the Irish and savored the warmth on the back of my tongue before swallowing it down. The alcohol struck me straightaway and only then did I realize I hadn't eaten a thing in eight hours.

Over the past three months I'd been losing weight. It wasn't the type of weight loss people pointed out and complimented you on. It was the type of weight loss people looked away from, tried to keep themselves from staring at, wondering all the while whether you were sick or doing too many illicit drugs or both.

I'd lost muscle in my arms and chest because I'd quit going to the gym. My cheeks were a bit sunken in and I was constantly pale, even this past summer, which was one of the hottest on record, not just in D.C. but on Earth.

To make matters worse, I couldn't sleep. Oh, I'd get the occasional two or three hours here and there, but I couldn't seem to get on any type of schedule, and I seldom dreamed. The days simply ran into one another, and the Beers of the Year calendar hanging over the register here at Terry's was the only thing I could count on to keep me grounded. That and the abrupt change in weather were the only reasons I knew I'd been at this for nearly a year.

Even though by now it felt as though I'd never done anything else. Ever.

As I sat there I felt the BlackBerry grumbling in my right pants pocket. I fished the device out and stared at the screen for several seconds before finally registering that I'd received an e-mail not a phone call.

Something that looked like a lightning bolt flashed in the upper left-hand corner, alerting me to a low battery. I thumbed the mouse and opened the e-mail client.

It was a message from Kati Sheffield, a former FBI computer scientist who now stayed at home caring for her three children while working on the sly for people like me. The message read, *Finder* (her codename for me), *open the two attachments and call me right away.*

Call you? I glanced at my watch. It was too damn late to call her; I'd wake the kids, not to mention her husband, Victor, a detective with the Connecticut State Police, who was suspicious enough about her online activities as it was.

I scrolled down to the first of the two attachments, clicked on it. The screen went blank and a blue bar crawled across the top where the time banner would normally be. As I waited I drank down most of my coffee, savored the heat in the pit of my stomach. Drew a deep breath and took in the blended fragrance of hard booze and polished wood that complement most Irish pubs in the District.

Just before the blue bar reached its final destination a red light blinked and suddenly I was staring at the logo for Verizon Wireless.

Casey said, "Everything okay, Simon?"

"Battery went dead."

"You can use the house phone if you want."

I shook my head. "It was an e-mail, Case." I dug into my pocket and pulled out a twenty, laid it on the bar. "Thanks for the drink," I said.

"See you tomorrow then, Simon."

"See you tomorrow."

I pushed open the door and threw my arm up against the fierce wind, heavy flakes of snow still slapping me full in the face.

As it turned out, I wouldn't see Casey tomorrow.

In fact, I would never see Casey O'Connell again.

Chapter 2

By the time I reached the door to my apartment building on Dumbarton, I was frozen, the exposed flesh on my face burned raw. I dug into the pockets of my jacket searching for my keys, but came up empty. Like a drunken teenager, I cursed and kicked at the door. Clenched my scarlet hands into fists and punched at the brick until my knuckles opened, dripping crimson down my fingers, spotting the newly fallen snow.

Christ.

To top it all, I was suddenly struck with the awful headache-nausea combination that often accompanies drinking on an empty stomach.

I folded myself into a ball and dropped onto the top step, leaning my back against the black iron rail. My neck ached like hell—a cervical herniated disc exacerbated by stress. I packed some snow on my wounded knuckles to keep them from swelling. Then closed my eyes and wished I would drift off. For a few days at least. Maybe for good.

Forty-one years old. At least half my life gone and no cause but a twelve-year-old cold-as-ice case to find the person who took and murdered my daughter. After eleven months I knew damn well that it was an impossible mission, yet I couldn't let go. Even if I could, there was nothing to move on *to*. Searching for the stolen—whether mine or other people's children—was something I simply couldn't do anymore. Something inside me had withered and died this winter, something had all but extinguished the flame that had been keeping me alive—the desire to find Hailey's killer.

It was possible he was already dead, of course. In which case, I'd spent the past year chasing a ghost. It was tough enough to locate the living. Looking for a corpse was an utter waste of time. Of that I was finally sure.

As sure as I was that Hailey had been murdered within weeks, if not days, of her abduction. I'd known that all along, never truly suffered under the delusion that my daughter might still be alive. Not since the FBI began taking agents off the case. Certainly not since Tasha's suicide.

No, I'd started my own chase much too late. I'd never sought to find Hailey while she was alive. Instead I'd sat on the sidelines, let the Bureau do its goddamn job, just as they'd insisted. I didn't begin looking for my daughter until she was dead.

And even then, I couldn't find her. Couldn't find the monster who'd taken her. Couldn't find her body, couldn't find her bones.

And sitting on that top step to my apartment complex, shivering in the freezing cold and scudding snow, I decided that I had known long ago that I never would.

Decided that I'd been deluding myself all this time after all.

Someone shook me awake. I searched the darkness for a face but all I saw was a crimson scarf wrapped around a hood, an indistinguishable pair of eyes hidden deep within.

Whoever it was unlocked the door, then held it open. When I didn't attempt to rise, he or she lifted a doormat from the lobby and placed it in the frame so that the door wouldn't close.

I mumbled some thanks but shut my eyes tight again. When I opened my eyes a few moments later, the man or woman who'd opened the door was gone.

Finally I pushed myself to my feet and slipped inside, kicking the doormat away behind me. I tried to shake off the cold but it had already burrowed itself deep in my bones.

I opened the door to the stairwell and started up, only now realizing I couldn't get back into my apartment anyway. Without my keys I'd have to spend the night curled up in the hallway. Still better than the freezing cold, I supposed.

When I reached the fifth floor I leaned over the railing, hoping to relieve a bit of the nausea. Instead I dry heaved, nearly vomited onto the stairs leading down to the fourth.

I stood and shoved my way out of the stairwell and lurched the fifteen steps to my door.

There waited my keys, still dangling from the knob.

I tried to remember leaving them this morning but my mind drew a blank. But then, what did it matter? Either *I* was too sloppy to continue living, or whoever was waiting for me inside my apartment was about to get what he deserved. Only one way to find out.

Before removing the keys I tried the knob, felt it twist between my fingers. With my other hand I pushed the door open and waited a few seconds before crossing the threshold. The flat was dark and quiet.

I slapped the light switch. Everything seemed to be just where I'd left it, and there weren't many places to hide. Quietly, I snatched my keys and closed the door behind me. Poked my head into the bathroom and exhaled. No one was waiting for me.

An irrational pang of disappointment struck my nauseated stomach.

I went to my desk and opened my laptop, pressed the power button and removed my old black leather jacket as I waited for the computer to boot.

As I tossed my jacket onto the bed my eyes fell on the refrigerator door, fixed on a photo that had been held there by a Jefferson Memorial magnet for as long as I could remember. The photo was of me,

Tasha, and Hailey, standing in front of Cinderella Castle at the Magic Kingdom in central Florida, smiles all around. It was taken on our last vacation together, mere months before Hailey went missing.

The twelve-year-old photo was faded, curled on all sides from age. I'd stared at the picture so often that any new thought it conjured punched me in the gut with surprise. Yet now I thought, *That week may have been the last time I truly felt happiness.*

"Quit pitying yourself," I muttered aloud.

I fell into the chair in front of my desk and clicked on the icon for Firefox. The browser immediately opened and I pulled down my history and tapped on the address to my in-box.

Kati Sheffield's e-mail was waiting for me, right at the top of the bin.

No subject line.

I opened the e-mail and quickly reread the message: *Finder, open the two attachments and call me right away.* It occurred to me that I'd have to charge my cell phone before I called anyone. My landline had been shut off two weeks ago for failure to pay. Not because I didn't have the money, but because clicking on their e-mail and downloading the bill and entering my payment information had seemed like too much bother.

In recent months I'd been weighing every action I took, no matter how minor. The only question I asked myself was, *Will this help me figure out what happened to Hailey?* Far more often than not, the answer was no.

So doctor and dentist appointments had been missed. Haircuts became fewer and further between. Clothes were worn for two or three days straight without a proper washing.

I downloaded the first attachment, saved it to a desktop folder marked KATI. I clicked on the icon to open the file, and a face materialized on the screen.

It was a face I'd seen many times before. The visage of a beautiful young woman with long chestnut hair and warm brown eyes opened wide. It was a face that existed only onscreen, a computer-generated fantasy no more real than the cowboy from *Toy Story.*

On the bottom right-hand corner of the screen were several familiar words: *Hailey Fisk at 18 years of age.* The corners of my mouth lifted as they always did when I stared at this image of what Hailey might have looked like if she'd survived to this day.

My eyes watered. A familiar lump caught in my throat.

Quickly I minimized the screen and clicked on the second attachment. Once it downloaded I saved it to the KATI file folder and opened it.

Another female face appeared. This visage didn't have the smooth skin of the girl in the other picture. The cheeks were blemished. Thinner, scarred, almost the color of ash. The eyes weren't nearly as wide or as bright; they were narrow and dark, one slightly larger than the other, reminiscent of Lucky Luciano's infamous mug shot. The hair was chopped short and dyed jet-black.

This was a real girl, probably in her late twenties or early thirties, a young woman who'd struggled with the world. She appeared tired and angry, almost ugly with hatred.

Here too there was a small caption: *Wanted on suspicion of murder: Garda.*

My first thought was that Garda was the name of a local police chief or district attorney somewhere here in the States. Then it struck me. An Garda Síochána was the name of the police force in Ireland.

I stared at Kati's message again. *Finder, open the two attachments and call me right away.*

I was confused. I lined the two images up side by side on the screen and compared. One looked nothing like the other. Nothing at all.

Except maybe the nose.

I lifted the laptop and held the monitor a few inches in front of my face.

Just the nose.

But no, there was more. The chin, maybe? The distance between the eyes? Since the second image was somewhat grainy—probably captured by a closed-circuit camera, then enhanced and magnified—it was difficult to tell.

I set the laptop down and decided to call Kati after all, the hell with the time.

The BlackBerry died as soon as I pulled it from the charger. I cursed then thought maybe I could make the call while the phone was still plugged in.

I was speechless when Kati answered on the first ring.

"Simon?" she said in the voice of someone who had clearly been awake. It was the first time she'd ever used my real name over the phone.

"Kati," I said quietly.

"Have you seen the pictures?"

"Just now. Kati, what is this?"

I endured a silence that lasted an eternity.

Then: "Simon, don't you see?"

My eyes remained glued to the screen. I felt stunned even though I was in no way convinced. My mouth became dry. So dry that I couldn't speak.

"Simon, I know this sounds crazy. But the geometrical features in the two images are nearly identical. Bottom line: I'd bet my life that the girl in that picture—the girl wanted for murder in Ireland—is Hailey Fisk."

Chapter 3

Let's see. Got four pairs of jeans, six T-shirts, eight pairs of socks, an inordinate number of boxer shorts—*Thank you, Tasha, very much.* Backup shoes, shaving kit, toothpaste, and toothbrush.

"You have *everything*," Tasha says as she blows through the door into our bedroom. She's wearing a light cotton dress, one of my favorites, with a multicolor knit cardigan covering her milky shoulders and bare upper arms.

I pull her close to me, breathe in the floral scent of her shampoo, say, "Everything, huh?"

"I packed a jacket in your duffel." She pecks me on the lips, adds, "You are cleared for takeoff, Marshal Fisk."

I brush aside a handful of her shimmering blond locks and find the sweet spot on her elongated neck and nuzzle. Feel her shiver in my arms, the gooseflesh quickly advancing upward from her wrists.

Still does it for her, I think with a thrill.

Next through the doorway with a unicorn backpack on her head is Princess Hailey.

"Mommy says if I wear this over my face, I can sew away."

"*Stow* away," Tasha corrects her.

I pull the backpack from atop her tiny noggin and toss it on the bed, drop to one knee and wrap my arms around her tightly, then press her shoulders back just a bit to take in those fresh and inviting big brown eyes.

In my periphery Tasha parts her lips, most likely to remind me of something, but defers when Hailey shoots her a look that says, you know better than to interrupt our Daddy-daughter ritual.

I pull Hailey even closer and, squirming, she giggles and says, "Let me go," as she always does, and I hold her to me even tighter, say, "Never, baby. Never," as I always do.

Alas, no hug lasts forever, but this is a particularly good one, and as she finally pulls away I'm satisfied that I've got enough of her in my lungs to carry me through the next few days, until I fly back from Romania.

"You gonna catch the bad guy?" Hailey says.

Still on my haunches, I say, "Yes, of course. You know that. Your daddy always gets his man."

I stand, take my wife, Tasha, into my arms and give her a PG-13 kiss on the lips, my tongue tempted to carry the embrace much further.

"*And* his woman," I add, if for no other reason than to give my lips a much needed distraction.

"We're gonna miss you," Hailey complains. "Why can't we come with you?"

"Budgetary issues," I say. "Besides, you don't want to go to Bucharest. Romania's a nation in transition. They rid themselves of a cruel dictator just a decade and a half ago, and civilization hasn't quite caught up yet."

A horn honks in our driveway.

"That would be your ride to the airport," Tasha says.

"What would I do without you, babe?"

I grab my navy suitcase and heave it onto my shoulder so that I can carry it down the carpeted stairs without taking a vicious spill.

"Call us," Tasha says.

"Call *me*," Hailey says.

When I hit the bottom of the stairs I lift my royal blue duffel off the marble floor in the foyer and hang it over my arm. Dragging my suitcase behind me, I open the door and step outside. Nod at the driver who's leaning against his black Lincoln with his hands in his pockets, staring up at the high window.

One last look behind me at the massive house, paid for by the in-laws so that their daughter can continue to look like money, even though she's married to a broke federal cop.

Christ, I resent that house. Probably always will.

But hey, the house makes Tasha happy, and that's what truly matters, right?

Her and Hailey.

Long as I have them I've everything in the world.

Chapter 4

Hours after speaking with Kati, I was seated in coach on an Aer Lingus flight bound for Dublin. I'd boarded the plane at Dulles at dawn but it took nearly an hour for the wings to de-ice. During the downtime I tried to doze, but was repeatedly slapped back to consciousness by the squawk of the PA, the pilot seeing fit to advise us every six minutes that he'd received no further news regarding our impending departure.

Luckily, I had the aisle. Next to me sat a tiny, silver-haired woman who'd kept her face buried in a worn copy of *The Spy Who Came in from the Cold* until takeoff. I typically avoided chatting with strangers on planes, but there was a warmness coming off this old woman the likes of which you hardly found anymore. So when she turned to me and said, "Are you traveling on business?" I replied, "The business of my life, I suppose you could say."

She set her book down and looked up at me. Said, "My name's Edie," and offered her hand. She possessed a lovely British accent, not much heavier than my own.

"Simon," I told her.

"I hope you don't mind my saying so, Simon, but you look like a man carrying the weight of the universe. May I ask why you're heading to Ireland? Or is Ireland home?"

Sometimes it takes the sound of another's voice to realize just how lonely you are. It occurred to me then that the only person I'd regularly kept in touch with over the past few years was Kati Sheffield, and my relationship with Kati was pure business. There was Casey, of course, but he worked for tips, and I'd never once seen him outside Terry's. I sometimes wondered whether he slept there.

"I'm looking for my daughter," I said.

"Oh, dear." She paused. "Has she run off?"

"She was taken twelve years ago, when she was six years old."

Edie flinched as though I'd made a fist. Her eyes fell away, her jaw hung open. A look I'd seen countless times before.

"Abducted?" The word emanated from somewhere deep in her chest. Pushed past her dentures like a puff of smoke. She leaned back in her seat, raised her fingers to her forehead as though to cross herself, then lowered them and shook her head as if to clear cobwebs. "I sometimes forget I broke away from the Church long ago."

I nodded but said nothing.

"So, tell me about . . ."

"Hailey," I said.

I told her. Told her what I'd told so few people over the past eleven months. Told her how I'd returned to D.C. one day a dozen years ago after chasing down a United States fugitive in Bucharest and learned that my daughter, Hailey, had been taken from our Georgetown home. Told her about my wife, Tasha, poor Tasha, how she'd looked, eyes enveloped in scarlet spiderwebs, hair a fright, spew dripping from her lips, mucous running from her nose; how she'd sounded; how she'd broken down over the following weeks and ultimately taken her own life.

But mostly I told Edie about Hailey herself, how she'd been the most perfect little girl, always worrying about others' feelings more than her own. I told her about the beauty she'd been, the hints of brilliance she'd shown. Told her how Hailey's disappearance left a crack in my world that nothing could repair, a gaping hole that nothing and no one could ever refill.

And, of course, I told her about the search. The early days when the FBI made a home in our home and instructed me to sit by the phone in case the kidnappers called. To sit there and wait, do nothing but think and wait and think and wait until something happened. Told her that nothing ever did. One day, there were simply fewer feds hanging around our house, the next day fewer still, and so on and so on, until there were none. Like Hailey's favorite nursery rhyme, the one about the ten little Indians.

Then Tasha was gone. Overdosed on prescription pills. Painkillers, muscle relaxers, tranqs. The works.

I told Edie about the business I subsequently went into, searching the globe for children kidnapped by their estranged parents; how I circumvented foreign laws, and brought those children home. How always, no matter where in the world I was, I searched for Hailey.

Then this past year.

And finally ending with my call to Kati a few hours ago.

"The world can be terrible sometimes," Edie said.

She said it in such a way that I knew she meant it. She'd witnessed the world's terribleness firsthand. I asked her about it and she didn't hesitate. Described for me in great detail how she'd lost her son in a senseless shooting at a Burger King in downtown Baltimore forty years ago. The killer took off with $267 and was cornered by police in an abandoned warehouse four hours following the armed robbery. Eleven months later he was convicted and sentenced to die in Maryland's gas chamber. Thanks largely to Edie, however, the killer's sentence was eventually reduced to life without the possibility of parole. Edie had spent the years since then traveling the country, fighting the death penalty in states such as Virginia, Georgia, Florida, and Texas. She was now seventy-eight years old and still going strong.

What are you going to do?" Edie said roughly halfway through the flight. "Once we land in Dublin, how are you going to go about finding your daughter?"

I winced. In my head, I'd been referring to the wanted woman as *the girl* because I didn't quite know who I was thinking about, my daughter or some nameless stranger, some *murderous* nameless stranger.

"I spoke to the authorities," I said. "An officer graciously offered to meet me at the airport in Dublin, then take me directly to the crime scene."

After phoning the Garda and being shuffled from one unit to the next, I was finally given a man who, very much unlike the others, seemed anxious to speak with me.

"This is Detective Chief Inspector Damon Ashdown of the National Crime Agency," he'd said.

"*Britain's* National Crime Agency?" I asked, incredulous. "Not to sound ungrateful, Detective, but why in hell am I speaking to you? Unless Her Majesty quietly annexed the Republic of Ireland in the past twenty-four hours, the crime I'm calling about falls well out of your jurisdiction."

"I'm a liaison," he said evenly. "I was told you're a British citizen."

"Dual citizenship," I said. "U.S. and the UK."

"And you say you're the girl's father?" He had a gruff voice, the voice of a cop who'd spent much of his life on mean city streets.

"I can't say that for certain," I told him. "I haven't seen my daughter in twelve years."

There was a long silence on the other end of the line and I thought I'd lost him. But then he said, "Tell me if I have this right, Mr. Fisk. You were born in London but moved to the States with your father as a child?"

I froze. That was something I didn't recall telling anyone in the past half hour and it sent a sudden chill through me. Was I wanted somewhere in the EU? Was this all a ruse? Was this going to go down the way it had in Paris two years ago?

But then, maybe I *had* told someone earlier. After all, I was exhausted, on no food and little sleep. The Irish coffee had gone straight to my head. Sure, Kati's e-mail had spurred me into action but much of the past hour was still a blur.

"That's right," I finally said.

"And your father's name?"

"Alden Fisk."

I could hear him scratching something down on a pad then tapping away at a keyboard.

"Your mother's maiden name?"

I allowed a bit of edge into my voice. "I'm sorry, Detective, but this is relevant how exactly?"

"Please, sir, bear with me just a little longer." He paused. "Any siblings?"

"A sister."

"Her name?"

I sighed, long and loudly. "Tuesday. Like the day of the week."

"Please hold."

I held. I held for a damn long while, wondering whether this entire evening was a setup. I couldn't imagine Kati taking part in any plot against me. But then, I hadn't asked her how she'd obtained this photo of the wanted girl; I'd been too taken with its possible meaning. And even if she wasn't in on it, it was fathomable that someone had discovered I was working with her. Maybe even her husband, the detective in Connecticut. Who knew what connections he had in Europe? It's a small world after all. And getting smaller by the minute.

Was Interpol running the show?

Had a Red Notice been issued for me?

Did this have something to do with the mess I left at the gangster Kazmer Chudzik's lake house in Poland two years back?

My mind took me down several possible roads, each darker than the last. Ashdown seemed to know about my childhood, something I rarely volunteered. I wasn't so much *brought* to the United States by my father as I was *taken*. Taken from my mother, Tatum, and my sister, Tuesday, neither of whom I'd seen or heard from since.

Had I uttered something about my background to one of the Irish cops I'd spoken to previously? Had the information been passed on down the line to Detective Chief Inspector Ashdown? Or was Ashdown reading from an exhaustive investigative file on me and my overseas activities?

In the end, I knew it didn't matter. Any chance I had of finding Hailey—or even discovering what happened to her—inevitably passed the test of risk versus reward.

Finally Ashdown reappeared on the line.

"All right, then. Let's plan on meeting as soon as you arrive."

"I'll catch a taxi to Garda Headquarters," I told him. "Are the Guards still located off North Road in Phoenix Park?"

"That won't be necessary," he said. "Just provide me your flight information. I'll meet you direct at Dublin Airport as soon as you land."

Chapter 5

Seven and a half hours after takeoff our 777 touched down in Dublin. As we sluggishly taxied toward the terminal, I kept my head down, my belt buckled, did my damnedest to remain calm.

I was seated in the rear of the plane. Soon as we reached the gate, I watched dozens of passengers spill into the aisles and open overhead bins to retrieve luggage that should have been checked. I remained seated, my breathing quickening, pulse racing, legs shaking as if there were a band. Edie slipped me a page torn from her book.

"My mobile," she said. "I'll be three days in Dublin visiting friends then retiring to my flat in London. Do please contact me if there's anything in the world I can do."

I thanked her. Folded the page and stuffed it in my wallet.

When the aisles finally cleared I stood and raced toward the front of the plane, knowing damn well there might be a pair of handcuffs waiting for me in the terminal. It was a risk I'd often calculated and had always been willing to take.

But when we emptied into the terminal I found no uniforms waiting.

I swept the area to get my bearings. Dublin Airport had been a frequent stop these past twelve years, but rarely a final destination.

After a few moments, I followed the crowd. The airport was clean and modern and bustling as usual. During the day this terminal was brimming with sunlight (or at least what passed for sunlight here in Ireland). But due to the time difference and the seven-and-a-half-hour flight, it was already full dark when we arrived, and the artificial light felt unusually harsh on my eyes. I was still tired, I realized; in fact, I was downright exhausted.

As I approached Customs, I pulled my weathered passport from my pocket. Stepped to the back of the line and prepared for another grueling wait.

Soon as I did I felt a hand on my shoulder. I turned ninety degrees and found a single man in a heavy black overcoat. He looked to be around forty, though I was a hell of a poor judge when it came to guessing the age of adults.

"Mr. Fisk," he said without flashing identification, "I'm Detective Chief Inspector Damon Ashdown."

Neither of us extended a hand. I at least for good reason; I was half expecting Ashdown to produce a set of cuffs to take me in.

He had a hard face framed by dark hair, his mouth a narrow straight line, the kind you can't imagine ever turning up at the corners. He stared at me with piercing blue eyes, as if challenging me to speak.

I scanned the masses moving around Customs but didn't peg anyone else for a cop.

"I'm alone," Ashdown said.

I didn't believe him, not for one second. It made no sense that he was alone.

"Why?" I asked him.

"Because if we officially involve the National Crime Agency to any extent, we'd have to bring her in as soon as we found her, whether it was here or in the UK."

Not so, I thought. My plan was to find her first, get her out of the

European Union as quickly as possible, and make for a country like Moldova, where we wouldn't have to worry much about extradition. I needed information, but once I had it, I intended on ditching Ashdown and finding the girl myself.

"If it's not to arrest her," I said, "then what's your interest?"

He hesitated, furrowed his brow as though locked in an internal debate. Finally, he said, "I'm here to help you, Simon."

"Help me, huh?" I scoped the area again, certain we were being watched. "And why would you want to do that?"

"Because we have a mutual friend."

The first face that popped into my head was Davignon, the French lieutenant I'd aided in Paris two years ago. No doubt he'd want to help if he knew the connection. But then, how the hell would Davignon have found out?

"A friend?" I said, probing.

Second face to pop into my mind was Kurt Ostermann, a private investigator I'd worked with in Berlin. We had a long history. He knew all about Hailey. He'd seen her photos, including the computer-generated likeness that Kati had sent.

"A woman," Ashdown said.

At that point I was sure he was referring to Anastazja Staszak, a Warsaw lawyer who'd accompanied me through Eastern Europe during the Lindsay Sorkin investigation. At the mere thought of her I felt movement in the pit of my gut, a flutter that immediately vanished when I pictured the wanted photo of Hailey.

Or whoever the girl in the photo might be.

"All right," I said. "Who is she?"

I'd told myself on the plane that I wasn't going to volunteer anything. I was coming to Dublin to gather information, not to relinquish it.

Ashdown hesitated again, a growing look of discomfort on his face. "Someone I think you need to meet for yourself."

"If this is some kind of game—"

"It's no game, Simon," he said with an air of impatience. "Let me take you to her. After that we'll head to—"

"No," I said firmly. "It's my daughter we're searching for. My daughter, my rules. I want to see the crime scene before anything else."

Chapter 6

A s we pull up to the curb in front of my house in Georgetown the white haze returns and I feel myself falling into a
faint. Terry slaps the left side of my face, gently yet firmly.
The haze disappears, replaced by spinning red and blue lights. There
are four—no, five—black-and-whites surrounding my house. One sitting in the driveway, three idling in front of us, and one parked
around the corner, facing my backyard. All Metropolitan PD.

In his cockney British accent, Terry says, "You want I come in
with you?"

By the time he finishes the question I'm already out the door, hur-
rying up the drive. A uniformed officer holds his hand up but another tells him, "No, it's all right. This is the dad."

This is the dad.

Next thing I know I'm being helped over the threshold and then
suddenly without thought I'm pulling away, shoving aside a plain-
clothes cop standing in front of me.

My eyes fix on Tasha. She's being held up by another uniform. I
feel an unprovoked urge to throw him through a wall but I know
Tasha can't stand on her own, so I fall into a kitchen chair sitting just
a few feet in front of her. I'm hyperventilating, my knees turning to
rubber, just as they did back at Dulles. I can't seem to pull myself

together and it's killing me. In times of crisis, the strong think clearly. Yet here I am, a professional, and I'm falling apart. Crumbling like a pile of dead leaves.

"Where is she?" I say.

Tasha shakes her head, tears coming off her like a wet dog. She's vomited, I can tell, puke still visible around her lips, the scent still coming off her in waves. Her whole body is shaking, like a volcano threatening to blow.

I want to stand and hold her but know that I can't. If I try to rise, I feel as though I'll fall through the floor.

A few moments of silence pass before I hear someone come up behind me. I turn and find a man with prematurely stark white hair and pale blue eyes. He's dressed in a high-end navy suit that might as well say *Bureau* across the left lapel.

"Marshal Fisk?" He extends a hand. "I'm Special Agent John Rendell."

Once he shakes my fingers in his, he steps aside to introduce his female partner, Special Agent Candace West, a thirtysomething brunette who looks more like a fresh-faced corporate lawyer than a cop.

West offers her eyes instead of her hand, a gaze that reaches straight into my soul. She has children, I know it right away from the look on her face. She has children and she's placing herself in Tasha's shoes at this very moment. She's looking at me and wondering where her children are right now, what they're doing, whether someone's out there watching them, whether they're truly safe.

That look makes her appear a little older than I originally thought. Now I can make out a few worry lines around the eyes, her bangs probably concealing slight creases in her forehead.

Rendell steps forward again, suggests we take the meeting to the living room, where we can all sit.

"We have a number of questions," he says. "We're hoping that the answers will help us find your daughter."

Find your daughter, I think, as Rendell helps me to my feet.

No, it's all right. This is the dad.

It occurs to me now, as Rendell guides me through the kitchen like a Boy Scout aiding an invalid, that regardless of how this all turns out, our lives—Tasha's and Hailey's and mine—will never be the same again.

Chapter 7

Twenty minutes after leaving the airport in Ashdown's midnight-blue Nissan crossover, we arrived in the heart of Dublin. We parked along the south bank of the River Liffey and entered a maze of cobblestone streets. Though it was biting cold and still early in the evening, nightlife in the Temple Bar area was already in full-swing, the frigid air thick with Irish ballads and the malty aroma of beer.

"The pub where it happened is called the Stalemate," Ashdown informed me. "Just a couple more blocks."

I stepped over a puddle of vomit and brushed shoulders with an intoxicated kid no older than twenty.

"Watch where you're going, Eurotrash," the kid shouted at me over his shoulder.

"Bloody Yanks," Ashdown mumbled.

The term *bar* of Temple Bar actually meant "riverside path," but the sheer number of pubs in the area could easily throw off anyone a smidgeon less Irish than Dylan Thomas or James Joyce.

Minutes later, Ashdown pointed at a corner structure that appeared somewhat older, definitely seedier, than most of its neighbors. "There she is," he said. "The Stalemate. She's been shut down since the murder, but the owner's applying pressure to have her reopened as soon as possible."

"Who is the owner?" I asked.

"I've no clue. I'm just passing along the information that's been given to me."

Amid a sea of lights the Stalemate stood in total darkness. As we approached, a figure emerged from the shadows, a woman, middle-aged, with hair the color of fire.

Ashdown said, "Simon Fisk, meet Detective Inspector Colleen MacAuliffe of the *Gardai*."

"Pleased," I said, taking her proffered hand. "Do I call you Detective or Inspector or Detective Inspector?"

"How about Colleen?" Her brogue was queerly refreshing; it reminded me of a girl I'd once known, though I couldn't recall her name, only her face and that voice, as light as air. In a Rhode Island elementary school maybe, back when I was still grasping for my European roots.

With a thin blade produced from her jacket pocket, Colleen sliced through the white-and-blue police tape covering the frame. She unlocked the locks, opened the door, and stepped aside, allowing first me then Ashdown to enter. From behind us she summoned the lights.

"This is about how bright they keep the pub during business hours," she said.

The interior smelled like Terry's on a Sunday morning after a particularly rough Saturday night. The bar itself, solid wood painted black, ran nearly the full length of the pub along the wall to our left. The tiled floor, not surprisingly, was modeled after a black-and-white chessboard, though we were spared any hint of rooks or bishops or knights. Hanging from the walls were the usual mirrors and posters and neon signs, touting this or that brand of beer or liquor, the occasional cola or energy drink.

"It happened in the rear of the pub," Colleen said. "Just outside the lavatories."

It wasn't difficult to imagine the pub packed with merrymakers, live music emanating from the makeshift stage set off to our right. Colleen removed a manila folder from her handbag and offered it to me.

As I accepted it, my stare froze on the human outline taped to the floor tiles in front of the gents' then gradually shifted to an evidence marker several feet away.

"That was where we found our murder weapon," Colleen said. "As you'll see from the photos, it wasn't terribly difficult to identify."

I gripped the folder tightly between my fingers, apprehensive about opening it. When I looked down my hand was trembling.

"Fingerprints?" I said.

I suddenly had a sour taste in my mouth, an ache in the back of my throat.

"On the murder weapon, yes," Colleen replied. "But no match to anything in our database or the UK's. No hits with Interpol. Nothing yet from the FBI."

When I finally deigned to open the file I grimaced. The photographs depicted a particularly gory scene, more blood than you'd think the human body could hold.

From the images it appeared that the victim was a Caucasian male, between thirty-five and forty-five years old, the blood spilled from a deep cut to the left side of his throat, probably an opened carotid artery.

"The vic is another ghost," Colleen said. "Had false identification on him. A driver's license issued in a suburb of Detroit. His prints aren't in our system either. The fake name he used was Ramsey Little. But what we have right now is a John Doe."

I flipped through the grisly photographs. The murder weapon was a broken beer bottle. No question of the brand.

"My goodness, my Guinness," Colleen said as I studied the photo of the shattered black longneck. "At least we know the girl had good taste."

Ashdown checked my face for a reaction, but of course Detective

Inspector Colleen MacAuliffe had no clue what my role was in all of this. Hell, even I wasn't so sure anymore. I felt severely in over my head, just as I had two years earlier in Paris. We knew nearly nothing about the killer or her victim, let alone a possible motive. And, bottom line, I'd never been embroiled in a murder investigation before. My duty as a U.S. Marshal was to hunt fugitives; my job since was to locate missing children abroad. This was the first time in my life I was starting with a dead body. The bodies usually came later, after I'd become involved.

"Do we know where John Doe lived?" I said.

Colleen shook her head. "Just where he was staying."

"A hotel?"

"The Radisson Blu St. Helen's Hotel just outside of Dublin."

"You found a key on him?"

"No, he made us work for it. We showed his picture round the entire city. He was registered at the Radisson under the name William Perry."

"Like the defensive lineman," I said almost to myself.

Ashdown appeared puzzled. "Sorry?"

"William Perry," I said. "They called him the Refrigerator. Played for the Chicago Bears back in the eighties."

Ashdown shrugged. "It's a rather common name where I come from."

He was right. The Fridge notwithstanding, the name was distinctly British. As was the vic's alternate alias, Ramsey Little.

"What type of identification did he provide the Radisson?"

"An older U.S. passport," Colleen said, "issued in Philadelphia, birthplace listed as the State of New Jersey. The passport itself was real, but the name and date of birth were altered. And the man the passport number originally belonged to is dead."

"We know anything about his death?"

"Only that it was likely of old age. The date of birth on the original passport was thirteen March 1927."

The files Kati had sent me suddenly clouded my mind.

"Where's the camera that captured the girl's image?" I asked.

"Just outside the pub."

"May I view the footage?"

"I have the digital file," Ashdown interjected. "I'll show it to you once we're in front of a computer."

Nothing since that first sip of Irish coffee at Terry's seemed real to me. The past eleven months, *they* fit well in the context of my twelve-year nightmare. But this, the e-mail from Kati, the conversation with Ashdown, the flight to Ireland, the tour of the Stalemate provided by D.I. MacAuliffe, this felt like nothing more than a figment of my imagination. This entire scene seemed like a mirage, like a drug-induced hallucination, one that filled my lungs with the cancer of hope, a high from which I would inevitably have to come down, and come down *hard*.

Breaking an interminable silence, Ashdown asked, "We about done here, Simon?"

I stared down at the marble tiles, intensely, as though they could speak to me, as though they could tell me whether my daughter, Hailey, had been here just forty-eight hours ago, whether she'd really killed John Doe, why she'd broken a beer bottle and gone for a man's throat, and where she'd run to afterward.

"We're about done," I said.

Ashdown thanked Colleen MacAuliffe, lavished her with praise, called her a saint, the whole nine. Then we followed her outside, watched her lock up, and said our good-byes.

Once she was out of earshot, Ashdown turned to me. "Well, old boy, may I now take you to meet our mutual friend?"

"No," I said evenly. "Now you're going to take me to the Radisson."

Chapter 8

Only once we arrived at the Radisson Blu St. Helen's Hotel did I realize I'd stayed here before, about ten years ago, when it went by a slightly different moniker. The main structure, which resembled a castle more than a modern hotel, sat on a sprawling green estate more than two centuries old. The gardens surrounding the castle were meticulously maintained and dotted with extravagant statues and fountains. But tonight, in the darkness, the castle appeared more ominous than opulent, like something out of a Shakespeare tragedy.

I'd stayed here for a brief May holiday following a particularly nasty case in Saint Petersburg, a retrieval that ultimately placed me on the Kremlin's radar. Following the job, I fled Russia and for a few days lay low in London. My allies in Washington had promptly washed their hands of me, so I didn't dare fly back to the States until the heat died down. A nice, rainy spring vacation in Ireland seemed at the time like the perfect escape. And it was.

Ashdown parked his crossover in the circular drive and waved off the valet. We pushed through the cold and entered the sumptuous lobby, which hadn't changed much since my stay.

"How may I be of service this evening?" the young man behind the front desk asked us. "Are you gentlemen checking in?"

Leaning over the rich wooden counter, Ashdown flashed his

credentials, which didn't do much to impress the clerk. Probably less to do with the young man's distaste for authority, and more to do with his innate disdain for the English.

Ashdown said, "Earlier this week, you had a gentleman staying here under the name William Perry. We'd like to pay a visit to his room. The *Garda* have had it preserved as part of their investigation into Mr. Perry's homicide in Temple Bar. We're here under the authority of Detective Inspector Colleen MacAuliffe."

"I see. Let me speak to my manager."

A few minutes later we were herded into a back office. A perky young woman in an expensive gray tweed suit greeted us as we entered.

"Dana Doyle," she said, offering her hand.

On the near wall hung an immense framed photo of the castle as it appeared a half century ago. As I passed it, I caught a glimpse of my reflection. Running a hand over several days of stubble, I was reminded of how Hailey would complain on days I didn't shave.

Daddy, my face gets all scratchy when I kiss you!

Dana Doyle motioned for us to sit then took a seat behind her broad desk. "I've already spoken with D.I. MacAuliffe. So what can I do for you two this evening?"

"We'd like to view your file on Mr. Perry's stay," Ashdown said, "and then if it's not too much trouble, we'd love to have a quick look round his room."

"Shouldn't be any trouble," she said. "I'd only ask that when you're upstairs you be discreet. Although it's a light-traffic season, we do have a number of guests on that floor this evening."

"Of course."

She offered Ashdown a thin blue folder that had already been sitting front and center atop her desk. As he leaned forward to accept the folder, Ashdown's coat opened just wide enough to reveal a holstered Glock 17, the NCA's handgun of choice.

The National Crime Agency, dubbed by the media as "Britain's

FBI," was still in its infancy. With an elite force of roughly five thousand officers, the NCA's purported mission was to take on the UK's most serious and dangerous criminals, including drug barons, pedophile gangs, human traffickers, and other organized crime syndicates. Why Damon Ashdown had decided to insert himself in *this* investigation remained a mystery to me. But I was determined to figure it out, and soon, before things went sideways.

Ashdown opened the file and handed me the photo of Perry's passport as he studied the invoice.

"Do you happen to have this image scanned into your computer?" I asked Dana Doyle. When she nodded, I added, "Would you mind e-mailing it to me?"

"Not at all."

I provided her my e-mail address, and she forwarded the image from her desktop right away. As we waited for her to retrieve the key card to Perry's room, I sent a message to several private investigators I kept close ties with: Kurt Ostermann in Berlin; my old friend Gustavo in Tampa; Wendy Isles in London, among others. I hoped someone would be able to dig in and identify John Doe before the Guards did.

Once I'd sent the image, I turned to Ashdown and said, "The Guards interviewed the staff here at the hotel, I presume?"

Ashdown nodded. "MacAuliffe told me no one observed John Doe anywhere near the bar. No one witnessed him conversing with anyone. In fact, no one other than the clerk who checked him in heard him speak at all."

"Accent?"

"Indistinguishable. The desk clerk took his U.S. passport without questioning whether he was an American. So obviously, John Doe, wherever he actually hailed from, could have passed for a Yank." He paused a moment, then added, "Of course, given what we know, it may have been an act."

"Vehicle?"

Ashdown pulled a handwritten form from the folder and studied it. "None listed on the hotel registration. Nothing left behind in the car park. Doorman said he saw John Doe jump into the rear of a standing taxi that night round six o'clock."

When Dana Doyle returned, we rose from our chairs. She handed Ashdown the key and asked him for a business card. As he reached into his overcoat, I surreptitiously stole a glance at his reflection in the framed photo of the castle.

In the instant he opened his billfold to retrieve his business card, everything changed.

I immediately made a decision. Once we viewed the room, the detective and I would be parting ways. That was for damn sure. The only question was, would he give chase?

Chapter 9

As Ashdown and I headed, unescorted, up to Perry's room, I wondered how many hotels I'd stayed in over the past twelve years. It seemed impossible to comprehend. How many cases? How many children? How many worried-sick parents had I consoled over the phone? How many kids had I taken to private airports in the dead of night? How many made it back to the States and went on to college? How many later committed crimes or overdosed and died, the victims of the broken or dysfunctional home to which I'd so zealously returned them?

On the fifth floor we stepped off the elevator and searched for number 506. Outside the door, Ashdown slipped on a pair of latex gloves and handed me another. Then he worked the key card and allowed me to enter.

The room was spacious and well-appointed. Clean and orderly. The king-size bed was not only made but turned down for the evening of the murder, a mint chocolate in a green foil wrapper placed atop one of the half-dozen pillows.

"What did the Guards remove from the room?" I asked Ashdown.

He consulted his notes. "According to MacAuliffe, they found nothing of a personal nature except for his clothes and a few toiletries. His reservation was for a week. But there was a note in the file that he may need to leave early or extend his stay, depending on circumstances beyond his control."

"So he was here on some kind of business," I said. "Alone."

Witnesses at the Stalemate on the night of the murder had offered little. No one had noticed the victim until he hit the floor with blood gushing from his throat. No one witnessed an argument. Because of the victim's positioning and proximity to the restrooms, it was assumed the girl had just stepped out of the ladies' room when the attack took place. Perhaps there had been an earlier confrontation, but no one could say for sure.

I opened the closet. Three nondescript suits hung alongside several Oxford business shirts and a number of ties no louder than an octogenarian's whisper.

"Whatever he was doing he wanted to remain inconspicuous," I said.

I poked around. Neither the suits nor the ties contained any tags.

"And," I added, "entirely untraceable should his wardrobe be searched."

"You think he was following her?"

"I think he was following *someone*. It may have been her. It may have been someone she was with."

"Witnesses at the Stalemate said she was alone."

"Alone at the bar," I said softly. "Maybe not alone in Dublin."

"She may live here for all we know."

"She may," I said. "But then why do we have a John Doe as opposed to a John MacNamara or a Joe O'Malley?"

"Bit of a jump, wouldn't you say?"

"With the girl on the run and the Guards on her tail, jumps are about all we have time for." I stepped over to the nightstand and stared down at the phone. "Downstairs you looked over John Doe's invoice. Any calls made?"

"Not a one. None incoming either."

"And yet no one discovered a mobile phone," I said. "Not on his person and not in the room."

"The girl might have taken it from him. I mean, who today walks round without a mobile?"

"The same type of people who walk around with false identities, I suppose. The same type of people who cut the tags out of their suits."

Several seconds of silence were punctuated with a smirk. "What are you thinking, Simon? That this bloke was MI6?"

"Would we necessarily know by now if he was?"

Ashdown thought on it for a moment. "Not likely."

"Then we can't rule it out," I said. "On the other hand, if he was with SIS, I don't think we'd be standing in this room right now. Do you?"

Ashdown shrugged. "I don't know the answer to that."

The hell you don't, I thought.

Since before its inception, the NCA had boasted about its intelligence hub, the so-called Organized Crime Coordination Centre, which amalgamated and analyzed intel not only from every other police force in Britain but from the Security Services, MI5 and MI6.

At that moment I felt a vibration against my right leg. I removed my gloves, plucked my BlackBerry out of my right pants pocket, checked the screen, and pressed it against my ear.

"Magda just opened the photo you sent me," Kurt Ostermann said in his stiff German accent.

"And?"

"And your John Doe's an international."

"You're sure?"

"Of course I'm sure. I've worked cases with him before. He's a career private investigator. Takes jobs all over the world."

"British?"

"As the Beatles. Main base of operations is in London. Whitehall to be specific."

"What types of jobs?"

"Anything and everything so long as the money's right. Missing persons, divorce, insurance fraud, the whole lot. He's good. *Damn* good. And he's expensive."

"His name?"

"Legal name is Elijah Welker, but everyone knows him as Eli."

"Wife?" I said.

"Four children. All still in the nest. Why?"

"Christ," I muttered with a sigh.

I told Ostermann that Eli Welker had been murdered and provided him with a few of the pertinent details.

Following a brief period of quiet he said, "So the Guards still have him down as a John Doe?"

"Yes."

"Can you keep it that way for twenty-four hours? I know his wife, Becky, rather well. I'd like to go to London and break the news myself. I can be there first thing in the morning."

"I assure you, if the Guards learn John Doe's true identity, it won't have come from me."

"If you don't mind my asking, Simon, what are you doing in Dublin? Is this something you're mixed up in?"

"Maybe, maybe not." I gave him the short of it, filled him in on Kati's e-mail and my visit to the Stalemate earlier in the evening.

"All right," he said. "Then while I'm visiting with Becky I'll see if I can't gain access to Eli's files. Maybe I can find out for you who hired him. Maybe more, depending on Becky's state."

"I'd appreciate that," I told him. "One last thing . . ."

"Oh, yes, the other name." Ostermann ruffled some pages. "Your host is indeed with Britain's National Crime Agency. However . . ."

"However?"

"However, he's currently stationed at Interpol Manchester."

Once I disconnected I found Ashdown working his iPhone with practiced thumbs. He too had removed his latex gloves.

I cleared my throat.

He held up an index finger, said, "I'll be just another minute. Sending a text."

As I waited, I considered my options. Interpol, of course, wasn't a police force in its own right. Rather, it was an organization that fostered international police cooperation. Each member nation maintained a National Central Bureau, which worked with local authorities to investigate and prosecute criminals according to national laws. So Ashdown couldn't arrest me here in Dublin, not on his own. He'd require assistance. Perhaps from the "mutual friend" he was so eager for me to meet.

"So what's the story?" Ashdown said as he pocketed his phone.

"Before I say anything," I said, slowly moving toward him, "I need to know that information flows only one way, unless I say otherwise. I'm not here to solve a crime. At least not *this* crime. I'm here to find my daughter."

Ashdown didn't hesitate. "You have my word, Simon."

I nodded once and extended my right hand, ostensibly to seal the pact. When he took my hand in his, I immediately twisted his wrist hard to the right, then kicked his left leg out at the knee.

As soon as he dropped, I reached inside his coat and snatched his Glock 17.

"*Why?*" I demanded with the gun pointed at his head.

"Why *what?*" he cried in obvious pain.

"*Why* do I have your word? *Why* are you involved in this? What do you *want* with me and Hailey?"

Ashdown's face grew red and defiant. "You're making a mistake, you nutter. I'm trying to *help* you."

"The hell you are," I said. "I saw your identification when you produced your business card for Miss Doyle downstairs. And I just received confirmation from my friend in Berlin. You're not just with the NCA. You're *Interpol*."

"*So what?*" he shouted from his knee.

"So you *lied* about it."

"I didn't *lie*," he insisted. "It just isn't bloody relevant."

"It's relevant to me."

"Look, I didn't want to scare you away, make you think there's a Red Notice issued for you."

"Then why travel all the way up from Manchester to meet me?"

Ashdown drew a deep breath, cradling his wrist in the palm of his other hand.

"Simon," he said, looking me squarely in the eyes from his spot on the floor, "it seems it's well past time you met our mutual friend."

"If you think I'm getting back into your vehicle, Detective, you're badly mistaken."

"You don't have to. She's already here. That was her I texted. She's going to meet us at the bar just downstairs."

I took a step back but kept the gun aimed at his center mass.

"Let me guess," I said. "A detective from the Garda Crime and Security Branch to help you effect an arrest, since you're out of your jurisdiction."

Ashdown shook his head with vigor. "She's not a cop, Simon. Not even remotely."

I took another step back and allowed Ashdown to pick himself off the floor. He took a step forward, gingerly, clearly favoring his left leg.

He said, "You can hold on to my gun if you still don't trust me."

"Believe me, Detective, I intend to." With my head, I motioned for him to move past me toward the door. "And make no mistake. If you so much as breathe too hard in my direction, I intend to use it."

Chapter 10

Despite my warning, by that point I *did* trust Ashdown. Because had he in any way considered me a hostile, he would have been ready for me. Even if he hadn't considered me a substantial threat, he would have at least been prepared to put up a struggle. Relieving him of his firearm would have been no simple task. Especially considering the shape I was in after eleven months of skipping not just the gym but meals and full nights of sleep. Right up to and including the previous twenty-four hours. Not only had I lost significant muscle, I was practically dead on my feet. A sleepwalker. That I was able to disarm him at all was owed to pure instinct. But had an elite officer like Ashdown executed the simplest handgun retention technique, he'd still have possession of his weapon, and I'd have been riding the down elevator in cuffs.

Given Ashdown's lack of preparedness, I had been certain that when we arrived downstairs at the Orangerie Bar, I would see a woman I instantly recognized. Maybe the Warsaw lawyer Anastazja Staszak. Maybe the London private investigator Wendy Isles. Maybe someone I hadn't thought of in ages. But surely someone I'd be able to identify the moment I laid eyes on her.

Not so.

When we entered the bar I turned to Ashdown, expecting him to say, "Let me give her a buzz; maybe she stepped outside for a cigarette," or "Let's have a seat at that booth; she probably just went to the ladies' to powder her nose."

But no.

Ashdown instead looked back at me in silence, anticipation evident in his cold blue stare. I scanned the room a second time. An older couple sipping gin and tonics in the far corner. Three boisterous businessmen in shirtsleeves with untied ties hanging from open collars, throwing back shots of whiskey at a tall bar table. Two Middle Eastern women sipping tea in a booth. A young man nursing a black and tan at the bar. Next to him a woman somewhere in her late thirties or early forties, flirting with the well-built bartender who probably had first-year college classes scheduled early the next morning.

Then there was the cocktail waitress, a fit young lady with short, dark hair. Before I could get a good look at her face, she turned her back to us to collect the empty shot glasses being stacked like a house of cards by the rowdy business boys.

"You don't recognize her, do you?"

"Should I?"

"No," Ashdown said, "I don't suppose you should."

He led me to an intimate round table where we each took one of the plush green chairs. I slipped a hand inside my black leather jacket and gripped the butt of Ashdown's gun, just in case. But I knew by then I wouldn't need it.

I eyed the empty lounge sofa, wondering who was about to sit across from us.

A second, older waitress came by to take our orders.

Ashdown said, "A pint of Smithwick's."

I said, "I'll have an espresso."

As she walked away, Ashdown asked whether I planned on sleeping tonight.

"Sleep will come when it wants me bad enough," I told him.

Our drinks arrived before our guest. My impatience began clutching at my throat. My nerves were raw, my skin tingling. I removed my hand from inside my jacket. Took a bite of the biscotti then downed half my espresso.

I set the cup down on its saucer and leaned back in the chair, pinching the bridge of my nose and squeezing my eyes shut because I felt a monstrous headache coming on. When I opened my eyes, I glanced at my watch without noticing the time. I exhaled audibly, lifted my cup of espresso but didn't take a drink. Instead I tilted my head back and gazed up at the high ceiling.

When I looked down, the thirty- or fortysomething woman from the bar was seated directly opposite me.

She stared at me, though I wasn't sure whether it was to scrutinize me or to avoid Ashdown's gaze. The tension between them was immediately obvious—and thick enough to smother someone.

"Hello, Simon," the woman said in a heavy British accent. She was lanky, wore a bright red dress she couldn't quite fill out. She may have been pretty, perhaps even beautiful, but it was impossible to tell under the dense layers of paint on her face. Her eyes were brown, possibly black, their color lost in a whirlwind of electric-blue eye shadow and brightly colored mascara.

I glanced at Ashdown.

"Simon," he said, "I'd like you to meet Zohanna Carlyle."

As I sat in silence trying to associate this woman with a case, with a cause, with something, anything, the cop added, "She is also the former Mrs. Ashdown."

I turned to him. "Your *wife*?"

"*Ex*-wife," the woman said, crossing her long, black-stockinged legs.

"I don't understand," I said to Ashdown. "You told me we were meeting a mutual friend."

Ashdown rocked his head from side to side. "A figure of speech, old boy."

"But I don't even know her. . . ." I started to say.

Then it struck me like a sledgehammer to the chest.

Slowly, I said to the woman, "I take it Carlyle isn't a return to your maiden name."

She shook her head.

Impossible, I thought. *After more than three and a half decades . . .*

"Tuesday?" I said so quietly I wasn't sure I said it aloud.

She parted her ruby red lips in a smile. "I never much fancied that name. *Tuesday.* An awful day, isn't it? Stuck there between Monday and Hump Day like the meat in a *bleh* sandwich. Not to mention I was actually born in the wee hours of a Wednesday morning." She shook her head but never once took her eyes off me. "No, Tuesday's not for me. Since you and dear old Daddy left us, I've always gone by Zoey."

Chapter 11

We went out to the backyard," Tasha says breathlessly, "to have a kind of picnic. I'd put together ham and cheese sandwiches and made a pitcher of sweet tea. We threw a blanket down on the grass and set it all up then sat down to eat. We'd each taken just a few bites when the telephone rang. I ran inside to get it because I thought it might be Simon. I thought maybe his plane had been delayed or he was landing sooner than expected. I don't know . . ."

Sitting on the sofa next to Tasha as she tells Special Agents John Rendell and Candace West what happened this morning, I want to lift my arm and place it around her shoulders, but I don't have the strength. But no, it's more than that, I realize. I *don't* want to hold my wife. I don't want to hold her because I'm angry. I'm angry at *her*. I don't want to be, but I can't help myself. How the hell could she let this happen? How the hell could she allow Hailey to be taken right from under her nose?

"But it wasn't Simon," she says, "it was my mother. She was just calling to check in with me, see how Hailey and I were doing. She calls a lot while Simon's away. While I was on the phone with her I looked out the window. Hailey was fine. She'd finished half her sandwich and she was sipping her sweet tea. The kitchen phone's a cordless, so I was about to take it outside. But I noticed a little puddle on the floor. Just a splash of Hailey's orange juice from this morning. I didn't want to step in it, so I grabbed a paper towel off the rack and wiped it up. Then I threw the paper towel in the garbage under the sink."

I don't want to be sitting here. I want to launch myself off this couch and jump into our Ford Explorer and start combing the streets looking for Hailey. But Rendell insists that I can be of the most help by staying here and providing him and West with the information they need to find my daughter.

I lean forward. The more I listen to Tasha tell her story the angrier I get. I don't *want* to get angrier; I want to sympathize. We need each other right now, more than we have ever needed each other before. I realize that. But part of me wants to—nearly *needs* to—stand up and shout, "What the hell were you *thinking,* leaving Hailey out there all by herself? You're her *mother,* goddamn you. How could you take your eyes off her even for a second? She's only *six years old.*"

"When I looked out the window to check on her again, I didn't see her," Tasha says through her tears. "But I thought she'd just moved to another part of the yard. Or maybe she was heading inside. I listened for the door. When I didn't hear anything I looked out the window again. Then I walked outside and looked around the yard. The gate was closed, so I thought maybe she was hiding. On the phone, my mother was telling me some ridiculous story about my father fighting with their neighbors over some landscaping issue. I didn't want to interrupt her or shout in her ear. So I kept looking. After another minute or so, I finally told my mother to hang on and I started calling out Hailey's name."

I know it's useless to point fingers just now. All that matters is that Hailey is found. But I can't help but feel as though Tasha's to blame. She says nothing else in the yard was amiss. That the sandwiches and sweet tea were still on the blanket. She listened and listened and heard nothing but silence. Finally she told her mother she had to go.

Didn't say why, didn't mention that she couldn't find Hailey, just said, "Let me call you back, Mom, I've got to check on something." *Why?* I think. Why not say, "I don't see my daughter." Maybe then her mother hangs up and dials the police, sends them to our address. Maybe it saves fifteen minutes. Maybe that fifteen minutes is all the time it would have taken to reverse this hell we're facing right now.

"I ran across the street to the neighbor's," she says. "They have a daughter a little older than Hailey, and a puppy Hailey loves to play with, a little basset hound named CJ. I rang their bell. I heard the dog barking, but no one came to the door. I was still holding the phone, so I tried to call nine-one-one, but I was too far from the house for the cordless to work. So I ran back to the house and called."

Rendell nods his head. "What did you tell the dispatcher?"

"I said, '*Someone took my daughter!*'"

"Why?" Rendell cuts in. "Why did you say that? Why did you think that right away?"

I look at my wife and for the first time since I arrived she fumbles for words.

"I don't . . . I just *knew*. I mean, she wasn't in the backyard and the gate was closed. It was *locked*. Even if Hailey left—which she'd never in a million years do—she couldn't have reached over and locked the gate."

Rendell makes a face I've seen before, a face only cops make when they're skeptical of something someone is saying. "Couldn't have?" he says. "Or wouldn't have?"

Tasha has to think about it. I wait for her to look at me, but she doesn't. She's barely looked at me since I arrived home, in fact.

"I don't know," she says finally. "I guess she's tall enough now. But she *knows* better than to leave the yard when I'm not there."

How often are you not there? I nearly shout.

"All right," Rendell says in the voice of an ER doctor about to deliver bad news. "We and the D.C. Police have every available human resource out there looking for your daughter. We'll watch the phones and hope we receive a call that Hailey's safe and sound, that she just strolled away and got lost. But it's been a few hours now since she went missing, so our job, mine and Special Agent West's, is to operate under the assumption that she's been taken. If she has, this first twenty-four hours is crucial. So I'm going to ask you a series of questions, some of which may seem completely irrelevant and some of which may make you uncomfortable. But it's all standard operating procedure, and the more you cooperate, the faster we're going to find Hailey and bring her home."

"We understand," I say.

"Good," he says, opening a small notebook. "Then let's start with family and friends who live in the area."

Chapter 12

I woke on the sofa in the sitting room of an elegant suite on the top floor of the Radisson. Daylight was squeezing through the razor-thin opening where the curtains were supposed to meet. I glanced at my watch and sighed. It was nearly eleven o'clock in the morning. I was disappointed with myself, but not the least bit surprised. After viewing the surveillance footage from the Stalemate, Zoey and I had stayed up most of the night, attempting in our own strange way to catch up on the past thirty-six years of our lives.

When I sat up on the couch, I noticed that Ashdown had retrieved my Swiss Army suitcase from his vehicle. I decided to shower and dress before knocking on the bedroom door and waking them.

I walked into the bathroom. Shed the clothes I'd been wearing since I spoke to Kati back in the States nearly thirty-six hours ago and stepped into the shower. As the scalding water beat down on my chest, I thought about last night.

Over the past couple of years I'd often daydreamed about what it would be like to meet my sister, Tuesday. (I still hadn't fully adjusted to the name change and seriously doubted that I ever would.) In any event, my sister was nothing like the woman I'd fantasized meeting. I'd expected a demure woman, refined in the ways in which most Americans imagine the British to be. But this woman was crass, even crude at times. She wasn't the modest, soft-spoken little girl I'd lost thirty-six years ago. She was blustery and garish; she drank like a sorority girl and cursed like a stockbroker witnessing a career-ending crash on the floor of the New York Stock Exchange.

At one point during the conversation here in the suite, I'd asked her how she met Ashdown. She raised her lip in a snarl as her ex-husband looked on. "Damon was working at the Met at the time. I'd been a dancer. After work, me and some of the girls would hit the car park for a bit of dogging and a wee taste of Charlie. . . ."

Ashdown casually averted his eyes.

"The car park was in a secluded spot," she continued, "and no one round there raised much of a fuss, so it was rare for the filth to make an appearance. But one night, he and his partner roll up like bloody Starsky and Hutch, and this one taps on our window and flashes his badge and tells us, 'Out of the car.' My girlfriends think we're right fucked because of the drugs, but from the way this one was looking at me, I could tell straightaway he was as randy as a schoolboy, and that if I gave him half the chance he'd bend me over the hood for a quickie. So, I ask him, 'Fancy a shag?' and he turns all red in the cheeks and says as coolly as he can under the circumstances, 'How about a date to start?' So, I say, 'Sure, whatever floats yours, ya know, long as you let us go,' and the next night he picks me up from my flat and takes me to this club, only he doesn't dance, so instead we grab a few bevvys and get pissed and end up snogging like a pair of teenagers right there in the middle of the lounge. This goes on for over an hour before he finally realizes, *What the fuck?* and takes me back to his place to have it off straight through the morning." She shot Ashdown a look. "Now, of course, he regrets the whole bloody episode."

Ashdown turned to her. "I don't regret a single minute of that night, love. It's my cock-up the next morning I'll never live down, isn't it?"

She looked at me and smirked. "The wanker falls for me straightaway, asks me to move in with him after breakfast. A bit dodgy, wouldn't you say, little brother?"

Little brother. Simply hearing those words returned me to the London of my childhood, where Tuesday and I alternately laughed and fought with each other, she a fan of flicking my large five-year-old ears, me a master at pulling her longish brown hair. Both of us lousy little tattletales to boot.

When I stepped out of the shower I found Ashdown standing on the balcony, smoking a cigarette, gazing out over the lush grounds.

"Didn't take you for a smoker," I said, stepping outside to join him.

"I'm not. The trollop just draws it out of me." He quickly looked over, said, "Sorry, mate. I didn't mean to . . ."

I shrugged it off and moved back inside. It wasn't me to whom he owed the apology.

Ashdown flicked his butt over the railing and followed me in. "What's the first order of business this morning?"

"A double shot of espresso," I said.

"And then?"

I stared at myself in the mirror, took in my own hooded gaze. Truth was, I didn't know what came next. The crime scene hadn't spoken to me; the dead man's hotel room had said even less. I told myself it didn't matter. It felt vital for me to remember that I was looking for Hailey, not Eli Welker's killer. As far as I was concerned, this wasn't an investigation; it was a search.

I started to respond to Ashdown's question but was saved by the bell on my BlackBerry. I hurried over to the desk and picked it up.

The screen was lit with Kurt Ostermann's mobile number.

"I've got good news and bad," Ostermann said. "Which do you want first?"

"Give me the bad news."

"Well, I'm in London and Becky's a mess. I tried to explain to her why she hasn't been contacted by anyone official yet, but she doesn't want to listen to it, Simon. So don't be surprised if she calls the Guards and spills the beans about the vic being her husband."

"What's the good news?" I said.

"Well, I haven't quite finished giving you the bad yet. The really bad news, as far as I'm concerned, is that Becky has no idea who hired her husband, and the information isn't in the thin files she allowed me a look at. She says Eli made his client's privacy top priority. Maybe some good old-fashioned police work—tracking down phone numbers, pounding the pavement, knocking on doors—will help us figure it out, but it's possible that the identity of his client is a secret he'll take to his grave in a few days."

I cursed under my breath. "And the good news?"

"Well, Becky wouldn't consent to me having a look around his home office, so I sent her off on a walk, you know, to clear her head. Then I picked the lock and had a see for myself. No physical finds whatsoever; everything's locked tight. Nothing on his hard drive either. But I scoured his recent e-mails and found a few photos he'd recently sent to himself."

"What kinds of photos?"

"I'm forwarding them to you now. Have yourself a look, then call me back if you still have questions."

"Thanks," I said.

"I'm staying in London a few days, Simon. Just say the word if you need me up there for anything, anything whatsoever, you understand?"

"Perfectly. Where are you staying?"

"The Corinthia. I have a corporate client here; I figure it's high time I started billing him what I'm worth."

As soon as I disconnected, I let Ashdown in on the conversation. Meanwhile, I opened Ostermann's e-mail, clicking on the attachments one by one.

It was the girl. The young woman in the photographs was the same woman caught on tape outside the Stalemate in Temple Bar following Eli Welker's murder. She appeared in the photos with a guy, a big fellow in his early thirties, I guessed. His arms and neck were heavily inked, his head completely shaven. His ears were pierced—

gauged, actually, the lobes stretched to accommodate half-inch plugs. From the looks of him, I doubted they were the only part of his body that contained man-made holes. From the images, it appeared that he and the girl were intimate; lovers certainly, perhaps even boyfriend and girlfriend.

"Clearly they didn't know they were being photographed," Ashdown said, his eyes locked on my BlackBerry.

"The backgrounds," I said, "do you recognize any of them?"

Ashdown scrolled through the pictures, zoomed in on a few of them then nodded his head. "You can make out the street signs in a few of these. Balornock. Keppochhill. Edgefauld Road. No question; the photos were taken in Glasgow."

"There are a number of pictures there that were shot in and around pubs," I said. "Seems to me, we talk to a few barflies, there's a good chance we get a lead on the guy, whoever he might be."

"I'm inclined to agree."

"Happen to have any contacts in the Police Service of Scotland?"

"I do," Ashdown said, handing me back my phone. "But no one I trust near as much as Colleen MacAuliffe. Trouble in Scotland—and Glasgow in particular—is that it's often difficult to tell the cops from the crooks."

"Any suggestions?"

"Glasgow's the most violent city in the UK. We can't just run down there asking questions. We need to have a plan."

"We?"

"You didn't think I was going to let you go this alone, did you?"

I said nothing.

"Thing is, you and I, we're going to stick out like sore thumbs down there. And the only folks they like less than the English are English law enforcement."

"You've already helped me plenty," I said. "I can take things from here."

Ashdown shook his head. "You'll get yourself stabbed or slashed first pub you enter, Simon. There aren't many guns in Scotland, but Glasgow's the knife capital of Europe."

"You just said so yourself; you're not going to fare much better than me. Not with that accent."

"I might not," he said, "but I know someone who'd be accepted in Glasgow straightaway, regardless of accent or creed or country of origin."

"Did I hear somebody mention Glasgow?" Zoey said, entering the room in her underwear, a mismatched set of bra and panties.

"Simon and I are heading there now. Want to come along?"

"I'd like to see the two of you try to stop me." She returned to the bedroom, muttering something about getting dressed.

I looked a question at Ashdown.

He shrugged. "I had a feeling she'd come aboard. Glasgow has the best bloody skag in all of Great Britain, she says."

Part Two

THE BARONS OF GLASGOW

Chapter 13

Figuring we wouldn't have much success finding the character in the photos during daylight hours, we decided to drive from Dublin to Glasgow rather than fly and arrived in Scotland's largest city shortly before dusk.

Well-rested and well-fed—and charged with a fair amount of adrenaline—I felt stronger than I had in nearly a year. During the five-and-a-half-hour drive in Ashdown's rented Nissan crossover, I'd stared at the photos on my BlackBerry until I'd etched every feature of the girl (and the man she was with) into my mind. Whether I'd been struck with a rare bout of optimism or a devastating case of wishful thinking, I didn't know. But I was beginning to believe that the young woman in the photos could conceivably be Hailey Fisk.

Fortunately, all the photos Eli Welker had taken of the couple were set in the same area. *Unfortunately,* that area was Springburn, an inner city district in northern Glasgow, best known for its drug trade and abundance of violent crime.

"Well, there's certainly no shortage of dive bars to choose from," Ashdown muttered as we cruised north along one of Springburn's desolate roads. "We may as well park and hoof it from here."

"No shortage of spaces either," I noted. Even on Springburn's main drag, traffic was nearly nonexistent. The few cars that were on the road were early model sedans that had surely seen better days.

Ashdown pulled the Nissan to the curb. "That's because two-thirds of Springburn's population can't afford a motor vehicle," he said, yanking the parking brake and killing the ignition. "Poverty has plagued this area for decades."

I turned and nudged Zoey, who'd spent the past couple of hours sprawled along the backseat, sleeping.

"Here already, are we?" she said, yawning as she gazed out the windshield. "*Shit.* It's beginning to snow. Some holiday you boys are taking me on."

"At least it's not brutally cold," I said as I stepped out of the vehicle. I'd opened the door expecting to shiver, but unlike my final night in D.C., there was no wind. Not so much as a breeze.

"Can't last though," Zoey cautioned.

I turned to her. "You know Springburn. Where should we start?"

"Bishop's, Highland, Shevlanes," she said with a shrug. "Makes no difference, really. They all attract the same sort."

Along with dive bars, the road was littered with rundown churches. Black iron gates discouraged trespassers from trampling their overgrown lawns, defacing their cracked and crumbling tombstones, their statues of saints thick with bird shit.

In the distance stood a group of cement blocks, thirty-some stories tall.

"Projects?" I asked.

Ashdown said, "Here in the UK, we call them council houses. Sounds more sophisticated, doesn't it?"

In the past couple of years I'd witnessed poverty in so many of its ugly forms, from the Podil district in the Ukrainian capital of Kiev to the La Carpio slums in the Costa Rican capital of San José. Watching needless human suffering in a world where so many have so much never got any easier.

"Let's start there," I said, pointing to a brown brick cube on the corner. A collapsing sign hanging against the side of the structure read THE OLD SOAK, which Ashdown explained was British slang used to refer to drunkards of long standing.

Zoey said, "I fancy it already."

As I gazed across the street, I laid out the plan. "I'll head in first, order a beer. Zoey, you come in after ten or fifteen minutes. Act like you don't know me."

"Shouldn't be much of a challenge, should it, little brother?"

I ignored her comment for the moment but damn well meant to address it later.

"Detective," I said, "you'll keep an eye on the place in case we need backup. You all right for an hour or two?"

"Of course."

As I turned and started toward the bar I heard Zoey asking Ashdown for money.

"Since when do *you* pay for your own drinks inside a pub?" Ashdown sneered.

"Oh, bugger off," she shouted. "Maybe it's not *drinks* I'm bent on paying for. Ever think of that?"

Once I stepped onto the curb on the opposite side of the street, I was mercifully out of earshot. I opened the metal door to the Old Soak and was immediately greeted by an odor I couldn't define. That and a middle-age male bartender who eyed me up and down as though I'd just told him I meant to rob the place.

There were only two other patrons in the pub, both elderly gentlemen seated at the bar, staring into tall glasses of ale. I flashed on a street sign I'd seen just a few blocks back. Depicting a pair of stooped-over stick figures, it read: WATCH FOR THE ELDERLY. Implied in that warning, I now realized, was that Springburn's elderly might well be drunk out of their gourds. At least the two old soaks seated at this bar clearly were.

As I took a barstool I motioned to the tap and said, "Pint of Tennent."

The bartender didn't say a word, didn't crack half a smile, just grabbed a cloudy pint glass from the drain board behind him and started the pour.

I drank down half the pint in a swallow. What I really craved was a double espresso, something to sharpen the senses rather than dull them. But when in Rome, and all that. And from the looks of the place, had I ordered anything sans alcohol, the bartender would have swiftly tossed me out on my British-American ass.

Ashdown was right. Had I come to Glasgow alone I'd never have gotten answers. At least not without a gun. And a willingness to use it.

But now we had a far more effective weapon in our arsenal.

And several minutes after I finished my first pint, she stepped inside the pub with a disarming smile painted across her ruby-red lips.

"Shot of your cheapest whiskey," Zoey called across the bar.

"Right away, lass."

Was it me? Or had the bartender's mood just vastly improved?

Chapter 14

As night fell, the pub began to fill. I'd tossed back about four pints and flushed another couple down the toilet so as not to arouse suspicion or draw the ire of the grizzled bar-keep. As long as I kept tossing money on the bar, I figured he'd continue serving me. But I also had the distinct impression that the Old Soak strictly enforced at least one unwritten rule: *If you're not drinking, you're leaving—by force, if necessary.*

Which wasn't an issue for Zoey. By close of Happy Hour, my sister had consumed an almost unthinkable amount of liquor, and there seemed to be no stopping her. Not that anyone but myself was trying. The pub's patrons, the great majority of whom were male, encouraged her like we were at a frat party. Not that she needed much encouragement either.

Best I could do was keep an eye on her, step in if some boozer began misbehaving.

But she didn't make it easy, repeatedly parading outside for smokes with plastered teenagers. I clung to the hope that Ashdown could monitor her from his crossover, which conceivably remained parked on the opposite side of the street, though I hadn't really instructed him to stay put. He, too, had the photos on his phone and could feasibly be touring the innumerable dive bars along the road, his English accent be damned.

One pub called Bishop's was on this very block.

Shortly after my sister returned to the bar following a smoke with a trio of teenage boys, the door to the pub opened again, and the atmosphere suddenly transformed. Like a rowdy classroom suddenly gone silent. From my spot at the end of the bar, I craned my neck to make out our newest reveler. A kid, somewhere in his early twenties, sporting a goatee and a badly receding hairline. Skinny, scrawny even, yet with the strut of a professional footballer.

Dressed in a navy tracksuit straight off the set of *The Sopranos*, the kid sauntered through the throng, which parted in a way that would have made ambulance drivers jealous.

To some he offered a nod, others a look that made them instantly shy away, like mares from a rattlesnake.

The bartender stopped mid-pour, turned, and snatched an ice-cold rocks glass from the freezer. Then he reached for the top shelf, opened a fresh bottle of Dalmore, and decanted three fingers, neat.

Sliding it carefully across the bar to his latest guest, he said, "On the house, mate."

The kid in the tracksuit swallowed the Scotch in a single go. Slapped the empty glass onto the bar, said, "Another, then," and slid over a pile of cash half as tall as the pour.

The chatting, which had briefly ceased, rose again, and the mood for the most part returned to normal. Yet a palpable air of trepidation lingered, like tear gas over a peaceful assembly.

I raised my brows in Zoey's direction. She replied with an inebriated shrug and a single finger that slurred, *I'm on it,* then she turned back to her current companion with a salacious grin and a question on her lips.

Several minutes later she strolled over to me, said in my ear, "The tracksuit's name is Kinny Gilchrist. He's the son of some local gangster known as The Chairman."

I stole a glance over at the kid and his newly arrived entourage.

They were seated in the back corner booth, which had been occupied by a different group of hooligans only a few minutes earlier.

"Any luck otherwise?" I said.

Zoey shook her head. "I showed the photo to a few of the blokes I took outside for a fag. Not a one claimed to recognize the girl. Or the wanker she's with in the pic."

"It's possible he's not local," I said, partially deflating. "But I'd like to confirm it with the Gilchrist kid. If he's as connected as your friend over there suggests, he'll know everyone in the neighborhood, if only for purposes of self-preservation."

"Want I go over and present him with the photo?"

I shook my head. "Not right away. And not alone. Too risky. Think maybe you can lure him outside?"

"I can try."

"Let's call that plan A, then."

"And plan B?"

"I'll let you know plan B soon as I think of it."

Twenty minutes later, Zoey was alone in the back corner booth with Kinny Gilchrist. I was anxious for her to draw him outside so that he and I could have a word, but she seemed to be enjoying his company, which shouldn't have come as much of a surprise. Ashdown notwithstanding, my sister clearly had a thing for bad boys. The younger the better.

Finally I glimpsed her lift a pack of cigarettes off the table and motion toward the door. Kinny shook his head, wrapped his bony arm around her bare shoulders, and dug a platinum Zippo out of his tracksuit. I glanced at the bartender, who seemed to be paying them no mind—even as the kid lit Zoey's cigarette a foot or two below a conspicuous sign that read: NAE SMOKIN OR YER OOT ON YER ARSE.

Enough, I thought. *I need to move things along.*

I drained my pint of Tennent and abandoned my barstool. But just as I started toward the corner booth, the Gilchrist kid stood up and signaled a couple of his boys. Then he turned toward the restrooms. One of his boys, the brawnier of the two, followed him to the toilet. The other took Gilchrist's seat in the booth beside my sister.

I continued toward her. As soon as the Gilchrist kid vanished behind the door marked BOG, I leaned across the table and said, "My apologies, Miss. But do you happen to have an extra smoke? I left mine at home, under the delusion that I'd actually be able to abstain for a few hours. But I'm a lost cause. Now I'm afraid it's either bum one or head home early."

With the lit cigarette clasped between her lips, Zoey lifted the pack to offer one to me. But the boy pressed her hands back down to the table and said, "That last part sounds like an idea, mate. Have a safe ride home an' all."

As I leaned in a bit closer, my eyes instinctively narrowed. Calmly I said, "Nothing against you, but I think the decision is hers. Mate."

His hands moved away from Zoey's and clenched into fists, his nails biting into his palms. In the vicinity of his left temple, a prominent vein pulsed. The outer corner of his left eye twitched. I could see in his gaze that he was fantasizing about doing violence to me.

He said, "Naw so long as she's sitting in Kinny Gilchrist's booth, it ain't." His Scottish burr apparently swelled with his sense of indignation.

I leaned in closer still.

"Who the fuck," I said slowly, raising the volume of my voice with each syllable, "is Kinny Gilchrist?"

Several of the surrounding patrons fell silent at the mere mention of the Gilchrist name.

I waited as the young Scot took my measure, his lips curling up in a canine snarl, revealing a set of rotting teeth and an advanced case of gingivitis.

The answer to my question finally came from just over my shoulder.

"*I* am, aren't I?"

I straightened my body and half turned to look into the kid's eyes. I sensed fire behind them but little else. Thought, *The hell with it. If Zoey can't get the little prick outside, I will.*

"Well, Kinny," I said, "you might choose your friends more wisely. Wouldn't want someone sullying your good name now, would we?"

He took the bait, stuck his skeletal face in mine. "Do you not ken who you're fucking with? Or are you totally mental?"

He was grinding his teeth, though I wasn't sure whether it was a physical manifestation of his anger or a result of the lines of coke he'd just snorted in the men's room.

"Look," I said, "I came over here to bum a cigarette. But if it's a fight you want, why don't we step outdoors?"

His face drained of color. Beads of sweat formed on his upper lip, which had started to tremble. He didn't understand how someone could possibly be calling him out in a public house in his hometown. Clearly he wasn't used to mouthing off to strangers. Springburn probably didn't see many to begin with, especially not in dives like this.

"Raymond," the Gilchrist kid finally said to the much larger guy standing behind him, "I don't have time for this shite. Glass this cunt, will you?"

Kinny Gilchrist stepped aside as Raymond made a show of pouring the remainder of his pint on the floor. Several more patrons fell quiet and formed a loose circle to observe.

Once the pint was empty, Raymond stepped forward. Then, with the glass gripped tightly in his hand like a weapon, he threw a powerful right hook aimed at my jaw.

It came fast, but he'd telegraphed it in such a way that he might as well have gift-wrapped it too.

With a sharp *smack,* I caught Raymond's wrist in my left palm.

Then I leaned back, clenched my teeth, stiffened my neck muscles, took aim, and lunged forward, delivering a Glasgow Kiss, quick and dirty.

Raymond's head snapped back like he'd been shot, his nose shattered, his nostrils spewing blood down the front of his shirt like faucets.

I turned to Gilchrist, but he'd spun on his heels and darted for the exit before his buddy even hit the floor. The kid from the booth, the one who'd been so protective of my sister's cigarettes, was right behind him.

Shaking off the head butt, I grabbed hold of Zoey's hand and we scrambled toward the front of the pub.

In a show of appreciation, the crowd parted as quickly for us as they had for Gilchrist earlier.

Just before we hit the door, I told Zoey, "Make straight for Ashdown's crossover. Get in and lock the doors. Tell him there's no need to shadow me; I'll be fine."

As soon as we pushed through the door, we were hit head-on by a hard, cutting wind. Gales so mighty they were like living things. Living things that had just been playing dead before.

"Told ya," Zoey shouted as I let go of her hand.

I turned left, ran straight into the gust. Thanks to the reflective stripes running up the arms and legs of his tracksuit, Kinny Gilchrist was visible from a block and a half away. Even with my eyes reduced to slits from the wind.

Which remained every bit as brutal as the moment I'd first stepped into it.

On the bright side, the frigid air sobered me up right off. And after the first few strides, my legs seemed to be carrying me just as fast as they had a year ago in the jungles of Central and South America.

Running hard, I found myself consistently gaining on them. Trying to predict their movements along the way.

If they'd had a car, I thought, surely they wouldn't have parked this far from the pub. Which meant they were probably making for one of their homes.

Far behind me I heard an engine roar to life and imagined Ashdown ignoring the message I'd passed to Zoey.

Just as well, I thought. If the Gilchrist kid had reinforcements somewhere nearby, I might well be needing backup after all.

The Gilchrist kid and his remaining buddy skirted a fallen trash bin and turned left down a side road named Mollinsburn.

I leapt over the bin and maintained pursuit, the headlights from Ashdown's crossover crawling up my back as I took the corner.

Behind me the vehicle's tires screeched.

As it tore a left after us, I chanced a look over my shoulder.

And realized it wasn't Ashdown's crossover, but a dark green SUV with windows tinted blacker than the street.

The SUV gained speed as it blew past me.

Shit, I thought. *They'll snatch up Gilchrist and his pal and I'll be right back at square one.* I pushed myself harder.

But a few seconds later, when the Gilchrist kid stole a glance back at the SUV, I caught a look of fresh terror in his eyes. He lowered his head like a sprinter and went for the burn.

That's when I noticed the SUV's rear driver's side window gliding down.

A thick arm reaching out.

At the end of the arm was a gun.

And on the trigger, a pale finger just itching to fire.

Chapter 15

Fifty feet ahead of me, the SUV passed Gilchrist then swerved to the left, banking onto the sidewalk, blocking his path.

Gilchrist stopped on a dime. But his friend's reflexes weren't quite so cooperative; his momentum carried him well past Gilchrist, nearly to the door of the SUV. And a single blast from the .45 damn near blew his head clean off.

His corpse struck the wet pavement with a gory *splat*. Blood immediately began seeping into the paper-thin layer of just-fallen snow, tinging it raven black in the moonlight.

Gilchrist let out a shriek worthy of a young Jamie Lee Curtis as he spun, slipped, picked himself up, and bolted toward me.

I scanned the block. Halfway between us was an alley. I had no idea where it led, but it looked like Gilchrist's only out. So as the dark green SUV started to reverse off the curb, I darted forward and grabbed him by the tracksuit before he could fly past me.

Sounds of gunfire erupted all around us. Loud. The kind of cannon-like explosions that'll cause you to wake with tinnitus the next morning. Accompanying the shots, shattered glass, chipped bricks, the cry of metal on metal from doorways.

I covered Gilchrist with my body, pushing him forward into the alley, which was dark and narrow and—*Christ, no*—a dead end.

I surveyed the space. If not a back exit, I'd been hoping to find a ground-floor window to duck into or a doorway to use for cover, but nothing. Not even a few loose bricks we could use for weapons. The alley was empty save for a single scummy gray Dumpster that wouldn't stop a bullet fired from a BB gun.

With the SUV turning toward us, I had no choice. I reached for the filthy rubber lid of the Dumpster and flung it open. Over his protests, I hoisted Kinny Gilchrist onto my shoulder and heaved him into the trash. Slammed the lid shut just moments before the SUV's headlights flooded the alley.

To throw them off, I turned and made for the opposite end of the alley until I couldn't. Once I was forced to stop, I stood stock still, trying to catch my breath, staring dejectedly up at the massive brick wall before me as though Gilchrist had gotten over it but I hadn't. Hopefully the occupants of the vehicle were too dumb to realize that the wall's elevation made scaling it a physical impossibility for either of us, even working in concert.

Behind me the SUV idled in the maw of the alley.

When I wheeled around, two young men were spilling out of its doors, one from the passenger seat, the other from behind the driver.

Both held weapons but only the latter appeared to be carrying a gun, the .45 caliber Heckler & Koch that had killed Gilchrist's pal from the booth in the pub.

As they approached, the one with the gun leveled it at me.

I thought about the girl who may be Hailey and cursed myself inwardly. I didn't give a damn about the Gilchrist kid. What was I doing protecting him? I tried to reassure myself that he was my best chance at identifying the man in the photo with my daughter. But it was more than that; I couldn't deny it. I'd chased the kid out of the pub and now, right or wrong, I felt responsible for him.

"Where *is* he?" the gunman shouted.

The other, who was carrying a metal pipe, cried, "Just give him up, auld man, or we'll do you too."

In the distance the faint hum of another engine caught my attention.

"Come on, then," the gunman said. "Dinnae be a tube. You're naw his minder, are you?"

I stared hard at the two men. Even in the dim light of the moon, I could tell the gunman had bad skin, a permanent victim of the lethal combination of teenage acne, untrimmed nails, and a lack of discipline. The other one, the one with the pipe, was a good-looking kid. Tall, well-dressed, probably from money. Most important for my purposes, both had distinctive looks I would have remembered. Which meant I could be relatively certain that neither of these two were at the Old Soak a few minutes earlier. And that afforded me options.

Slowly, I raised my hands in the air. Spoke the first words in the first language that popped into my head.

"*Je ne comprends pas,*" I said as innocently as possible. "*Parlez-vous français?*"

The one with the metal pipe said, "Are you taking the piss?"

"Naw," the gunman said, shaking his head. "He's a bloody *frog,* isn't he? A feckin' cheese-eating surrender monkey."

The sound of the second vehicle was growing closer. If it was Ashdown, the situation would come under control. I just needed to buy a few extra seconds.

But before I could say another word, the driver of the green SUV shouted from his window: "Ewan, I think the bastart chucked the Chairman's boy into the rubbish."

The one with the metal pipe seemed to consider his options. Then he nodded to the gunman, who spun toward the Dumpster.

As the gunman raised the .45 and took aim at Gilchrist's hiding spot, I charged at him.

Spotting me in his periphery, the gunman held his fire and swung the weapon in my direction.

In that instant I was as large and as vulnerable a target as I could be. My only hope was to reach the handgun before he squeezed the trigger.

Desperately, I swiped at the air in front of me. Felt the metal of the muzzle beneath the fingers on my left hand and squeezed it tightly, guiding it to the side as I did.

The gun went off.

A hot blast scorched my palm.

Using my momentum, I threw my right hand up near my shoulder blade and raised my elbow in an uppercut that connected with the gunman's chin. His head snapped back, harder and faster than the one I'd head-butted back at the pub.

He dropped flat on his back and didn't move.

Meanwhile, the one with the pipe slumped forward, clutching his stomach.

I remained still as the pipe *clanged* against the blacktop, the sound echoing off the brick walls like a church bell.

I looked down at the gunman, who lay at my feet. He was conscious but barely. Muttering something about Inverness, the kid had no clue as to where he was.

The driver of the SUV sat slack-jawed, his eyes flicking from me to his fallen friends and back. Then finally settling on the good-looking kid who'd been carrying the pipe.

Following his gaze, I locked on the moaning, groaning form as he tried to slither in one direction and then another, all to no avail.

In the black of the alley, it was difficult to tell, but he appeared to have taken a gut shot. One from which he wouldn't recover.

In the next few moments, several things happened at once. The driver of the green SUV finally gathered his nerve and jumped out of his vehicle. He looked more like the kid with bad skin than the one who was dying.

I remained frozen as the driver reached into his jacket and drew a second handgun. Another HK .45, which he immediately trained on me.

The squeal of tires from behind him caused him to turn just in time to see Ashdown's Nissan crossover skid to a stop, effectively blocking the SUV from any chance of escape.

The gunman swung his weapon around. But Ashdown was already out of his vehicle, aiming his Glock 17, and shouting for the driver to drop the weapon and get to his knees.

The driver followed Ashdown's instructions.

"You all right, Simon?" Ashdown called out without looking at me.

Before I could answer we heard the bleating of sirens. Maybe as close as three or four blocks away.

"We need to get the hell out of here," I said, already moving toward the Dumpster.

Ashdown said, "Am I to take it that this would be a bitch to explain?"

I said, "Unless we want to spend the next seventy-two hours in a holding cell, we're not even going to try."

I lifted the lid of the Dumpster. A hand gripping a switchblade materialized out of the rubbish and took a swipe at me, slicing my left palm.

I swallowed the scream forming in the rear of my throat.

As I drew back, the knife and hand vanished into the trash.

I squeezed my bloodied left into a fist and stuffed it into the pocket of my old black leather jacket.

With my right, I dug into the garbage and fished around for a head, a neck, an arm, something.

Finally I felt flesh. A forearm. I slid my hand downward, gripped the kid's wrist and, with a sudden jerk, snapped it.

As he cried out in pain, I pulled Gilchrist free of the Dumpster and set him down on his feet.

His eyes widened as he fixed on the fallen figure, who now lay still in a pool of blood beside the pipe.

Battling my own agony, I shook Gilchrist out of his daze and ushered him quickly toward Ashdown's crossover. On the way, he glanced at the SUV's driver, who remained on the ground with his hands on his head. He also stole a glimpse of the kid with bad skin, but his gaze kept returning to the dead man.

I shoved him forward.

Zoey opened the rear door of the crossover and I tossed Gilchrist onto the backseat and climbed in after him.

Ashdown tucked his Glock into his jacket and jumped back into the driver's seat. The sirens were closing in, fast. Ashdown threw the transmission into drive and finally slammed on the accelerator.

We peeled away just as the sirens and flashing blue lights rounded the corner.

Chapter 16

I hurry down the stairs with photo albums and shoe boxes of videocassettes under my arms. I dump everything onto the dining room table and immediately begin flipping through the photo albums, searching for the most recent pictures of Hailey.

"Do you have any that were taken this year?" West asks.

I nod my head as I tear through the pages, certain now of what I'm looking for but completely unsure where to find them. "We took a vacation to Disney World just a few months ago. We still use a thirty-five-millimeter camera. We went through a half-dozen rolls of film."

"Those will do great," West assures me.

I twist my neck and peer into the living room where Tasha is on the couch holding her head between her legs. "I could use my wife's help," I say.

West says, "Let's leave her be for now. I'll help you find what we're looking for."

I close one album and move on to the next, muttering, "Tasha fills these albums. She knows where everything is."

"It's all right." West lifts the lid off one of the shoe boxes. "What are these?"

"Home videos," I tell her. "Your partner said we should turn some over to the media."

"Any recent ones?"

It takes me a moment. "Her sixth birthday party."

"Perfect."

I finally land on the photos taken during our most recent trip to Orlando. "Here they are," I say, pulling the pictures free of their sleeves one at a time. "Hailey in our hotel room at the Polynesian. Hailey in front of the ball at Epcot Center. Hailey with Donald Duck." A strange giggle emanates from my throat. "Donald's her favorite character for some reason. Tasha and I never understood it. To us he's just a bare-assed duck who always seems to be pissed off."

West chooses the best representations of Hailey and hands them to a uniformed officer along with instructions.

Meanwhile, I sort through the videocassettes. Most are labeled but in Tasha's atrocious handwriting. I crane my neck to see if she's recovered, but she hasn't moved an inch.

"This one," I say, plucking a cassette marked HAILEY'S 6TH B-DAY out of the shoe box.

"When did this party take place?"

"Just a few weeks ago."

"Where?"

"Right here. In the backyard. We hit on a nice sunny day in April."

"Do you happen to have a guest list?"

"A guest list?"

"A list of the people who came. It'll help us eliminate some sets of fingerprints, especially on the gate."

I hustle into the kitchen and grab a pen and a piece of paper then return to the dining room table. As I jot down the names of the people who were here, my hand trembles and I can barely recognize my own handwriting.

One of West's agents pulls her away for a private conversation while I try to think back to Hailey's party.

West sidles up next to me, says, "There's a locked safe in your bedroom closet. What do you keep in it?"

Puzzled, I say, "Important papers. My service weapon. Things like that."

"May I have the combination?"

I glance at the stairs and remember that West's team is conducting a search of the entire house. Earlier I saw agents coming down the stairs with small plastic bags carrying Hailey's hairbrush and toothbrush, presumably to obtain her DNA. Articles of Hailey's clothing—shirts and shorts and underwear—presumably for scent-tracking canines. But what the hell are they looking for in my safe?

It doesn't matter. I give West the combination.

"What else do you need?" I ask.

West says, "Why don't you sit down and take a breather? We have everything we need for now."

"And what's happening? In the investigation, I mean. What steps are being taken to find my daughter?"

"We've broadcast Hailey's description. We're reviewing sex offender registries to determine if there are any sexual predators in the area. We've initiated a neighborhood canvass using a standard questionnaire. We're contacting Hailey's pediatrician and dentist for her medical and dental records. And we've already set up a hotline to receive tips and leads."

"Shouldn't I be out there looking?"

"No, you need to be here, Mr. Fisk. In case there's a call. In case there's a ransom demand. In the meantime, our people are out there looking. Not just on the streets but in shrubs, crawl spaces underneath houses, in swimming pools, parked vehicles, in tree houses, on rooftops. Everywhere."

I turn and stare out the window. Say, "I feel like I need to be out there looking for my daughter."

West lays her hands on my shoulders and gently turns me in the direction of the living room. "You need to be here, Mr. Fisk. You need to be home. Loving and supporting and taking care of your wife. She needs you tonight. She's devastated. She won't get through this without you."

Chapter 17

Despite a right wrist that was clearly broken, Kinny Gilchrist refused to go to the hospital.

"They'll get to me in hospital, won't they? Especially after you killed one of them."

"I didn't kill anyone," I said quietly, sitting next to him in the back-seat of Ashdown's crossover. "His friend did him. His gun, his shot. I wasn't even carrying a weapon."

Meanwhile, with respect to the hospital at least, I found myself in a bleakly similar situation. My left palm, wrapped tightly in a clean white T-shirt Zoey had liberated from my luggage, continued bleeding profusely and felt like it was on fire. Though I hadn't yet been able to examine the extent of the injury, I knew the cut was long and deep and that there was possibly nerve damage. Because in addition to the agony, my fingers had gone numb. But making an appearance in the emergency room wasn't an option after what had happened in the alley off Mollinsburn. I might as well head straight to the prison infir-mary for all the good a visit to the local hospital would do me.

The kid said, "Except that's not how they'll tell it, will they? I'll be the one to catch the blame."

"Who are *they* anyway?" I said. "And why do they want you dead?"

"If not to hospital," Ashdown cut in from the driver's seat, "then where to?"

"*Home,*" the kid said. Only with his Scottish accent, it sounded like *hame.*

"Where's home?"

"East Kilbride."

"And where's that exactly?"

"South Lanarkshire, innit? Take the A727 west to Busby and on to Clarkston Toll."

I tried flexing my fingers with mixed results. Since the nerves in the hand are located in close proximity to the tendons, damage to one could well mean damage to the other. And the flexor tendons control movement from the wrist down to the fingers. Which meant that the knife wound Kinny Gilchrist inflicted on me may well have put my entire left hand out of commission for the duration of the search for Hailey. If not permanently.

Without a proper examination, only time would tell.

As we headed west, I used my remaining hand to remove my BlackBerry from my pocket. I pulled up the photo of Hailey and held the screen up to the kid's face.

"You know this girl?"

"Shove that phone up your arse," he cried, knocking my arm away. "I'm in blinding pain, aren't I? You broke my bloody wrist."

"I *saved* your bloody life."

On the other side of Gilchrist, Zoey was digging in her purse. "Here," she said, pulling out an unmarked pill bottle and twisting the cap. "Take two of these, you'll be right as rain."

"What are they?" Gilchrist said, holding out his uninjured hand. He popped the pills in his mouth and dry-swallowed both rather than wait for an answer.

"Hydromorphone," Zoey said, before popping two herself.

"*Banging,*" Gilchrist said. "This is potent gear. How'd you get your hands on it?"

She smiled. "Shagging a script writer; how else? For a tit-wank the quack will write me a taste of anything."

"Anything?"

"Blues to leapers and everything in between."

Ashdown's eyes blazed in the rearview.

"Brilliant, innit?" the kid said, laughing. "You *hoor*. I knew you were a class bird right from the start."

Ashdown made a sharp right.

Zoey looked over at me and shook the pill bottle. "How about it, little brother? Something for the pain?"

I turned away, muttered, "How about something for the kid's smell?"

Kid smelled like I'd just fished him out of a Dumpster.

Ashdown turned onto a residential road.

"My gaff's just two blocks down," the kid said. "Cut the next left, will ya?"

Ashdown pulled to the curb. "I think it's best we let you off right here."

"No way, mate. They'll *kill* me out here. They know where I live, don't they?"

"Who are *they*?" I said again.

Nearly a full minute of silence followed.

"Tell you what," the kid finally said to Ashdown. "You drive me right up to my front door and I'll tell you who the bloke in the photo is. Deal, mate?"

Ashdown's eyes locked on mine in the rearview.

I bowed my head yes.

The Gilchrist house was an L-shaped Dewar that didn't stand out among its neighbors. I'd been expecting a mammoth black iron gate or stone wall, maybe a moat, but there seemed to be no security at all. No men standing out front with guns, no bodyguards hustling outside to receive the Chairman's son following the kid's call to his father, explaining the situation.

"Our gangsters do things differently," Ashdown said by way of explanation.

Yet the scene outside the Old Soak was something straight out of New York or Los Angeles.

We pulled into the driveway and sat in silence.

"We're at war," the kid said quietly, staring down the street as we idled in the drive, waiting for his father. "Us and the Maxwells, I mean."

A flash of recognition crossed Ashdown's face in the rearview. "Tavis Maxwell?"

"None other."

From the glazed look in the kid's eyes, I assumed the hydromorphone had already kicked in and was doing its business.

I looked at Ashdown. "Who's Tavis Maxwell?"

He stared back at me with a pained expression. "Last King of Scotland, they call him. The Pablo Escobar of the UK. Only Maxwell's got more blood on his hands. And not just because he's lived longer."

The kid drew an audible breath. "He's a head case is what he is. And you . . ." He stared at me with what could only be described as pity. "You just topped his only son."

In the rearview, Ashdown's eyes widened in horror. "The one who got shot in the alley? That was Ewan Maxwell?"

"That was the punter, all right."

"Bloody hell."

"The one with the metal pipe?" I said, incredulous. "The only one without a gun?"

"He'd never carry a firearm," the kid said. "Why would he risk it? He's always got at least two gits around to carry *for* him."

"Another British thing?" I said.

Ashdown nodded. "Different culture. Firearms are a serious business in the UK. Get caught with one, you do serious time."

I said, "I don't mean to sound like a broken record, but it was one of Maxwell's two friends who shot him. Not me."

The Gilchrist kid shook his head. "Those two from the SUV, they're brothers. The MacBride brothers, Duncan and Todd. They have each other's backs, don't they? The MacBrides have already gotten their bloody story sorted. Believe me, mate."

"We've got to get the hell out of Glasgow," Ashdown said to me. "*Now.*"

With my good hand, I pulled up the photos on my BlackBerry. Held the screen in front of the kid's face again. Was about to ask him once more who we were looking at when Ashdown suddenly said, "Bullocks."

I glanced up. Several men were casually circling the crossover. At least two were carrying double-barrel shotguns.

One was aiming his through the windshield, directly at Ashdown's head.

Chapter 18

What you did, Mr. Fisk," the Chairman said in a voice that sounded uncannily like Sean Connery's, "you stepped right into the middle of a blood feud."

We were seated around his large but simple dining room table, the five of us: Gerry and Kinny Gilchrist, Zoey, Ashdown, and myself. The men outside had extended us an invitation. At least that was what they'd called it, though I suppose that an invitation with a double-barrel shotgun pointed at your head might well be considered a kidnapping or an unlawful imprisonment in some less sophisticated circles.

"The Gilchrist clan and the Maxwell clan," he continued, "go way back to a time when drugs were too dirty a business for our hands, to the days when prostitution, gambling, and loan-sharking represented ninety percent of our income. And the other ten percent was derived by collecting items fallen off of trucks."

The doorbell rang. Ashdown and I exchanged nervous glances as the Chairman rose from the table.

"Nothing to fear, boys," he assured us.

I watched Gerry Gilchrist step through the family room, nodding to his bodyguards along the way. I waited for him to stop, to step aside, to allow one of the guards to open the door so that he was well out of any potential line of fire. But as Ashdown said, gangsters do things differently in the UK. Gilchrist walked right up to the door and opened it wide without so much as a glimpse through the peephole. On the doorstep, he greeted a ragged middle-aged man with a mop of red hair and invited him inside.

The guest stumbled over the threshold but caught himself in the nick of time.

"Did I catch you on the piss?" Gerry Gilchrist said to him.

"'Course ye did. But it's naw a surgery, is it?" His Scottish accent was thicker than most I'd heard since arriving in Glasgow.

"It is though. My boy's willy got nicked."

A horrified expression washed over the guest's face. "Dae talk shite."

"I'm telling you," the Chairman said with a straight face, "Kinny was at the Old Soak, jaked on lager. At chucking-out time, he solicits a gobble from some weegie hoor. Only afterwards, he cannae find his wallet. So she pulls out a chib—and *snip*—takes his knob in lieu of payment." He motioned to his guards. "I had to send the boys here to retrieve the organ."

"Well, bugger *me*," the guest said. "He's lucky she left him his bawbag in case he wants bairns."

The two men stopped in the entryway to the dining room. The redheaded guest stared at Kinny, said, "Ye still have your willy, mate?"

The Chairman slapped the guest on the back. "Of course he does. It's just a wee thing, isn't it? The hoor would have required some serious tools; I'm talking *precision* medical instruments."

While the host and his guest howled, Kinny looked over at Zoey, shook his head. "My auld man's just having a laugh."

Finally, the Chairman settled down and made the introductions. "This, gents and lady, is Dr. Rory Lochhead."

"Well," Lochhead said, "nae really a doctor naw more."

"Bullocks," the Chairman said. "You're more of a doctor than anyone else in this room. And that's good enough for me."

Christ, I thought, looking down at the bloody T-shirt wrapped around my hand. *Maybe I should have taken my chances at the prison infirmary after all.*

Aside from your gammy hand," Lochhead said to me, the odor of cheap Scotch coming off him in waves, "do ye have any other health worries, like say, the HIV or AIDS, the diabetes, ye ken? Crotch critters? Anything like that?"

"My health's fine, doctor."

He chuckled. "All my mates just call me Doc."

"That's generous of them," I said.

Doc was examining my hand from his knees at the dining room table. He'd already seen to Kinny's wrist. After icing it and elevating it and icing it again, Doc had recommended Kinny take a trip to the hospital. When he was told the hospital wasn't an option, Doc iced the wrist again, then wrapped it in a makeshift splint. Kinny bitched and moaned until Doc finally handed him a bottle of dihydrocodeine. Kinny popped a couple of tabs, washing them down with three fingers of Dalmore, neat. He'd been quiet ever since.

Ashdown set his own glass of Scotch on the table, said to the Chairman, "So Tavis Maxwell put a hit out on your boy?"

"Aye," Gerry Gilchrist said, stroking the sides of his neatly trimmed snow-white beard with one massive hand.

"But Maxwell's son, Ewan, caught the bullet meant for Kinny, right?"

"That would seem to be the course of events, Mr. Ashdown."

Ashdown, Zoey, and I had just listened to the Chairman's tale of how the Gilchrist-Maxwell feud came into being and I'd begun to regret turning down Gilchrist's offer of whiskey.

Gerry Gilchrist and Tavis Maxwell were once best mates. They'd grown up together, swiped the local churches' donations together as tykes, raided post offices together as teens. They'd served as best man at each other's weddings, Gilchrist's in Glasgow; Maxwell's in Guadalajara, Mexico.

Inevitably, as adults, they became partners in crime.

Built an empire.

Struggled for power.

Split but remained allies in the drug trade, exploiting Scotland's heroin epidemic of the nineties.

"Then I got robbed," Gerry Gilchrist said. "A shipment of high-quality smack was diverted to a small group of Yardies in Manchester. All well and good, right? The price of doing business. But then, who goes and buys the product from those Manchester tossers? Tavis Maxwell is who.

"No big deal, you're probably thinking. And you're right; it wasn't. Sure, I had a head of steam for a while. I made some threats. But in the end, I was willing to let sleeping dogs lie. But then, just weeks later, my top lieutenant gets pinched. So I pay a visit to a mate who works with the bizzies."

"The bizzies?" I said.

"You know, the polis. The fuzz. The filth. Whatever you want to call them."

I refrained from glancing at Ashdown, who'd earlier told Gilchrist he was a used car salesman in North London. "Certified *pre-owned* vehicles, we prefer to call them," he'd said to help prop up his backstory.

"You don't say," Gilchrist exclaimed. "I own a dealership next town over."

Ashdown froze but Zoey quickly came to his rescue, explaining that the three of us were in Glasgow on holiday and hoped to pay a visit to a young girl Zoey had recently met in rehab in Essex. "Unfortunately," she added, "all we have to go on are a few photos on our mobiles. Rehab's bloody anonymous, you know. I can't even guess at her first name."

"Anyway," the Chairman said, continuing his story, "I asked my mate what the hell happened. Turns out, Maxwell's son-in-law, an eejit named Lorne Trask, had got *himself* pinched a few months earlier. And, what do you ken, the sod had turned informant.

"So, I went to Tavis and told him what had happened. Warned him that if he didn't take care of the problem, I would."

We waited as Gilchrist took another hit of whiskey.

"Well, let's just say, he didn't take care of the problem. And so I had to."

Chapter 19

The Chairman said, "Clan feuds like ours are nothing new, of course. You've probably heard tell of Arthur Thompson, another son of Glasgow. Another son of Springburn, in fact."

Ashdown nodded. "The Godfather, they called him."

"*Before* there was a book and movie by that name, if I'm not mistaken. Thompson made his mark in the fifties and remained on top for thirty years. Began as a simple money lender. Only he crucified those who failed to pay their debts. *Literally*, crucified them. Nailed them to doors or floors and watched them die slow, painful deaths."

"Christ," I said.

The Chairman nodded. "Exactly. Next Thompson went into the protection rackets. Even invested in some legitimate businesses. Ironically, it was those legitimate businesses that made him a wealthy man. But where's the bloody fun in that?"

Ashdown said, "He had a son, didn't he?"

The Chairman nodded again, this time staring down at the table, reflecting. "Thompson's son, Arthur Jr., he took over the drug trade in the eighties. Junior, of course, was his father's pride and joy."

Kinny lowered his head. Gilchrist didn't so much as glance in the kid's direction as he said it.

"Thompson's rival was the Welsh clan," the Chairman continued, "two members of which one day planted a bomb under Thompson's car. Only the goons planted the bloody explosive under the passenger seat instead of the driver's. Fucking thing blew and Thompson escaped without a scratch. Killed his mother-in-law though. Killed her to fuck. Which I suspect would be a blessing for most of us."

He cackled at his own joke. This time Zoey joined him. Purely, it seemed, in order to irritate Ashdown.

"But Thompson didn't have much of a sense of humor when it came to attempts on his life. So when he saw the two men he suspected of planting the bomb—Patrick Welsh and James Goldie— together in a van, he drove his car directly at them and ran them off the road. The van went straight into a lamppost killing them both instantly.

"As for Thompson's wife, Ruth, she was naw too pleased with her mother exploding. So a couple years after the incident, she forced her way into the Welsh home and stabbed Patrick Welsh's wife in the chest. Did a few years for her efforts.

"Of course, that was only the beginning. Junior, who everyone knew as Fat Boy, had taken his earnings from the drug trade and converted his council house into a luxury palace, a fortress he affectionately called The Ponderosa. That raised some brows, of course, and the polis started nosing around. Wasn't long before they caught Junior in a massive heroin bust.

"Junior served some eleven years. Of course, that kind of time isn't good for business. While Junior was inside, his men fell in with another clan and attempted a hostile takeover."

"Hostile how?" I asked.

"Junior got himself shot in the crotch. Just hours after he got out of prison. Right outside his beloved Ponderosa. He did the smart thing though. He checked himself into a private clinic and told the filth he'd accidentally hit himself in the dick with a drill bit.

"But Junior's luck at the Ponderosa never got any better. A few years later, someone ran him over on his own sidewalk. He survived the attempt and again he did the right thing. When the polis started asking questions, he told them to bugger off. And bugger off they did.

"Then a couple years later, Junior was back in the joint. Came home from prison on a furlough one weekend. Was home just six hours when he got himself gunned down. Died right in his father's arms. Outside the Ponderosa." He looked up at me. "If you're a father, it's a thing you can only imagine. The worst pain in the world, losing a child, and it's a pain you know will last forever. Right up through the day they put you in the ground."

On the table, the Chairman's cell phone started buzzing. I couldn't tell for certain, but it looked to me like a burner, a prepaid hunk of plastic that you can get for cash at your local convenience store.

"Aye," he said into the phone. "Well, that's naw much of a surprise now is it?"

When he ended the call he looked directly at me, said, "It seems you'll be spending the night with us, laddie."

I shook my head. "That's not necessary."

His eyes narrowed. "Don't presume to tell me what's necessary and what isn't. The three of you, you'll be bunking here tonight. End of story."

"And why's that?" I said.

"Because Tavis Maxwell has predictably lost his bloody head over the death of his boy. He's got dozens of men on the streets of Glasgow just waiting for you to show yourself."

Ashdown said, "Then it's best we leave Scotland altogether."

The Chairman shot him a look. "Naw, Mr. Ashdown. I'm afraid that's impossible at the moment. See, Maxwell's got men surrounding South Lanarkshire as well. They ken you're here. They don't dare approach my house; it's part of the pact we have with the old bill. But as soon as you walk out that door, you're fair game, all of you, including the lass."

Ashdown rose. "I think we'll take our chances."

Gerry Gilchrist slammed his fist down on the table. "Look, I don't need this aggro. I'm doing you all a bloody favor, and I expect some fucking gratitude for it." He turned to me. "Now, I'm sorry if I'm pissing on your strawberries. But you saved my boy. Which means, like it or dislike it, you're under my protection tonight. You three get yourselves killed, it's my reputation that's at stake. And I don't intend to be perceived as weak. Because when you're perceived as weak, that's when they come for you, the fuckers."

The Chairman stood from the table and stepped out of the room.

Kinny Gilchrist, who'd sat silently the entire time, shrugged his bony shoulders. "Guess that means meeting's adjourned. My father's mates will show you to your rooms."

Chapter 20

I was too wired to sleep. So was Zoey, though for an entirely different reason, I suspect. Following our discussion with the Chairman, she had gone off to another part of the house with Kinny, who'd hinted at having an ample and varied supply of party favors.

"So," she said as we sat alone in Gerry Gilchrist's sizeable library, "we chatted a bit about our adult lives back in Dublin, but neither of us really touched on our childhoods."

"We reminisced some," I said, leafing through a hardcover copy of *Madame Bovary*. I was searching for a quote I was fairly certain wasn't within the pages of any of Flaubert's works. Despite a poor memory for such things, these words had remained emblazoned in my mind since the day I'd first read them:

"One mustn't ask apple trees for oranges, France for sun, women for love, life for happiness."

"I'm not talking about the part of our childhoods we spent together, Simon. I'm talking about our childhoods after we'd separated."

I sighed, my eyes pinned to a random page. "When it was just me and dear old Daddy?"

"And me and Mum."

Her newly pensive tone unsettled me. I'd just gotten used to Zoey as she was, just hours ago completely erased from my mind the sister I'd expected her to be. Now she sounded like someone else entirely. Someone sober, figuratively if not literally. Someone earnest with serious questions that demanded serious answers. And my childhood, my years spent with Dr. Alden Fisk, weren't something I readily spoke about with anyone.

I glanced at the door, suddenly wishing Ashdown would materialize in its frame. But he was upstairs, asleep by now, or at least close to it. He'd looked exhausted (and more than a little intoxicated) when he wished us good night a half hour earlier.

"Did Daddy ever remarry?" Zoey asked.

I shook my head as I gazed up at the spines of the hardcover classics lining the Chairman's bookshelves. Bram Stoker, Mary Shelley, Robert Louis Stevenson, Charles Dickens, Edgar Allan Poe. Poe never failed to remind me of college at American University, of lying in the grass on the edge of campus reading stories alongside Tasha. My favorite had been "The Tell-Tale Heart."

"How about Mum?" I said

"She had someone for a time. During my primary education. He lived with us for a bit." She paused. "Was very clingy, like."

I looked at her and saw the little girl I'd played leapfrog with, the child who used the threat of brute force to persuade me into games of hopscotch and jump rope and tea party and dress-up when none of her darling girlfriends were around to entertain her.

"Not in that way," she said. "He was affectionate, he was. Not sexually though, not with me. More . . . *fatherly*, I suppose. More fatherly than Father ever was at least."

"What happened to him?"

"I don't entirely recall. I know he'd done time. I remember us visiting him in the nick. Shortly after you left."

My brow furrowed. "In prison?"

Since our chat at the Radisson last night I hadn't thought anything my sister said from then on could surprise me.

"He was a violent man," she said. "Although, as I recall, I was only occasionally on the receiving end."

"He beat Mum?"

She winced. "Hit her, sure."

"Often?"

"Often enough for her to take me and run."

"Run? Where did you run to?"

She shrugged. "Not far, actually. We remained in London. Mum could never have left London, not in a million years. I guess 'hid' is a more accurate term. We didn't run. We hid. Hid from him."

"How so?"

"Well, we did move for one." She rolled her eyes. "To Leyton of all places. And Mum changed our names."

"*She* did."

I thought about our exchange outside the Old Soak, when Zoey made a dig about how it wouldn't be much of a challenge for her to act as though she didn't know me.

I said, "You know, I tried to find you once." The words I spoke sounded far more defensive than I'd intended.

"Did you?"

I nodded but said nothing.

"I suppose changing our names didn't help in that respect," she said. "When was this?"

Two years ago, I thought. *Only two years ago. And only after a woman I fell in love with, the Warsaw lawyer Anastazja Staszak, convinced me it was "terrible" that I hadn't searched for my mother and sister before.*

I was ashamed to tell Zoey I'd waited all those years, couldn't bring myself to form the words. So I changed the subject. Or, more accurately, returned to the previous topic, which continued to sting.

"This man Mum dated, he was in prison *before* he moved in?"

She nodded, her eyes fixed on the plush carpet as though in deep thought. I was trying to piece together the timeline, but I needed more, and I could tell she wanted to move on from that particular subject. So I didn't probe. Instead I viewed her silence as an opportunity to escape the conversation altogether. Cowardly, sure, and I would deeply regret it later. But at the time I seized it like a junkie seizes the chance to get his hands on a fix.

"Speaking of prison," I said, setting the book down and rising from my chair with a theatrical stretch, "I have an early day tomorrow."

It was the truth. Kinny Gilchrist had been as good as his word, as Dickens might have said. Immediately after our meeting with his father adjourned, he'd identified the man in the photo with Hailey. Well, sort of.

"I don't ken *him* exactly," he said. "I ken his cousin, though."

"His cousin, then? Who's his cousin?"

"Cousin's Rob Roy Moffett, innit?"

"Where can I find him?"

"Naw far. Between here and Edinburgh."

"Can you take me to him?"

He lifted a bony shoulder nearly to his ear. "Naw tonight, I'm afraid."

"Why not?"

"Because there are naw visiting hours after dark."

"He's in hospital?" Ashdown had asked.

The kid shook his head. "HMP Shotts."

With that the kid had motioned to Zoey, who nodded and followed him upstairs.

I looked a question at Ashdown, who frowned.

"Shotts is a maximum-security prison," he said.

Chapter 21

TWELVE YEARS AGO

Can't sleep. Neither can Tasha. Now that we're lying in bed staring up at the ceiling, it seems foolish to have thought we might drift off.

In the darkness Tasha says softly, "This is the first night Hailey and I are apart. The first night since she was born."

What do I say to that?

Seconds pass. I know the longer I remain silent, the longer she'll dwell on that fact and the longer she dwells on it, the more pain she'll feel.

Hell, maybe that's what I want.

"We are going to find her," I try.

I don't know why I use the word *we*. *We* are not going to find her, not Tasha and I. We're not even allowed to leave the house. At least that's how we've been made to feel. If anyone's going to find Hailey it's Rendell and West or one of their people.

But Rendell and West went home for the day.

They're sleeping, Special Agents Rendell and West.

I glance at the digital clock on my nightstand. It's five A.M. Rendell and West have been sleeping for hours already. Maybe West had some difficulty. Maybe she rolled out of bed to check on her children once or twice. Maybe woke her husband to do it. Maybe she even invited her youngest into their bed as Tasha is wont to do when either of them is feeling frightened or sad or lonely. Maybe she eventually surrendered and swallowed a pill.

Maybe.

But she's asleep by now, West is. In her bed. Head sunken into her soft pillow. Maybe dreaming. Maybe warding off nightmares. Nightmares of stolen children like Hailey. Nightmares of the ones she's found; in her subconscious gone missing again. Nightmares of the ones she never found; in her subconscious found tortured or dead.

"Rendell will find her," I say in order to silence my thoughts. "Rendell and West, they'll find Hailey. I know they will."

Quietly, Tasha scoffs. "They don't even *know* Hailey."

I force my eyes shut. "They know their *job*."

"That's not enough. They're looking . . ."

I open my eyes. "They're looking . . . what?"

"They're looking in all the wrong places, Simon."

I glance at her in the darkness, probably the first time I turn my head in her direction in hours. I can't look at her in the light. I hate to admit it, even to myself, but it's the truth. I can't stomach to look at her. I can't stomach to look at my own wife.

"What do you mean, 'they're looking in all the wrong places?'"

Not only am I ashamed but I'm afraid. I don't want to hurt her. But for the first time in my life, I'm not sure I'll be able to control the words that come out of my mouth. I'll say something. Something subtle at first. And she'll catch it because Tasha's many things, but stupid isn't one of them. And if she doesn't catch it, I'll keep at it, I know I will. In time I'll openly blame her for Hailey's disappearance. Because any way you look at it, it's her fault, isn't it? It's Tasha's fault Hailey is missing. Tasha's fault my daughter's not sleeping under my roof tonight. Tasha's fault Hailey was . . .

Hailey was what?

Taken?

"All this bullshit," she says softly, "about the abductor being someone we know, someone who lives in the area, it's just statistics, right? And for the feds that's just a safe zone. What else are they going to say? I mean, the abductor being someone we know, that's the only way we'll possibly get her back, isn't it? If it's someone we don't know . . ." Her voice cracks mid-sentence. "If it's a complete stranger . . ."

She doesn't finish the thought. Doesn't need to. Stranger abductions are a completely different animal. We both understand that.

She's right, I think. *It's no one we know.* Because I've thought of everyone we know and ruled out each of them, one by one.

"They never reached your father," Tasha says, seemingly out of the blue.

It takes me a moment to catch her meaning. "They talked to a nurse at his practice," I say. "He's away on vacation."

"Which is oddly coincidental, don't you think?"

I turn toward her a second time, maintain the calm in my voice. "No. No, I don't think. It's May, for Christ's sake. He always goes away in May. He hates crowds, he hates heat."

He hates everything, I think but don't say. *Everything and everyone.*

Tasha digs in. "And the fact that his nurse says he went to Virginia Beach?"

"He owns a timeshare," I tell her. "He goes every year."

Is she serious, I wonder, or is she grasping for straws?

Or is she trying to get under my skin?

"Besides," I add, "Virginia Beach is over four hours from here."

She hesitates. "They weren't able to reach him at the timeshare either."

"Not yet," I say as casually as possible. "Which means nothing. He works hard all year, he takes a week off, remains in complete isolation."

"He's a doctor."

"So?"

"He can't be reached in case of an emergency?"

"He's not that kind of doctor, Tash. He's not a cardiologist or a neurosurgeon. He has a general practice and he has another doctor covering for him. A doctor he's known for more than eleven years."

She's quiet for a moment, then: "I don't believe in coincidences, Simon."

She *is* serious.

"Well then, you should pay more attention." My voice rises despite my efforts to control its volume. "Because the world's fucking full of coincidences."

There it is, I think. I said it. Subtly. Out of context. *You should pay more attention.* I knew it would happen.

From the resulting silence, I know she's caught it.

In the immediate aftermath, I ponder why the hell I'm lying here defending my father anyway. Why?

Because Alden Fisk's a complete waste of Rendell's time.

A complete waste of Hailey's time.

A complete waste of mine.

"My father is a piece of shit," I say, "but he's not a kidnapper."

Silence, and I think that's the end of it. I close my eyes. Listen to the twittering of the first birds of morning. Their chirps are soon drowned out by the huff and puff of a sanitation truck laboring up the street.

Once the truck's chugging is reduced to a faint grumble, Tasha mutters something under her breath. Three words, each as sharp as knives—and true.

"He kidnapped you," she says.

Chapter 22

Ordinarily, visiting an inmate in a maximum-security prison wouldn't have proven much of a hassle, at least not for me. As a U.S. Marshal, I'd spent plenty of time escorting violent prisoners to and from federal courthouses for their hearings or proffer sessions, their depositions or trials. But here in Scotland, I had a bit of a problem. Well, two problems actually.

For one, I was wanted by the Scottish Police for questioning in the deaths of Ewan Maxwell *and* Sean Turnbull, the late friend of Kinny Gilchrist whose body had been found splattered along the sidewalk near the alley on Mollinsburn Street.

Secondly, there was the issue of Tavis Maxwell, the so-called Last King of Scotland, who'd apparently put a contract out on my head worth one million British Pounds Sterling, which worked out to roughly $1.6 million U.S.

But I wasn't about to let any of that stop me from talking to Rob Roy Moffett at HMP Shotts this morning. Because finding Hailey continued to be a race against the clock. Last time Ashdown had spoken to D.I. Colleen MacAuliffe in Dublin, she'd told him that the Guards had positively identified the victim at the Stalemate as Elijah Welker and that visits to his home and office in London were imminent.

While MacAuliffe interviewed Welker's widow, a team of investigators would be working with New Scotland Yard to learn as much as possible about Welker's private investigation firm, especially with respect to the case that brought Welker to Dublin. It wouldn't be long before the Yard's computer geeks located the photos Welker had e-mailed to himself. Once they recognized Hailey, they would follow the same trail that led *us* here, searching for the man standing with Hailey in the photos. Only they'd have the distinct advantage of being able to contact the Scottish Police Service, which could well lead them directly to the man we'd already spent the better part of a day trying to identify.

We arrived at HMP Shotts a little after nine o'clock in the morning, after ditching Ashdown's rented Nissan crossover in favor of a black Jeep Grand Cherokee leased under the name of one of the Chairman's more legitimate businesses. Head-on, the exterior of the prison looked like a state-of-the-art library on a fancy university campus back in the States. One circular building (which I assumed held the prison's administrative offices), was flanked by two long rectangles encased in black bulletproof glass and red brick.

A couple of hours ago, while we were eating a hearty breakfast (of bacon, eggs, sausage, scones, fried mushrooms, grilled tomatoes, and hot porridge) in Gerry Gilchrist's kitchen, he gave us a rundown of the prison.

"Shotts is midway between Glasgow and Edinburgh, almost to the mile. The prison houses over five hundred of Scotland's most dangerous inmates, more than half of whom are serving life sentences for murder." He turned to Zoey. "Are you sure that finding your mate from rehab is worth this much trouble, love?"

"We were close," Zoey said in a way that sexualized the relationship. "*Very* close. And I fear she's prone to relapse."

Nonplussed, Gilchrist's eyes drifted toward the second floor, where his son had fed Zoey herself a buffet of drugs only hours ago.

"Unlike myself," Zoey added, "she *can't* handle her drugs. Especially when she's on her own. Without me, she'll OD. And when she does, I know I won't be able to live with myself."

He finally nodded his understanding. "So you want to bring her back to London with you."

"That's the plan."

"All right, then," he said. "But let me give you a little background on Rob Roy Moffett. Because he's naw your average prisoner. He's naw even your average killer."

We pulled up to the second of two security gates and Ashdown presented our passports. The guard took a stroll around the Grand Cherokee, took down the plates, then circled again with a mirror that allowed him to inspect the undercarriage.

Once he was satisfied we weren't there to facilitate a prison break, he returned to his station and lifted the gate.

Ashdown, who insisted he'd interviewed hundreds of Moffetts in his career, graciously offered to meet with this Moffett on his own. But I declined to send a proxy. With the stakes this high, I needed a face-to-face with Rob Roy Moffett, and I wouldn't settle for anything less.

"Better if you don't come in with me, Detective," I told Ashdown as we pulled into the visitor's parking lot. "I don't want to make it look like we're ganging up on him. Besides, you'd be much more useful lying low here in the lot in case the Maxwell boys are planning an ambush."

"As you wish," Ashdown said, glancing in the rear of the Grand Cherokee, where Zoey again lay sprawled out, sleeping. "The princess and I shall await your safe return."

I stepped out of the Grand Cherokee and squinted into the moody silver sky. Then I hiked across the parking lot and was welcomed through the front door like a guest of honor at a royal ball. I scanned the lobby and discovered that the interior of the prison was every bit as modern as the exterior.

At the front desk, I was greeted all around by smiles. No doubt on account of my perceived association with Gerry Gilchrist, who'd arranged the meeting with Rob Roy Moffett at the prison earlier this morning.

"Let me give Whitehead a ring," he'd said after warning us of Moffett's nature. "The warden owes me a few favors, doesn't he?"

Ashdown's eyebrows rose. "The warden owes *you* a few favors, eh?"

The Chairman offered up a mirthless smile. "Of course he does. Don't be so daft, you bloody used car salesman."

After breezing through security, I was escorted to a small room with walls so immaculately white they nearly blinded me.

A nice place, I thought, *for a prison.* Hell, maybe getting pinched for Ewan Maxwell's murder wouldn't be the worst thing in the world. But my arrest would have to wait until I found Hailey and got her the hell out of Europe. In which case, I'd probably never return to the United Kingdom anyway. At least not by choice.

After waiting for all of six minutes, a large man wearing more chains than the ghost of Jacob Marley was led into the room by a pair of guards.

The Chairman had described Moffett as an absolute maniac, but Moffett certainly didn't look the part as he stood before me awaiting instructions. He looked like he might be heading out to fix your neighbor's cable box.

"Have a seat," I said.

He sat on an orange plastic chair positioned directly across from me.

When I asked the guards if Moffett could be unshackled for the visit, they looked at me as though I'd just asked if I could light a doobie in front of the Queen.

"You do ken who he is, don't you?" one of the guards asked.

I nodded.

The other guard laughed. "We let him out of those shackles, we may as well call you a priest right now so's that he can get here in time to administer yer last rites."

I ignored him. Waited for the guards to leave the room but soon realized they weren't going anywhere.

I said to Moffett, "Don't trust you much around here, do they?"

"They're a mistrusting lot," he said affably. "Must be in their nature."

Moffett's shaven head was large and as round as a melon. His skin was glowing and red, as though he'd just stepped out of a piping shower. Only he wasn't wet; except for a pair of watery eyes, he appeared to be dry as a bone.

I studied his clothes. A light blue polo with the logo of the prison, HMP Shotts, over khakis. Again I flashed on a university back home.

"What's HMP stand for?" I said, trying to make small talk in an effort to make him comfortable around me.

"Her Majesty's Prison, innit?" His voice was soft, his tone formal as though he was interviewing for a job.

"How old are you?" I asked him.

He shrugged a massive shoulder. "Twenty-nine, right?"

"And how long a sentence did they give you?"

"Twenty-five to life."

"For?"

"You mean the charges?" He had a thick Scottish accent like Doc's from the night before, so that *charges* sounded a hell of a lot more like *chairges*.

"Sure," I said. "What were the charges?"

"Double murder, then. One attempt. Kidnapping. Torture." He rattled off his convictions with all the gravitas of an English nanny reciting a grocery list.

I bowed my head in thought. "Quite a list."

"It is, innit?"

I lifted my eyes to meet his. Moffett's calm was beginning to unnerve me. This was one sadistic prick for sure, a psychopath all the way. Yet he expressed himself like an accountant a week past tax day, perhaps following a few Reef Runners and tabs of Ativan poolside in Barbados.

"You were a drug dealer, I was told."

He smiled. "A wee bit of one, yes."

"And the two murders," I said. "What happened?"

The smile didn't budge. "One, he fell off a bridge."

"And the other?"

"The other, he just died, didn't he?"

I widened my eyes, feigning surprise. "Just died, huh? How?"

"Choked."

"On his food?" I said lightly. "Maybe some haggis?"

Moffett laughed. "Naw on his food, mate."

"You gave him some help, then?"

"Maybe." He chuckled. "I gave him the rope, see. Helped him put it round his throat. Tightened it a wee bit. Next thing ya ken, his eyes are popping out of his skull."

"A bad guy?" I said, expressionless.

He shrugged. "He was my cousin. And I don't like to talk badly about family, you understand."

"And the dead?"

"Especially naw of the dead," he said, smiling. "But, truth be told, my cousin dinnae pay his debts."

"Drug debts?"

"Aye." Following a few seconds of silence, he added, "I gave him a choice though."

"A choice?"

"His life or his cock."

I swallowed hard, hoping he hadn't noticed. "Which did he choose?"

"Neither." He waited a few ticks. "So I chose for him."

"You chose to take his life."

He smiled again. "Well, when you think about it—I mean, *really* think about it—what am I going to do with a cock, right?"

I nodded, waited for my pulse to slow.

"You had a score to settle with this cousin of yours? Aside from the drug debts?"

"Naw really. It's just something that happened, innit?"

"Just something that happened."

"Live by the knife, die by the knife, right?"

"I suppose."

"Don't you ever argue with your mates?"

"Sometimes," I conceded. "Though those arguments don't usually end with my mate's eyes popping out of his skull."

He shrugged. "Guess you and I are just different, then."

"I guess we are."

Moffett shifted in his chair, the metal legs scraping against the linoleum floor. He leaned his head back and filled the ensuing silence by whistling a tune. Some sort of Scottish jig.

Then he turned back to me. "I played a bit of football with him though."

"Did you?"

"Aye."

"As kids?"

"Naw, after."

"After what?"

He smiled again. "After I sawed off his head. I kicked it round a bit with a mate of mine. Got some fresh air, the three of us did." He puffed out his chest. "Some exercise, they say, is good for the soul."

I looked down at my injured left hand to avoid his gaze. My hand was sloppily bandaged. The pain in my palm was unbearable and I'd refused to take anything for it because I needed to stay alert. What concerned me most, however, wasn't the pain; it was that the fingers remained completely numb.

"So," Moffett said, "what brings you by?"

I looked up. He wasn't in any rush to get rid of me, just curious.

With my good hand, I pulled out the photo Gerry Gilchrist had printed in his study. I unfolded it and held it out in front of Rob Roy Moffett.

"You know the girl in this photo?" I asked.

He shook his head slowly.

"How about the man with her?"

He nodded just as slowly. "Aye."

"You know him?"

"Aye."

"How so?"

His eyes remained glued to the photo. "He's a cousin of mine."

Unlike his cousin, Moffett wasn't inked, at least not anywhere I could see, and his earlobes remained intact. But he did have scars. Plenty of them. On his face, on his arms. Many from deep, deep cuts. Some clearly self-inflicted.

"Your cousin," I said.

"Aye. But naw the one who died."

"Good to know." I drew a deep breath, said, "What's his name, your cousin? The one in the picture, I mean." Kinny hadn't known. Or if he had, he wouldn't tell.

For the first time Moffett hesitated. "Why are you looking for him?"

"I'm not," I told him. "Not really. I'm looking for the girl."

He looked me in the eyes. "Why are you looking for the girl, then?"

"Because . . ." I suddenly found myself fumbling for words. I hadn't expected to get emotional in front of this lunatic. But now my throat was closing up, my vision becoming blurry with tears that would never fall.

"Twelve years ago," I finally managed, "someone took my six-year-old daughter."

He processed this, then: "Could naw have been my cousin, mate. He would've been, like, fourteen years auld his own self."

"No," I said, "I know he's not the man who took her. But he's my only lead to this girl. This girl in the photo. Who may well be my daughter."

His lips parted. "Oh, I see." Following a few moments of reflection, he said, "And if you find her?"

"What do you mean?"

"I mean, if you find your daughter, does it all end there? Do you pick her up, tell her 'Daddy's here now, everything's gonna be all right' and bring her home?"

"What do you care?"

"Enquiring minds wanna know, right?"

I stared at him, gazed into his watery eyes and saw nothing but darkness. Like the bottom of the blackest sea.

His motivations were simple enough, transparent enough. Maybe even fair. I wanted to extract something from his head; he wanted to extract something from mine.

"No," I said finally, "that won't be the end of it. I also want to find the man who took her. I want to find out why." I paused but his eyes insisted I go on. "And then I'm going to make him answer."

"To the polis?"

"Not to the police."

"To who, then?"

"To me," I said. "I'm going to make him answer to me."

"Answer what? Questions, like?"

I shook my head. "Not just questions."

"What, then?"

"I'm going to make him answer for what he's done. To my wife, to my daughter. I'm going to make him answer for what he's done to *me*."

Chapter 23

In Edinburgh, Zoey and I checked into the Tucker Guest House on Orchard Brae West. The Tucker was a two-story brick bed-and-breakfast less than one mile from the city center, which itself was compact and divided neatly in half by Princes Street with Old Town to the south and New Town to the north.

Family-run by a warm, old couple named Brenda and Alan, the Tucker was not exactly what I'd had in mind for this part of the operation. But Ashdown only knew top-end accommodations like the Bonham, the Balmoral, the Caledonian, the Le Monde; and when Zoey stayed in Edinburgh she slept wherever and with whomever she happened to be partying at the time. So we made our reservations sight-unseen and the Tucker was where we wound up.

At the desk, we hit our first speed bump.

"Cash or check in Pounds Sterling only," Brenda said as I set down my AmEx. "We cannae accept credit or debit 'cause we're naw set up for it. We're just a wee establishment, see?"

When she noticed my pained expression, she added, "Sorry fer the inconvenience, laddie. But there's a cash machine jus' about a hundred yards down the road."

"Not necessary." I reached into my pocket and pulled out sixty pounds. Problem was, I'd been saving the cash for the drug-dealing cousin of the murderous psychopath I'd just met at Shotts—the heavily inked brute in the photo with the girl who may or may not be my daughter. But I couldn't very well tell Brenda and Alan that, now could I?

As Brenda counted out the cash, I noticed a sign posted over her head. It read: NE'RE SPEAK ILL O' THEM WHOSE BREID YE EAT.

Alan followed my stare. Said, "That's a warning, laddie, naw to insult yer host."

When I turned to him, he wasn't smiling; he was dead serious.

Brenda slipped me a handwritten receipt. "Yer in the Lavender room, second floor as requested. Naw smoking whatsoever, but you do have free Wi-Fi."

"Thanks," I said.

"Our guests tend toward the quieter side," she cautioned me. "So please respect yer neighbors."

"Of course."

She eyed my left hand. "And Western General Hospital is but a ten-minute walk from here if you need it."

With my right, I pulled out my BlackBerry and said to the old woman, "This fellow in the picture, he's our cousin. Okay if he drops by later today?"

The old woman lifted the spectacles hanging from around her neck and studied the photo. She scrunched up her already wrinkled facial features, trying none too hard to hide her disgust. "I suppose. So long as he doesn't stay the night."

"He won't be staying long at all," I assured her. "But I'd be grateful if you could give us a heads-up when he gets here."

"A heads-up?"

"A courtesy call."

"I see." She picked up a pen and tested it on a scrap of paper. "His name, then?"

"Angus Quigg," I said.

*   *   *

Upstairs, I sat on the bed while Zoey toured the eight-by-eleven room. I pulled out the phone number Rob Roy Moffett had given me at Shotts prison and dialed. I listened to one ring followed by a sound I hadn't heard in at least a few years, and a much longer time before that. Three beeps then dead air. I entered the Tucker's number along with the extension to our room. Then I hung up and waited.

"What are we ordering?" Zoey said.

"Ordering?"

"Yeah, he's gonna expect us to order something, isn't he? He's a drug dealer, not a stripper. He's not gonna show up just to shake his bum."

"All right," I said. "What should I order?"

"How much cash do you have?"

"Less than I entered with, thanks to Brenda and Alan."

"So how much?"

"A couple hundred. Moffett said Quigg can procure whatever his clients desire. I figured I'd ask for some weed."

She considered this. "Let me pick up the phone when he calls. You sound too much like the filth. He'll be onto you in a second, little brother. Take it from me."

A few minutes later, the phone rang. I stood, but Zoey looked me back onto the bed, then answered.

I could only hear her side of the conversation. Which was plenty.

"Hey, Q, I'm calling to party. . . .

"Your number? From your cousin, the one who's starred up over at Shotts. . . .

"Yeah, that's right. . . .

"Wanted to invite some mates over, didn't I? Make this a bash . . .

"Well, Tina and Charlie, for sure. Lucy's if she's round. . . .

"Bafta. By the way, brown is my favorite color. . . .

"Oh, don't be so naughty." She paused for effect. "Least not till you get here."

As she spoke to Quigg, I inspected the HK .45 the Chairman had given me this morning. Two magazines, ten rounds each. Twenty shots.

"If I'm the fuzz," Zoey said into the phone, "then Amy Winehouse is alive and queening Great Britain. . . .

"Decent. Oh, and I'll need some artillery, love. . . .

"Yes, I think you'll find me quite fit. . . .

"The Tucker, then. You know it?

"Kicking. Two B. Or not to be, right?

"All right, then. See you soon, love . . ."

Zoey set down the phone.

"How long?" I asked her.

"One hour."

I paced from one end of the room to the other. A total of ten steps. "What do we do till then?"

"How about we continue that convo we started last night at the Chairman's?"

I suppressed a sigh.

"Tell me, Simon. Tell me about you and Daddy in the good ol' U.S. of A."

I gave her the abridged version of life with Alden Fisk. Hit on the highlights (few) and the lowlights (many). Described the back and forth on everything from his insistence that I lose my British accent (and my pushback) to his urging me to follow in his footsteps by going to medical school (and my adamancy about becoming a federal cop). Told her how he deflected questions about my mother and sister using every tool in the trade, from diverting the subject to punishment and rewards to emotional blackmail.

He used guilt, I said. When I asked about Mum he asked was he not good enough. Didn't he raise me? Sacrifice for me? Pay for my education? When that got old he resorted to anger. What business is it of yours, he'd demand. They're part of *my* history; you don't even remember their faces, so why do you care? What do they matter to you if they matter nothing to me?

"I visited her grave," I said some forty-five minutes later.

Zoey frowned. "Whose grave?"

"Mum's."

"When?"

"Roughly two years ago."

"You were in London? What for? Work?"

I hesitated. "To find you and Mum, actually. I didn't want to mention it earlier, because I was a bit embarrassed."

"Embarrassed, why?"

"Because I waited so long to come looking for you."

She shrugged. "We didn't exactly make a proper effort ourselves, you know."

"I know," I said quietly, with my head down. "And that's why it took me so long. Part of the reason anyway. I told myself if you and Mum wanted to find me, you could have. Dad's Rhode Island medical practice was always listed. Hell, I'm pretty sure our home address and number were listed as well."

Zoey shrugged again. "Wasn't really up to us, was it? I mean, you and me, while we were children. Would have been up to Mum and Dad to seek out their offspring." She paused. "But I suppose their hatred of each other was too great."

It was my turn to frown. "That's something I never understood. How hatred for your spouse could outweigh love for your child."

"I don't know, do I?"

"I pondered it for a while. But it really came home to me after I had my daughter, Hailey. Minute she was born I knew it was impossible for me to ever despise Tasha in such a way that I'd give up Hailey being part of my life."

Several minutes passed in silence.

"Did Dad ever talk about me?" she finally asked. "I mean, in the very beginning at least?"

"I don't recall," I lied. "And Mum?"

"She spoke of you all the time for a while. After we ran." She rolled her eyes. "I mean after we hid from our boogeyman."

I stared at myself in the mirror above the dresser. "I should have looked for Mum earlier, while she was alive."

"You didn't know that she'd died. She wasn't so old. You didn't know you'd find her at Streatham Cemetery when you arrived."

I nodded, but I was still disgusted with myself. "When I saw her grave she'd already been belowground a decade."

Zoey bowed her head. "How'd it look, her grave? I haven't been there in years."

"It looked fine. I'd noticed she'd used her maiden name. 'Tatum Fuller,' it read. 'Beloved Mother.'"

"The headstone was so small. I've always felt badly about that."

"Don't."

"So what happened after you found her? Did you think to come looking for me?"

I turned to her. "Of course I did. That had been the plan anyway. But after seeing her headstone, seeing how long she'd been dead, I didn't think I could handle a reunion with you. At least not right away."

I thought about the date of death on her headstone, how close it had been to Hailey's disappearance. Made me think of that first night, after Hailey was taken. When Tasha and I were in bed, arguing. Over my father no less. And whether he was a viable suspect.

At the time Hailey was taken, my father had been away. At Virginia Beach. Closer than Rhode Island but still four and a half hours from our home in D.C. The feds hadn't been able to reach him at his office or his timeshare.

That night Tasha told me she didn't believe in coincidences.

I'd told her, *"Well then, you should pay more attention. Because the world's fucking full of coincidences."*

Seeing the date on Mum's headstone at Streatham Cemetery caused that conversation to play out in my head all over again. Not just once, but dozens of times over the weeks that followed.

Now it was playing out all over again.

I parted my lips to ask Zoey how Mum died but never got out a word.

Because the room phone started to shrill.

Angus Quigg had arrived.

Chapter 24

Yer, uh, guest has arrived, Mr. Fisk."

I thanked the old woman and hung up the phone.

Zoey said, "Best you wait in the loo."

"Won't he check it out?"

"He'll be checking out other things, little brother, trust me. Besides, if he does, so what? Most he'll be carrying is a knife, won't he? You can handle one of those. At least according to poor little Kinny."

I held up my bandaged left hand. "And look what I earned for my troubles."

I stepped into the bathroom. Closed the door behind me and leaned against it, breathing in and out slowly, thinking about another struggle I'd had with a knife, two years ago in front of a clinic in Minsk. A Russian named Jov had attempted to drive the blade into my throat. I'd blocked the blow. But the knife plunged deep into my left forearm.

From my position on top of him, I'd howled in pain. Punched the Russian flush in the face, until blood spewed from both sides of his nose. Then I pushed hard under his chin so that the blood would stream into his eyes, blinding him.

I dislodged the knife from my left forearm. Meant to sink the blade deep into his chest.

Only there had been enough killing by then.

Now, as I stood against the bathroom door, I wondered if I could possibly show Hailey's abductor the same mercy. Or whether I meant every word I'd said to Rob Roy Moffett this morning at Shotts. At the time I'd told myself I was just feeding him what he wanted to hear. Like a politician tossing red meat to the masses. But maybe that was just me telling myself what *I* wanted to believe.

A few moments later, a knock interrupted my thoughts. I pictured Zoey padding across the small room and opening the door to find the man from the photos on my phone, the man with the head shaven like Moffett's, with the gauged lobes and heavily inked arms and neck. The man with the girl who may or may not be Hailey Fisk.

She'll be different too, I told myself. Even more dissimilar than Zoey was from the Tuesday I'd known. If it's Hailey at all, she'll be nothing like the little girl who I held in my arms before I left for Bucharest twelve years ago.

Clear as day, I saw Kati's e-mail in front of my eyes. *Finder, open the two attachments and call me right away.* First, the computer-generated fantasy. Then the real-world image of a harried woman who'd just committed murder by slicing a man's carotid with a broken beer bottle in a pub full of people.

I heard Quigg's voice.

He was with her, I thought. This man, he'd touched the young woman who may be Hailey. Had spent time with her, maybe even loved her.

Maybe used her.

I did my best to clear my head. Listened to Zoey and Quigg communicate in UK street slang but couldn't make out what was going on.

Sounded cordial enough, I supposed.

I glanced out the tiny bathroom window onto the street. During any other season the multitude of trees would have blocked any view. But not now, not in the heart of winter. Everything once green was now bare and dead or dying. Which allowed me to look out on the rustic city center, the Georgian urban architecture, the quaint cobblestone walks.

It was dusk. Snow continued to fall and was sticking to the ground. The wind wasn't so fierce but few Edinbronians had ventured out. Or if they had, they'd already found their seats in one of the dozens of warm pubs.

There were cars on the roads, especially on Princes Street, but not nearly as many as there were earlier.

I could live here, I thought.

It was an odd phrase to materialize in my head. I'd been in cities all around the world, and not once could I recall thinking something similar. Not even in Warsaw where Ana Staszak had taken a job as a criminal prosecutor. Maybe it was the circumstances, the stress. Maybe I actually felt close to finding Hailey. Maybe I was just getting old and tired of running from city to city, country to country.

I listened for Zoey and Quigg, could already smell the pungent aroma of crack smoke and thought Brenda would have a heart attack if she knew.

I'd promised Zoey three minutes. Only two had passed. So I continued gazing out the window. I recognized most of the landmarks but couldn't identify very many by sight.

Edinburgh Castle, however, was unmistakable.

And in the center of it all, North Bridge, which connected the New Town to the Old.

Somewhere out there was Edinburgh University.

Maybe Hailey would be interested in going there.

With thirty seconds remaining, I mentally swatted away that ridiculous notion and lowered my eyes to the street just below our window.

Headlights approaching.

Several pairs.

The vehicles large and dark in color.

"Rob Roy Moffett," I said under my breath, "you goddamn snitch."

The Maxwells had tracked us. And it had probably been cake. We'd left too simple a trail to follow. If Gerry Gilchrist had an in with the warden, no doubt Tavis Maxwell had ins too. When we entered the lot at HMP Shotts, the guard had noted the make and model of our Jeep Grand Cherokee, had taken down the license plate, had taken down our names.

Someone had phoned Maxwell.

Maxwell had asked who I'd visited.

Rob Roy Moffett, they would have told him.

Maxwell maybe paid Moffett a visit. Maybe he didn't have to. Maybe he just got him on the phone. Moffett would have told Maxwell he'd given us his cousin's name and pager number. No love lost between cousins in that family, we'd already established that.

Once they had Angus Quigg's name, they would have come to Edinburgh to follow him.

Or to seek out the Jeep Grand Cherokee, which I couldn't see from our window.

Christ. Maybe Ashdown was already dead.

I quickly scanned my BlackBerry. I'd received no calls, no texts.

Hell, maybe Angus Quigg was in on it too.

Didn't matter. Either way, the Maxwell boys were coming.

And Zoey's three minutes were up.

Chapter 25

I squeezed the polymer grip of the Heckler & Koch until it felt like an extension of my hand. My damaged left continued to be useless. So I lifted my foot, aimed just below the knob, and kicked out the door.

"Easy, Quigg," I hollered.

I trained the .45 on him, but all he had in his hands were a crack pipe and a cheap plastic lighter.

"*Sod* it," he shouted as he rolled off the bed. "What is this *shite*?"

"We're not the filth," Zoey shouted to him. "We're brother and sister. We just have a couple quick questions for you."

"Not now," I said, lowering my weapon. "We've got some uninvited guests coming this way."

Downstairs the bell jingled, which meant someone had entered through the front door. I listened and heard Brenda's voice, but I could make out neither what she was saying nor with whom she was speaking.

I threw a look at the far window but I'd already ascertained it wasn't a viable route of escape. A diversion at best.

To Quigg, I said, "Do you know the Maxwells?"

"Do I?" he shouted. "Do I fuck?"

"I'll take that as a resounding yes. And I'm assuming they're not friends of yours?"

"Competition, mate. But what the hell are they doing here in Edinburgh?"

"Looking for me," I said.

I took a long look at Angus Quigg. He appeared just as he did in Welker's photos. Was even wearing the same clothes.

"You two stay here," I said. "If they corner us in the room, we're all toast."

"Simon, *no!*" Zoey shouted.

But I'd already tucked the HK into my jacket and opened the door.

The hallway was clear, but there were feet on the stairs. Which meant the hallway wouldn't be clear for long.

I reached back and closed the door behind me and drew the HK.

Short hallway. Only two other rooms besides ours. Which meant I'd have to fire straightaway. No time to spare. No waiting for the whites of their eyes or things of that sort.

The door from the stairwell started to open.

I raised the HK, finger hovering around the trigger.

"Don't shoot!"

Ashdown's face suddenly appeared in the door frame. His cheeks were red. He was out of breath.

"Maxwell's boys are outside," he cried.

"You don't say." I lowered my weapon. "I thought you were one of them."

"No, they're parked all along Orchard Brae, waiting on an opportunity."

"They're not coming in?"

"No," he said. "We're in a bloody bed-and-breakfast. They wouldn't storm a mom-and-pop."

"Let me guess," I said. "Too polite?"

"British gangsters do things differently," he said.

* * *

What about the cops?" I asked once we were back in the room.

"They're bent, Simon." Ashdown ran to Zoey and grabbed hold of her by her bare upper arms and said, "You okay, love?"

She shoved him away.

"Bent enough they'll allow a shootout in Edinburgh's city center?" I said.

"You're a wanted man anyway. You killed Maxwell's son. The way the cops see it, Tavis Maxwell is owed blood. It's gangster justice, pure and simple."

"I didn't kill anyone," I said, though I knew by then it was pointless.

Zoey asked, "What do we do now?"

I turned to Ashdown. "Why the hell didn't you call me? Where's the Grand Cherokee?"

"I had no time. The minute I spotted them in my rearview, I had to make a run for it. I knew that if they'd found us, it meant they had our plates."

"So the Grand Cherokee?"

"Is done for. I heard them go to work on it as soon as I started running."

"Can't you call the NCA?"

"I could," he said. "But then the search for Hailey is over, and at least one of us is behind bars for the murder of Ewan Maxwell. Maybe the Turnbull kid as well."

At the mention of Hailey's name, I swung my head in Quigg's direction. Studied his face.

Saw nothing that wasn't there a moment ago.

I pocketed the HK again.

With dread crawling up my spine, I removed the BlackBerry from my jacket.

It could be that my search for Hailey was to end right here, right now anyway. If that was the case, Ashdown could call the National Crime Agency. I could turn myself in, admit to the murders of Ewan

Maxwell and the Turnbull kid. Clear Ashdown and Zoey of any wrongdoing and let them both return to London, safe.

I'd likely never make it to trial anyway. Maxwell would get to me inside Shotts. Hell, it might well be Rob Roy Moffett who receives the nod. Regardless, I wouldn't put up a fight. I'd take the chib in the gut or wherever Moffett chose to place it. I'd bleed out, and that would be the end, the end of all of this.

On my phone, I pulled up the photos of Angus Quigg and the girl. Looked hard at the young woman who could be my daughter one last time.

Then I held up the screen in front of Quigg.

"Who in bloody hell took that?" he said.

"Doesn't matter," I told him quietly. "Who's the girl?"

"Shauna," he said without hesitation. "Shauna Adair from Springburn."

"How long have you known her?" I asked.

"Forever, like. I've ken her since we was born."

Chapter 26

Quigg's words were like a knife to the gut. For nearly a minute I stood, wilting, like a weed waiting to be plucked from the earth.

The room spun around me, a white flame flared at the edge of my vision.

I shut my eyes and the world went bloodred.

When I opened them, tears I'd thought gone forever streamed down my face.

I swallowed hard and managed a breath. Looked at Zoey. I had to keep Zoey safe. I no longer cared how any of this ended, so long as Zoey and Ashdown made it out alive. Made it back to London safe and sound.

In my periphery I saw Quigg awaiting guidance. All the questions I'd had for him were falling away like feathers from my mind.

Where is she now?

When was the last time you heard from her?

What was she doing in Dublin?

To Ashdown I said, "It's your ball game now. We do whatever's best for you and Zoey. If that's calling NCA and allowing me to surrender myself, then that's the game plan."

"You're certain, Simon?"

"I'm certain."

Ashdown nodded. Walked over to the room phone and lifted the handset.

In a flash of motion that nearly knocked Quigg from his feet, Zoey leapt over the bed and ripped the phone from Ashdown's hand.

"The *fuck* it is," she screamed.

She swung the handset at Ashdown's head. He made a halfhearted attempt to bat it away, but it caught the left side of his forehead.

"Simon's *my* little brother," she shouted, "you bloody coward. Either we all walk out of here, or *none* of us do."

Ashdown's forehead was already turning red.

Christ, I thought. I hadn't anticipated this. Though she *was* a Fisk, after all, wasn't she? Good or bad or neutral, it didn't matter, Fisks were all stubborn as shit.

I realized then that it was stupid of me to even try to place the ball in Ashdown's glove. This was as much Ashdown's ballgame as it was Quigg's. From here on out, it would be Zoey who called the shots.

Come to think of it, I'm not sure it was ever any other way.

Hello," I said into the phone, "front desk?"

"Aye, this is Alan Tucker."

"Alan, this is Simon Fisk from room two-B. I've a bit of a problem."

"Naw with the plumbing, I hope. That toilet, you need to flush her with each wipe lest you want to be bathing in yer own shite. Didn't Brenda tell you?"

"Actually, my problem isn't shit-related, Alan." I paused. "Well, in a way it is, I guess. But as far as I know, the plumbing's fine."

"Then what can I do fer you, laddie?"

"I'd like to have a word with you in private, if that's possible."

"Door's always open fer a guest, Mr. Fisk."

With the HK tucked away in my jacket, I stepped into the hallway and took the stairwell down one flight. After nearly shooting

Ashdown in the upstairs hallway, I wasn't taking any chances with the gun. My heart had since sunk and my reflexes weren't what they were a year ago to begin with. I didn't want to risk mistaking Brenda for one of Maxwell's bruisers and sending her to an early grave.

Before I stepped out into the lobby, I stole a glance through the narrow glass window. Empty, but I couldn't be sure one of Maxwell's men wasn't sitting in the office waiting for me, with a gun to Alan Tucker's head.

When I'd asked Ashdown whether he was sure Maxwell's men wouldn't enter, he'd said: "Look, Simon, the fuzz here are bent. But even *they* have their limits. Gangland justice is one thing. If the Maxwells were to shoot up a bed-and-breakfast in the middle of the Scottish capital, the NCA couldn't just look the other way. Trust me. They're not coming inside. They don't need to. They'll wait us out. Long as it takes. Because the other thing about British gangsters, they're bloody patient. We're not dealing with some neurotic thug like Tony Soprano here. Tavis Maxwell is a man who may well outlive all of us."

I walked through the short lobby and stopped at the front desk. Alan waved me around and ushered me into his office.

The room was a tiny thing, large enough for two but not three. The walls were lined with well-kept filing cabinets and a small desk with an older model laptop computer and a printer that probably jammed if you so much as looked at it funny.

"Where's Brenda?" I asked.

"Back in our room, taking a nip."

"A nap?"

"Naw, a nip. You ken, a swally. She likes to get a wee bit squiffy in the evening, ever since our son Johnny got himself thrown in the lockup for armed robbery a few years back. Naw harm in that, is there?"

"Of course not."

Hell, I could have used a nip myself just then.

"Why do you ask, Mr. Fisk?"

I was trying to get a read on him, hoping to determine the proper tack to take. When I first devised the plan, I was sure I'd need to show Alan Tucker the gun. But I didn't want to. Alan and Brenda seemed like good people, and with Hailey no longer an issue, I could afford to attempt this with some tact.

"On the way in," I said, "I noticed you have an attached garage. You keep a vehicle in there?"

"Aye. What of it?"

"Let me be blunt, Alan. Outside there are at least four SUVs filled with men who are looking to kill me. Me *and* the woman I came in with."

I watched for a reaction but he hadn't so much as flinched.

"The men work for a gangster named Tavis Maxwell, who mistakenly believes I shot his son, Ewan, in an alley in Glasgow last night."

"Ah, so yer the one all the hoo-ha is about. I read about the twit's death in the paper this morn. Too bad you didn't take out the auld man as well. Those bastarts have had their way with Scotland fer far too long."

"I don't care about myself," I said. "But I want to get my sister and her ex-husband out of here safely. And to do that, I'm going to need a vehicle. Maxwell's men disabled the Grand Cherokee we came with."

He thought about it. "How you figure on getting past all them muppets in a five-year-auld Ford Fiesta, Mr. Fisk?"

"I don't," I said. "Not me, personally. My plan is to create a diversion. It's me the bastards want, it's me they're going to get. Only my sister and her ex don't need to know that just yet. They can puzzle it out once they're safe."

Alan Tucker scrutinized my face. "They won't kill you. You ken that, don't you? Not Maxwell's men. Not the Last King of Scotland's subjects, so to speak. They'll capture you. Take you alive back to their boss. Then they'll torture you like naw man's ever been tortured before."

I grinned. "Thanks for the uplifting message, Alan. But this is something I have to do."

"It ain't though, Mr. Fisk. See, you chose to stay at the Tucker Bed-and-Breakfast, rated four stars by the Scottish Tourist Board fer our friendly, relaxed, soup-to-nuts service. There's *nothing* Brenda and I won't do fer our guests."

"Look, we can't call the police."

"'Course not. The polis here, they'll bring you straight to Maxwell's doorstep."

"I'm not quite catching your meaning then, Alan."

"Let's just say, it won't be told that Alan and Brenda Tucker fed their guests to the wolves." He stood, snatched a set of keys off the wall, and tossed them to me. "These are fer the Ford Fiesta in the garage. She's auld, but she runs well." He laughed out loud. "Just like the missus, I like to say."

"Appreciate it," I said. "I don't have any more cash on me, but—"

"Nonsense, mate. You've already paid. But I will make you a trade."

"A trade?"

"Yer jacket. That ol' black leather thing yer wearing."

"You want my jacket?"

"Aye. I'm naw gonna be much use as a diversion without it. It's dark outside and I can make it darker by canning the outdoor lights. But we ain't exactly twins, you and me."

I shook my head vehemently. "I can't ask you to do that. I can't ask you to put yourself in that kind of danger."

"You didn't ask. I offered. And if you were to refuse my offer, I'd be mighty insulted. And you ken from our sign out there, you don't come to Edinburgh and insult yer host." He went to his closet and added, "Especially one who's good with a shotgun."

"Why?" I said. "Why are you willing to put your life on the line for guests who brought violence to your door?"

He looked me in the eye, said, "'Twas a Maxwell who corrupted our boy Johnny."

Chapter 27

I sat in the passenger seat of Alan Tucker's Ford Fiesta with the HK in my lap. Cold to the point of shivering because I had given Tucker my jacket. Ashdown was seated behind the wheel, Zoey and Angus Quigg in the rear. The garage door remained closed, so Ashdown kept the engine off.

"You sure about this?" Ashdown said.

I shook my head. "But Alan says he is."

And then Alan Tucker appeared in the doorway, a man twice my age or close to it, dressed in my black leather jacket and a matching fedora.

"Gotta admit," Zoey said from the rear, "he looks pretty badass."

It wasn't my jacket, but the double-barrel shotgun resting in his palms.

Alan held up five fingers. Ashdown acknowledged the signal. Then Alan returned inside.

"He's convinced they won't shoot him because Maxwell wants me alive," I said.

"And when they realize that he's not you?" Zoey asked.

"He told me to trust him."

The garage door began its slow automatic rise and Ashdown turned the ignition.

From the corner of my eye I could see Alan's form as he stepped out the front door, moved swiftly up the walkway, lifted the shotgun to his shoulder and fired the first blast, which for us, also served as a starting gun.

The blast took out the first SUV's front left tire and caught Maxwell's men completely by surprise. They hadn't been expecting incoming fire.

Ashdown slammed on the accelerator as Alan took out the second SUV's front left tire and a moment later we were out of the drive.

Ashdown aimed the Ford Fiesta toward the city center just as the remaining two SUVs roared to life.

One got its front right tire shot out as it attempted to turn around. The other made it out of Alan's line of fire just in time to give chase.

In the rearview I watched Alan Tucker duck indoors as a pair of Maxwell's men ran up the front path after him. With Brenda upstairs phoning the police, I had a feeling they'd both be fine.

We, on the other hand, had a tail.

And it was coming up fast.

Though I knew much more about motorcycles than I did cars, I knew enough about the Ford Fiesta to fear that Maxwell's men would catch up to us sooner rather than later. The Fiesta was an economy car, and unfortunately, fuel efficiency wasn't a virtue when it came to car chases. At least not brief car chases. And I fully expected this one to be brief.

The Fiesta boasted a four-cylinder engine with a five-speed manual transmission. Traveled zero to sixty in just under ten seconds. Not exactly the Bugatti Veyron that Edgar Trenton's driver used to pick me up last year on Mulholland Drive in Los Angeles after I watched the Dodge Charger I was chasing soar off a cliff.

So even though Ashdown seemed to be a fine driver, we needed an edge, some significant advantage to counter the disadvantage of running from a Range Rover in an old couple's early-model American hatchback. Something. Or we'd never make it back to Glasgow alive.

So as Ashdown turned onto Regent Road, I lowered my window.

"What the hell are you doing?" he yelled at me.

"Whatever I can," I said as I unhooked my seat belt.

I tucked the HK into my front waistband and struggled to pull myself up with my single good hand.

"Are you *mad*?" Ashdown shouted. "You're going to get yourself killed."

"You're going to get us all killed if I don't."

I turned my body, leaned out the window, the wind batting me hard in the back of the head.

I removed the HK from my waistband. Steadied my hand as I aimed for the SUV's engine, and fired.

And missed.

A moment later, the SUV's passenger-side window glided down and a gun materialized, just as one had the previous night on Mollinsburn.

I ducked back inside just as it fired.

"I need a better angle," I said to Ashdown.

"Oh, *right away,* sir!" he yelled.

"I'm serious!" I shouted.

"You're mental is what you are."

I turned and stared at him. "If we get out of this alive, you and I are going to have a grave conversation about cooperation."

He glanced at me, said, "You *are* serious, aren't you?"

"As death itself."

He gritted his teeth. "Let me ask you something, Simon. Do I rub you the wrong way?"

I looked away from him. "Everybody does. Now get me that angle."

"And just how do I do that?"

"A wide right turn. But first you need to slow down, let them come right up on us. Then accelerate roughly a hundred feet before the turn to put some distance between us and them. Got it?"

"Got it."

Two minutes later, he said, "Right turn straight ahead."

I lowered the window, pulled myself up again as Ashdown slowed the Fiesta. Once I had purchase, I told him to punch it, and punch it he did, curling to the right toward a freeway on-ramp, giving me a sixty-degree angle to take my shot.

Only we'd offered them a pretty decent shot ourselves.

And they took it.

The shot slammed into the passenger-side door, missing me by mere inches.

I took a long, deep breath.

Aimed at the SUV's engine.

And fired.

Smoke immediately billowed from under the Range Rover's hood on either side, effectively blinding them. The vehicle swerved one way then the other and finally began to slow.

And continued to slow until it was just a solitary dot of light in our rearview mirror.

I ducked back inside, glared at Ashdown.

Grudgingly, he looked back at me and muttered, "Jolly good show."

Chapter 28

Our dining room is set up like a war room. Rendell had offered to set up his team a few miles away at a Hollywood Video that had recently gone out of business. But I'd insisted they set up here so that I could play some role in the investigation.

Not that they have afforded me much of one.

I sit in the laundry room leafing through my copy of the file, trying to make sense out of what I'm seeing. As a federal marshal this is new to me. I've never before worked an investigation like this.

I'm certain they're keeping some things from me. And I'm equally certain they have their reasons. To them I'm a civilian. A broken father with a wife rapidly spiraling toward a nervous breakdown.

According to Rendell, eyewitness accounts have ruled out the possibility that Tasha willfully or negligently killed our daughter and disposed of the body. The forensics team has thoroughly searched the premises and found no traces of blood or signs of a struggle. Hailey was seen by a neighbor retrieving our *Washington Post* that very morning. That same neighbor confirmed that our Ford Explorer hadn't moved from the driveway in the previous twenty-four hours. So although Tasha's polygraph was inconclusive because of her deteriorated physiological state, her story, as she's told it numerous times, checks out.

Likewise they have been able to rule out all friends and family who attended Hailey's sixth birthday party. Tasha's parents were at home, one arguing with a neighbor, the other on the phone with Tasha. The parents of Hailey's friends all happened to be at the school auditorium taking part in a bake sale, of which Tasha had bowed out. Of the neighbors who attended, two were at the mall (and caught on video camera), one was at work (confirmed by her boss), and two had taken a road trip to the boardwalk in Wildwood, New Jersey (during which they had accumulated a hefty pile of receipts). Of my friends who attended, Jimmy the U.S. Marshal was in Bucharest with me, and Terry had opened his bar promptly at eleven A.M. as he does every Saturday morning. Thus, not a single fingerprint or fiber collected on our property has proven to be of use.

All delivery personnel—FedEx, UPS, U.S. Mail—who have been in the neighborhood over the past ninety days are being questioned, as are employees of our gas, electric, water, cable, and phone companies and the local sanitation department.

A map in the file shows that there are 903 sex offenders in the D.C. area, plus ninety-six "non-mappable" offenders for a total just shy of one thousand. I've been assured that each and every offender who meet the criteria will be questioned by local law enforcement. A list of the most likely candidates will then be passed on to the FBI for further investigation.

Meanwhile, I've downloaded a recent New York Times article that attempts to profile a child abductor and now that I'm alone I can finally read it without worrying its contents will cause Tasha to go into shock.

Ninety-five percent of child abductors, the article says, are men. They tend to be unmarried with few friends. Unlike the great majority of child molesters, who coerce their victims by winning over their trust, child abductors rarely have contact with children in their daily lives.

They have poor social skills.

Use child pornography.

And are willing to use violence.

Roughly forty percent of the time, men who abduct children for sex kill their victims.

I suddenly feel sick. I'm sweating and my head is swimming. I set the file folder on the floor and try to take deep breaths.

Think of something else, something positive.

With the aid of Tasha's parents, we've offered a reward of a quarter of a million dollars for Hailey's safe return.

It's no use.

I jump off my chair, scramble to the washing machine, open the lid, and vomit into it violently.

Chapter 29

Back at Gerry Gilchrist's house in Glasgow, the adrenaline wore off, and it felt as though I'd lost Hailey all over again. Sitting at the dining room table, I wanted nothing more than to close myself off in a room with a handful of Zoey's pills and a bottle of Dalmore. But the flurry of activity made that impossible, since I still felt responsible, not only for Zoey and Ashdown but for Kinny Gilchrist as well.

And Kinny Gilchrist was missing.

"He's not at the Old Soak," the Chairman said, slamming down the phone. "I have Kerr checking all the hospitals and listening in on his scanner. But if someone in Maxwell's pocket picked him up, we can expect nothing but radio silence."

"Kerr?" Ashdown said.

"Detective Chief Constable Gavin Kerr. He's one of mine."

Ashdown nodded but said nothing.

Meanwhile, Doc Lochhead dropped to his haunches in front of me. "Give me that paw," he said. "I'll need to change the dressings, won't I?"

"Forget it," I told him. "I'm fine."

Zoey stood a few feet away, her arms crossed over her chest. "Let him do it, Simon. Please."

I bowed my head, held out my injured left, and Doc Lochhead went to work.

Gilchrist finally took his usual seat at the table. One of his body-guards set a glass of whiskey in front of him and he pushed it away, then thought twice and put it to his lips.

Ashdown asked, "Mind if I take a quick shower? It's been a rough seventy-two hours."

"Help yourself," Gilchrist said.

Zoey moved to a corner of the room where Angus Quigg was chatting with one of Gilchrist's men. Since our arrival Quigg had made fast friends in the Gilchrist household.

"If Tavis Maxwell harms one hair on that boy's head . . ." Gilchrist said to no one in particular. He took a pull of whiskey and turned to me. "I never finished telling you about Arthur Thompson, did I?"

I shook my head. Doc finished his handiwork and moved off in the direction of the kitchen, no doubt for a drink of his own.

Gilchrist said, "I told you how Junior—Fat Boy, they called him— was finally gunned down outside his residence, the Ponderosa."

I nodded.

"Well, two of the hard men thought responsible for the killing were Bobby Glover and Joe 'Bananas' Hanlon."

I flexed my fingers as best I could, thought I felt a bit of life returning to them.

"A few hours after Junior's funeral, young Bobby and Joe Bananas were found outside a pub in east Glasgow. Each of the boys had a bullet in the back of his head. Plus an extra one fired up his fucking anus for good measure."

"Christ," I muttered.

Gilchrist shook his head. "There are naw saviors in Glasgow, Mr. Fisk. Not when someone brings harm to your boy. Naw, in fact, that wasn't even the full extent of their injuries."

As I listened I couldn't take my eyes off Angus Quigg and what might have been.

Gilchrist leaned back in his chair and took a drink. "Earlier that day, Bobby and Joe Bananas had been stuffed in the trunk of a car. One of the cars that took part in Junior's funeral procession, in fact."

"Dead or alive?" I asked.

"Alive, but barely." He emptied his drink, said, "In the middle of the procession, that car came to a complete halt. Four men exited the car and removed young Bobby Glover and Joe Bananas from the trunk. Laid them side by side in the middle of the road."

I didn't want to hear the rest. But Gilchrist was going to tell it.

He said, "When the procession resumed, Junior's hearse—driven by none other than Arthur Thompson, Sr. himself—ran the bloody fuck over his son's assassins." Gilchrist smiled. "Slowly," he added. "So as not to kill them."

In that moment I thought of the old woman, Edie, from my Aer Lingus flight from D.C. to Dublin. Her number was still in my wallet. Her boy had been killed too, shot dead in a Baltimore Burger King for a couple hundred dollars.

And what did she do?

Fought to save her son's killer from the death penalty, then devoted her life to ending the practice of capital punishment in the Western world entirely.

I looked up at Gerry Gilchrist. I knew who was right and who was wrong. But, staring into Gilchrist's eyes, I couldn't help but wonder which path I'd have followed had I found Hailey's abductor here in the UK, and gotten him alone in a room with me.

What would I have done?

I shot a glance at Quigg and thought, now I'll never know.

A *crash* emanated from upstairs. Then another. It suddenly sounded like we were seated below a bowling alley.

Gilchrist and I both rose from our chairs and started for the stairs.

As we neared the second-floor landing, the sounds became unmistakable. Human bodies smashing into hard wooden furniture.

When we hit the top of the stairs, a bedroom door swung open.

In its frame appeared two of Gilchrist's guards. Holding a battered Damon Ashdown, naked from the waist up, between them.

"What the hell's going on?" Gilchrist demanded of his men.

The smaller of the two men spoke. "While this one was in the shower, I poked through his wallet and—"

"Why the hell would you do that?" Gilchrist said. "He's a bloody guest in my house."

The guy didn't have an answer. But then, he didn't need one.

He held up Ashdown's badge instead.

"NCA?" Gilchrist said, incredulous.

"Naw just NCA," the smaller one said as he reached into his pocket and held out Ashdown's wallet.

The Chairman took the wallet in his hand, opened it, quickly scanned an identification card, then locked his eyes on Ashdown.

"Well, I'll be damned," he said. "Fucking Interpol, are you?"

Chapter 30

With guns to our heads, we were led back downstairs.

In the dining room, one of Gilchrist's goons slammed me face-first into a wall.

Gilchrist came up behind me, close enough that I could feel his breath on the back of my neck. Close enough that I could taste the Scotch coming off him.

"You'd better have a good goddamn explanation, Fisk, or you and your lot are going to die so badly, it'll make the deaths of Bobby Glover and Joe Bananas seem humane."

I closed my eyes and drew a deep breath. "Damon Ashdown is only here because of me," I said quietly. "It has nothing at all to do with you. Nothing at all to do with the National Crime Agency or Interpol."

"So it's some bloody coincidence, is it? Just some bloody coincidence that an officer with the NCA—the British agency that investigates *organized crime*—is sitting in *my* home, drinking *my* whiskey, listening to *my* conversations. Well, let me tell you something, Fisk, I don't *believe* in coincidences."

"Then you should pay more attention, Mr. Chairman. Because the world's fucking full of coincidences."

"Listen to me, you son of a bitch—"

"Your son Kinny told you how we met, didn't he? He told you what

I wanted from him. You yourself arranged the goddamn meeting with Rob Roy Moffett at Shotts."

"You *lied*. The detective here said he was a bloody *used car* salesman."

I thought about my confrontation with Ashdown in Eli Welker's room at the Dublin Radisson.

"Because we didn't think you'd take too kindly to his official position," I said. "And it appears we were right, weren't we?" I turned to face him. "But we're in Glasgow for one reason and one reason only. Because we were looking for the girl."

"*Were* as in past tense?"

My eyes flicked over to Quigg, who seemed to be a known quantity to Gilchrist and therefore not a threat. Hence, no gun to his head.

"Turns out," I said, "she's not who we were looking for."

"And just *who was it* you were looking for? Not Zoey's strung-out mate from Essex, I presume."

I sighed heavily. Said, "We were looking for my daughter."

Then I told him all of it, just as I'd told Edie on the Aer Lingus flight to Dublin. Told him about the abduction, about the investigation, about Tasha's suicide.

I told him about the past twelve years, went into some detail about the past eleven months. Then I told him about the e-mail I received from Kati back in D.C.

The conversation I had with Ashdown.

The tour of the Stalemate in Dublin.

The reunion with my sister Zoey at the Radisson.

The photos I received from Kurt Ostermann in London.

The question-and-answer session I had with Rob Roy Moffett at Shotts.

And finally ending with our brief stay at the Tucker Bed and Breakfast in Edinburgh.

"I can vouch for that last part," Quigg said in the moments of silence that followed my story.

Gilchrist's phone began ringing. He walked over to the dining room table and answered it.

Meanwhile, Quigg stepped over to me. "You says before you had a gaffe in Virginia, didn't you?"

"D.C.," I said softly. "Georgetown area."

"Basically same thing, innit?"

"Close."

I was terse. Because I was in no mood to talk. After laying out my story again, this time with a gun to my head, I would have been content never saying another word. I just wanted it all to end.

"I mean, if I was to tell you that the lass in the photo—Shauna—that she told me that she done part of her primary schooling in Virginia, you might want to hear more, wouldn't you?"

Something moved within my chest. "You said you'd known her since you were born."

"Since we was wee bairns, true. But . . ."

"But what?"

"I actually only recall meeting her a couple years ago at a dance club in London."

My pulse started pounding. "Why did you tell me you knew her since you were kids?"

"The night we met at the club, she says to me she grew up in Springburn, see? Then she asks me where I'm from. When I told her Springburn was *my* hometown too, she says, oh yeah, she ken me from way back when we were bairns. It was odd, like. But who's gonna question a bonnie lass like Shauna, right?"

"Where does Virginia come in?"

"Well, we started seeing each other, right? While I was letting a flat in London. And we'd get to talking in bed."

He shuddered, searched my eyes but I assured him it was all right. "Just go ahead."

"Anyway, Springburn starts sounding more like a cover, right? Then one night, we sees something on the telly, some spy show set in Virginia—or wherever those CIA blokes are located—and she talks about the area like she's been there. When I ask, she lets slip that she's done part of her primary schooling there. In Virginia, I mean. And . . ."

"And what?"

"And she told me something about her mother."

"Tasha?"

"She didn't tell me her mother's name, right? She just told me that she offed herself."

Chapter 31

They'd found Kinny Gilchrist.

"That was Gavin Kerr," the Chairman said when he hung up the phone. "Kinny's with him at our safe house in North Kelvinside. Badly beaten, but he's alive."

He stepped around the dining room table and approached me. Quigg moved off.

"My boy was set up," Gilchrist said to me. "By his own best mate, Raymond Aiken."

My eyes narrowed. "The kid from the pub?"

"The one you knocked unconscious with a Glasgow Kiss." He placed a firm hand on my shoulder. "After some *enhanced* interrogation, Kerr got a full confession from the kid. He'd planned on killing Kinny last night, as soon as they left the Old Soak. The SUV you encountered was just backup in case Raymond botched the job."

"What are you saying?"

"I'm saying, if you hadn't intervened at the pub, there is naw question, my boy would have been killed last night."

I bowed my head. Stared at his hand until he removed it from my shoulder.

"Well, he's alive," I said. "And according to Quigg here, there's a chance my daughter is too."

Ashdown lifted his head. He was in bad shape but nothing that appeared life threatening.

According to Quigg, Shauna had stopped by to see him just a couple of days ago on her way to Dublin. Said she was running an errand for her father. Something of vital importance. She was in a rush, only stayed with Quigg in Edinburgh the one night after hitting a pub called Bishop's in Quigg's hometown of Springburn.

Quigg knew little about her father. Only that he was a businessman. And that he was an older man. In Quigg's own words, "More like a grandfather, right?"

"And how about her?" I asked with a lump in my throat. "How old is she?"

"I don't ken. I have a 'naw ask, naw tell' policy, see."

"But could she be eighteen?"

He considered this. "She'd have to be an auld soul, I think. Because she's smart. Like, street smart, see. Worldly, I guess is the word I'm looking for."

He hadn't heard from her since she'd left Edinburgh. She'd had no phone and gave Quigg no contact number.

She'd told him that she only meant to stay in Dublin a night or two before returning home.

"Where's home?" I'd asked.

"Liverpool."

"Where in Liverpool?"

"I don't ken exactly. I've never been there, have I?"

"Why not?"

"Because she lives with a fella."

"A boyfriend?"

"Some bloke her auld man don't approve of, right?"

"Why not?"

He hesitated. "Well, 'cause he's a Yardie an' all."

"A Yardie? Part of a Jamaican gang?"

"British Afro-Caribbean is the politically correct term, innit?"

"A drug gang?"

He shrugged. "Few years back they were selling crack, right? But the Liverpool Yardies have moved on since then."

"Moved on to what?"

He lowered his voice. "Gun-trafficking, far as I ken."

You're gonna need assistance getting out of Glasgow," Gilchrist said when I told him I was leaving for Liverpool.

"I can make it out," I said. "I'm just going to need transportation."

He nodded. "I own a dealership next town over."

"You have bikes?"

"Dozens of them."

Chapter 32

Twenty minutes later Gilchrist, his men, and I were standing in his pitch-black showroom. Outside there was little wind and it had stopped snowing. Still, a three-hour motorcycle drive would be risky. I needed a solid bike with exceptional handling.

My eyes immediately fell on fifteen-hundred pounds of perfection.

"She's a beaut, isn't she?" Gilchrist said.

"But a half-million-dollar beaut," I said.

"My boy's life is worth at least that much, I think."

I looked at him. "I couldn't."

"You could. And you will. Otherwise, I'd be insulted. And the one thing you'll learn about Scotland, you *never* insult your host."

Especially one who's good with a shotgun, I thought.

"Is she street legal?" I said.

"Do you care?"

"No."

"With a top speed of over four hundred kilometers an hour, the filth won't be able to come near you anyway."

As we circled the machine, he said, "The Dodge Tomahawk was

built as a concept vehicle. Dodge called them 'rolling sculptures' never meant to be ridden. But who the hell are they to tell us what to do, right?"

"Right."

The five-hundred horsepower, 8.3-liter, V10 SRT10 engine, he said, was borrowed from the Dodge Viper.

"Zero to sixty?" I asked.

"From a standing start, two and a half seconds. At least in theory."

The bike had two front wheels, two back wheels pressed together for extra stability.

"I may not be able to return her to you," I said.

"I should hope not, Simon." He rested a hand on my shoulder again. "You find your daughter, I trust you'll throw her on the back of this beast and blow the bloody hell out of Great Britain for good."

A half dozen of Gilchrist's boys were straddling lesser bikes, ready to ride out of the dealership's massive garage as decoys.

"I'll get your sister and Mr. Ashdown safely back to London in the morning," the Chairman assured me.

The garage door started to open, letting in the cold.

I zipped up the black biker armor jacket Gilchrist had given me, adjusted the gloves, and lowered the helmet onto my head.

"And you'll have Kerr check in on the Tuckers in Edinburgh, right?"

"You have my word as a Scotsman."

I thanked him.

"Thank *you* for saving my boy."

I started the engine.

"And remember, Simon," he said over the roar, "be vigilant. Tavis

Maxwell's reach extends far south of Glasgow. Perhaps even far south of London."

I lowered the face shield.

Nodded my head.

Then rode out of Glasgow as though my little girl's life depended on it.

Part Three

THE LOVERS OF LIVERPOOL

Chapter 33

His name is Lennox Sterling," I said into the phone.

It was dawn. I'd reached Liverpool less than an hour ago and hidden the Dodge Tomahawk in an abandoned three-story car park on the outskirts of the city.

On the other end of the phone, I could hear Kurt Ostermann trying to kick the sleep from his voice. "And the girl's name again?"

"Shauna Adair." I spelled the surname for him.

As he tapped away at a keyboard, I took in my surroundings. Although the port city was steeped in eight hundred years of history and boasted one of England's more diverse populations, Liverpool remained best known for its title as the birthplace of the Beatles. I'd always been more of a Stones fan myself, but Tasha absolutely adored the lads from Liverpool, and by her sixth year of life, Hailey had come to love them too, especially the song about the yellow submarine. On road trips, she'd have me play it on a loop for hours on end. Drove me absolutely nuts.

But damned if I ever even considered refusing her request.

"Should be easier to find the guy than the girl," Ostermann said after several seconds. "There are about a half-million people residing in Liverpool and ninety percent of them are white. And the majority of black Liverpudlians are of African descent. Only five thousand or so are of Afro-Caribbean origin."

"He's a Yardie," I said, "so I'm hoping he has a sheet. You might want to check with the Merseyside Police first."

"I'm on it."

"Any luck tracking down the identity of Eli Welker's client?"

"Not yet. But I've tossed a few lures in the water. Magda spread word over the Internet that current clients of Eli Welker should contact me here in London, or something to that effect. She provided a phone number and an e-mail address to head off any privacy concerns. No bites yet. But I'm hopeful."

"All right, then."

"What do you intend to do first?"

"I'm going to find myself an espresso. Then I'm going to go looking for Sterling."

"And how do you intend to go about that?"

"By shopping for a gun."

I started in Everton, an inner-city district just north of the city center. After fueling up with a couple espressos at Smokin' Joe's on South Pine Road, I took a walk down White Street toward Teralba Park, where I hoped to find some of the city's homeless—a few trampled souls down in the mouth and eager to sell their sole asset: information.

But the weather was working against me. A hard Atlantic wind was blowing in over the River Mersey, and it was still too early for the shelters to have let out. So I finally hopped aboard the Merseyrail and headed west to Vauxhall then north to Kirkdale and east to Anfield.

No luck.

Although the streets by then were beginning to spark to life, I continued to meet with limited success. For some peculiar reason, your average Liverpudlian was reluctant to engage in conversation with a caffeinated stranger dressed in full black biker armor enthusiastically seeking out illicit firearms.

Go figure.

But as far as the biker armor went, I was unequivocally impressed.

"Designed by Miguel Caballero in Bogota," Gilchrist had told me back in Glasgow. "Not just to spare you from road rash either, mind you. It's bloody bulletproof. Can withstand a fifty-caliber round, if I'm not mistaken. Caballero has designed clothes for Prince Felipe of Spain, President Uribe of Colombia, the late Hugo Chavez, even President Barack Obama. Not just motorcycle gear, of course, but topcoats and blazers. Tuxedo shirts, if you can believe it. I think it's safe to presume that were James Bond not merely a fictional character, Miguel Caballero would be his personal tailor."

Bulletproof and all, the biker armor afforded me a full range of motion and was so comfortable it felt like a second skin. Dressed head to toe in such expensive and exquisite gear, it seemed almost criminal *not* to get myself shot.

Ten minutes before noon, I was about to call it a morning and grab a quick lunch when Ashdown called.

"Zoey and I are going to meet you in Liverpool."

"Not necessary," I said. "Besides, the Chairman promised to send you straight on to London."

Zoey apparently snatched the phone from him.

"We'll be in Liverpool in a few hours, little brother. Are you going to tell us where you are or are we going to have to come looking for you?"

No use, I thought. *She's a Fisk, right down to the bone.*

"Call me when you get here," I said. "I'll be in a different district by then."

I pocketed my phone. I hadn't yet puzzled out whether Damon Ashdown was helping me because he possessed the heart of a good cop or whether he was just aiming to get back into my sister's good graces. A bit of both, if I had to bet.

And I wasn't sure whether it should matter to me anyhow. Ashdown had gotten me into the Stalemate to view the crime scene, and gained us access to Eli Welker's room at the Radisson. He'd gotten me a look at Welker's hotel file, which netted me the passport picture, which Ostermann used to identify Welker and ultimately led to his sending me the photos of Shauna with Angus Quigg in Glasgow.

If not for Damon Ashdown, I might still be running around Dublin, trying to discern the identity of the dead man in Temple Bar.

Kurt Ostermann's callback came a few minutes after Ashdown's.

"No sheet on Lennox Sterling," he said. "But I have a good idea where you'll find him. Know a district called Toxteth?"

"Of the Toxteth riots? Sure."

"A friend of mine contacted a Merseyside cop. There's an open investigation into a group believed to be trafficking in firearms there."

"Are we talking about a crime firm," I said, "or a street gang?"

"A hybrid, it sounds like. Since the Yardies have a reputation for cold-bloodedness and resorting to extreme violence at the slightest transgression, crime firms are apparently quick to adopt the moniker. Scares off the competition *and* throws off law enforcement in the same breath."

"Do you have an address?"

"I'm afraid not. That's as far as he would go."

"Well, it's a start. Thanks."

"Before you thank me, please carefully consider what you're about to walk into, Simon. I'm only four hours away in London. How about you find yourself a local library and read some Bukowski until I can get there?"

"Not necessary," I said. "I have Ashdown and my sister on their way down from Glasgow."

Following a significant pause, he relented. "All right, Simon. Remember, though, I'm here if you need me."

"I know."

By the time I ended the call I was already standing at the entrance to the Anfield Merseyrail Station.

Slipping my hand into my jacket, I surreptitiously moved the HK to my waistband for ease of access.

Then I descended the steps to board the next train south to Toxteth.

Chapter 34

I'm staring out the living room window. The press is parked outside our home and I can't decide whether they're friend or foe. Oh, I know they're far more interested in ratings and selling newspapers than in finding my six-year-old daughter. What I don't know is whether all the attention is helping or hindering the investigation. Or whether it's having no effect whatsoever.

Rendell is ambiguous on the matter. "The best thing we can do at this point, Simon, is forget they're there. You and Tasha have done what needed to be done. You've made an appeal to the public. You've spoken directly to any potential kidnapper. And you've instructed Hailey on what she needs to do if she's watching. That's about as much as we can control with respect to the media."

I nod and close the drapes. Turn toward the kitchen where Tasha is seated with her best friend from college, Aubrey Lang. Aubrey has been in D.C. since the day Hailey was abducted. Flew all the way up from Costa Rica where she works as a nurse to provide Tasha some moral support. We offered her a room but she insists on staying at the Georgetown Best Western in order to remain out of the way. She drops by every morning to keep Tasha company. And I'm grateful beyond words. Because at this point I find myself unable to talk to Tasha at all.

She blames *me,* she says. Blames me for going off to Bucharest and leaving her and Hailey at home alone.

"Yes, *I* was in the kitchen," she shouted at me early this morning. "I was in the kitchen while Hailey was out in the backyard. And where the hell were *you,* Simon? On a goddamn plane somewhere over the Atlantic. At least I care enough about my daughter not to take off for the other side of the *world.*"

When I argued that it was my job, she became hysterical.

"*Why* is it your job? Why, Simon? Because *you* requested the assignment. You weren't content escorting prisoners to and from FCC Petersburg. You weren't content chasing down federal fugitives here in the metropolitan area. You *wanted* to work abroad."

"What are you *saying*?"

"I'm saying you weren't content with *us,* Simon. You wanted *more.* Your request for overseas assignments had nothing to do with advancing your career. Finding a federal fugitive in D.C. or Maryland is just as goddamn important as finding one in Lisbon or Madrid. But you wanted to be *away.* You wanted to be away from *us.*"

"Why would I want that?"

"Because you were *bored.*"

"The *hell* I was."

Even as I said it, I wondered whether she was right.

Is this all my fault?

I had told myself I was bored with my *job* at the D.C. field office. But was it more than that? Was I bored coming home to Tasha and Hailey every night? Bored watching the same inane television shows and Disney DVDs every evening? Was I bored with the same damn dinners night after night? Was I bored having sex with my wife even though I'd never so much as considered having an affair?

It's true that I requested the assignment shortly after Hailey was born. At the time my world had been changing so drastically, I'd figured one more modification wouldn't upend it. But had I ever really reflected on *why* I wanted to work abroad?

It's not as though extraditions are exciting. It's all waiting around and paperwork. It's working with foreign law-enforcement agents who resent your very presence. And in the nearly two years since September 11, air travel has become a living nightmare.

So why was I so insistent on leaving?

Christ, am I just like my father? Did I make a calculated decision to spend as much time as possible away from my wife and daughter without resorting to divorce? Did I find a way to walk away from my marriage without forcing Hailey to endure an ugly and protracted legal disentanglement? Am I just like Dr. Alden Fisk, abandoner of wife and daughter, callous breaker of lives?

Is Tasha a victim just as my mother was?

Is Hailey a victim just as my sister, Tuesday, was?

I stare into the kitchen and watch Tasha with Aubrey. I feel compelled to walk in and apologize. But I know that this argument has already gone too far. There may well be no coming back from it. Too much has been said. By both of us.

And I still can't be sure who's right.

Probably both of us are.

Probably neither of us, too.

That's the way the world works, isn't it? Everything infinitely gray, nothing at all black-and-white?

"Simon?" Rendell is saying. "Simon?"

I barely hear him over the storm brewing inside my head.

Chapter 35

Although the Toxteth riots occurred nearly thirty-five years ago, the reasons behind them are just as relevant in many major cities in the UK today. And in the United States for that matter. Such as Ferguson, Missouri, in the Greater St. Louis metropolitan area, where a young unarmed black man named Michael Brown was recently shot and killed by a Ferguson police officer, igniting months of mammoth protests and civil unrest.

So it was in 1981 Toxteth, where long-established tensions between the local black community and the Merseyside Police finally erupted into waves of full-scale riots. At the time, Britain was in recession, with unemployment at a fifty-year high. And not surprisingly, the inner-city area of Toxteth was plagued with one of the highest unemployment rates in the country.

Unfortunately, over the past three and a half decades, not much had changed. At least not with respect to the area's economic conditions. Whether police-community relations had improved or declined, I didn't know and hoped not to find out, at least not until I was clear of the city.

I remained the primary suspect in the murder of Ewan Maxwell in Glasgow, which meant I was a wanted man throughout the United Kingdom. Regardless of how things went from here, I wouldn't be seeking the assistance of the Merseyside Police. At least not directly. Not without Kurt Ostermann or someone else as a go-between.

With little to go on, I decided to begin my search of Toxteth much in the same way I began in Springburn. I took out my BlackBerry, opened the browser, and called up a Merseyside pub guide. First I scanned for Caribbean bar names, looking for words like *island* or *tropical* or *paradise* in the title. Next I hunted for spots that featured reggae music. Failing all that, I finally pursued pubs in which one of the main drinking attractions was either rum or Red Stripe.

Nothing.

Since there were no overtly Caribbean bars, I took the criminal angle instead. Rather than taking note of the four- or five-star pubs with rave customer reviews, I searched for the dives, the one- or two-star pubs with reviews featuring words like *tatty* or *filthy* or *scary*.

Much easier to find.

On the first site I visited, there were three dives to choose from. I settled on one called Down Your Neck (a variation, I assumed, on the American idiom *down the hatch*), which, according to MapQuest, was located only three blocks east from where I was roaming near the docks.

The reviews for Down Your Neck did the pub justice. Which was to say the pub was indeed a tatty, filthy, scary place. Precisely what I was looking for. I took a seat at the rough-and-tumble bar and ordered a bottle of Fuller's ESB. No glass, in order to lower my risk of contracting hepatitis A.

I was the only patron in the place, which worked well, since the bartender seemed like a talker. A young guy with a pierced nose and lots of facial hair, he reminded me somewhat of Casey O'Connell back at Terry's in the District, though this barkeep was skinny and slightly better dressed. He paced behind the bar as though he were debating whether to pick up and leave.

Which also served my purpose. I pulled a couple hundred pounds out of my pocket and set it on the bar. As he made a return run, his eyes fell on the cash and lit like stars gone supernova.

He wasn't dumb.

"On the hunt for something?" he said in his thick Liverpudlian accent.

I bowed my head yes.

"Puff? Gear? A good rogering?"

I made a gun with my thumb and index finger and fired.

The barkeep thought about it then shook his head. "Best I can do is a knuckle duster, mate."

He folded his arms and watched for my reaction but I offered none.

Finally, he nodded. Said, "You're looking to tool-up, then. How much is it worth to you if I could point you in the right direction?"

"That would depend."

"On what, exactly?"

I said, "I'm looking for a certain *type* of salesman."

"What type might that be?"

"A Yardie."

Yardie was essentially just a label. Slang spawned long ago from a Jamaican neighborhood called Trenchtown. The title had been slapped on residents of West Kingston's housing projects, which had been known to most as "government yards."

The barkeep stuffed his hands into his pockets and leaned back against the counter. "You'd have better luck in London, I'd think."

Back in the 1950s, after World War II, Britain's economy was in the crapper and cursed with extensive labor shortages. In order to fill these job vacancies, the UK encouraged migration from the Caribbean, especially Jamaica, which had once been a British colony.

Most Caribbean immigrants went to work in the UK capital for government organizations like the National Health Service, London Transport, and British Rail. But decades later, the population had spread widely throughout England and beyond.

"Let me be straight with you," I said. "I'm actually looking for a particular fellow who *does* reside in Liverpool. Friend of mine said I could trust him. That he'd set me up with whatever I needed at a competitive price. Unfortunately, my friend didn't have a current contact number for him."

"You have a name for him?"

"Sterling," I said. "Lennox Sterling."

The bartender frowned. "Never heard of him, mate. But for the right price, I might be able to connect you with one or two of his brethren."

I pushed the cash across the bar, said, "That's all I have. The rest is reserved for the merchandise."

He quickly flipped through the bills. Satisfied, he stuffed them into his pocket.

"Right, then," he said. "I'm gonna give you a name and an address, mate. But if things go pear-shaped, you didn't get either from me. In fact, you and I have never even met."

Chapter 36

We have a name and an address for the man who drove you to the airport," Rendell says. "But he has no criminal record, not so much as an unpaid parking ticket. And he's been with the limo company for eighteen years."

"But you'll check him out," I say, "you'll check his alibi. And if it doesn't pan out, you'll get a search warrant, right?"

"Of course. But just so we're clear, I don't like him for this. Neither does West. He's married with two teenage boys, one of whom is headed off to Duke on a full scholarship this fall."

We're seated across from each other at our kitchen table. I look over my shoulder to make sure that Tasha's out of the room and out of earshot.

"Where are we with the teachers at Hailey's school?"

"West and I have interviewed each of them. Twice. And not just the teachers but everyone on staff, from the maintenance workers on up to the principal. We're checking their alibis but so far every single one of their stories holds up. We haven't found a solitary crack."

I push aside a copy of this morning's *Washington Post*. Hailey's disappearance is the most sensational criminal investigation since the Beltway sniper attacks that took place over a three-week period last October.

I lower my voice. "Still no word from my father?"

"Not yet. But we have a pair of agents down in Virginia Beach looking for him. So far we've been able to confirm that your dad made it down there on the day he was supposed to. My people are canvassing the community to learn what, if anything, he's been up to since."

"Okay."

He looks into my eyes. "One of your father's neighbors suggested he may have an ongoing relationship with a woman down in Raleigh. You wouldn't know anything about that, would you?"

I shake my head. "Why wouldn't he have brought her up to Virginia Beach, then? Or told his staff he'll be in North Carolina for at least part of the trip?"

"Your father's neighbor suggests the woman may be married."

I nod. "Of course she would be."

"And affluent."

"She'd be that too."

"Actually, your father's neighbor thinks her husband is the one who is well-to-do."

As I flash on my recent arguments with Tasha I sink deeper into the table.

He places a hand atop mine. "Let's try to retain focus on what's important, Simon."

"Speaking of married women," I say in a near-whisper, "any progress on that other question?"

He lifts his hand and sighs. "We've looked at her computer, her phone records, credit card and bank statements. We've discreetly asked friends, family, and neighbors. We've even talked to some old high-school boyfriends. There is absolutely nothing to suggest an affair."

I don't know whether to feel disappointed or relieved. A bit of both, I suppose.

"It's a stranger," I say softly, staring down at my hands. "Isn't it?"

"On that front, we have officers combing Georgetown and the

surrounding neighborhoods, asking whether anyone's seen a strange vehicle parked or driving slowly around the area. So far, nothing. But that doesn't mean we won't catch a break."

I flash on the few people from our community that I've seen on the local news. They're terrified that their own children aren't safe. Some are keeping their kids home from school since it's so close to the end of the school year anyway. But there's more than just fear in those faces. There's a certain peace. They're not happy that Hailey was taken, of course, but they're thanking whatever gods or stars they believe in that it wasn't their child. They're grateful. And who can blame them?

Learning that your child is missing is worse than receiving your own terminal diagnosis.

Worse than anything that I can think of. Because every version of this story ends the same way in my head. With me finding out what happened to my baby girl. And then wishing like hell that I hadn't.

I know now. There will be no ransom demand.

I know now. There won't be a change in the heart of the bastard who took her.

I know now. There will be no hidden clue that leads us straight to her like in the movies.

"You look utterly exhausted," Rendell says to me. "Why don't you go upstairs, Simon? Shut the lights, close the curtains. Just *try* to get some sleep."

I look into his eyes, pale and blue like a swimming pool. Almost beautiful, I think.

"With all due respect, John," I say, "but are you fucking kidding me?"

Chapter 37

The address the bartender gave me was located on Lander Road, a few blocks east of the docks. It was a quiet road lined with aging two-story redbrick row houses that resembled sections of South Philly. This afternoon the area looked and felt like a ghost town, a long-unused set on a studio lot in Burbank. Even the shops at the end of the block—a barber, a pet groomer, a bodega—were shuttered as though in preparation for a category-five storm.

Closed, I thought at first. Then realized they were more likely out of business.

A number of pubs I'd passed had suffered the same fate.

I checked the numbers on the buildings (only one of every four or so still had one hanging), and found the address I was looking for directly in the center of the block. I stepped back to try to gauge whether any lights were on in the second-floor apartment and, more important, whether there was any movement. But all the shades were drawn. Not just at the address I wanted but everywhere, it seemed. For a moment I thought the bartender had taken me for a mark. But if he did, it would be a first for me. One of my assets as an investigator, is that I had the look of someone who'd come back for you if you fed me bad information. Especially if I happened to pay well for it.

So I climbed up the six cracked cement steps to the outer door. Wasn't surprised to find that there were no name tabs next to the intercom. If there were, I'd have been looking for a Mr. Kordell Rickets.

I considered the buzzer, then thought better of it. With my good hand, I pressed firmly against the door near the frame. Then I pushed. When the door budged, I knew a kick wouldn't be necessary. A shoulder would suffice. Which was a plus because it meant significantly less noise. And, since I hadn't been going to the gym regularly for the past eleven months, no chance of pulling a groin.

A single shot to the green wooden door knocked it open and almost off its hinges. I caught it on the rebound and closed it behind me before starting up a flight of creaky, weathered stairs.

When I reached the second floor, I found only one apartment door. The hallway was thick with the stench of smoke, but I couldn't tell whether it was fresh or had developed over time by seeping into the yellowed walls and ceiling. Maybe a combination. I listened carefully but heard no music, no television, no ringing phones. No conversation, no pets, no signs of life whatsoever.

Not exactly a booming small business, I thought, even for a weapons dealer. But then, maybe Mr. Rickets was out to lunch. If so, I was sure he wouldn't mind my having a quick look around.

I tried knocking first.

When I received no response, I withdrew my handgun from my waistband and threw my shoulder into it again.

The door flung open. From the frame I could see the kitchen and the living/dining area. Tidy for the most part. But marijuana and tobacco were fighting it out for olfactory superiority. Near the windows where a bit of light was slipping through the shades, I could see the smoke hanging in the air, thick as the fog you'd expect to encounter in London. So dense that if not for the frigid air, I might have thought the flat was on fire.

Quietly, I stepped over the threshold. To my right was the kitchen area. To my left was a short hallway that ended with an open door.

As I moved toward it, I finally heard a sound. Faint, as though it might be coming from another apartment.

I poked my head into the room. Saw an attractive young black woman sleeping soundly across a double bed. She was wearing headphones, which was where the sound was emanating from. Music. The Beatles, whereas I'd been expecting Bob Marley. First Zoey, then Scottish gangsters too polite to enter a family-owned bed-and-breakfast, and now this. So much for stereotypes.

She opened her eyes. Which startled me as much as seeing a strange white man dressed in full black biker armor standing in her bedroom with a gun must have startled her.

When she opened her mouth to scream, I started toward the bed. Held my bandaged left hand to her lips and practically begged her to remain silent.

"I'm not here to hurt you."

She was shaking, either from terror or cold or both.

When I looked down, I realized she was wearing nothing but an oversized T-shirt.

I did my best to calm her. First by tucking my gun back into my waistband. Then by removing my hand from her lips.

Once she had settled down some and controlled her breathing, I grabbed random clothes from the closet and asked her to get dressed.

"Where's your boyfriend?" I said as she slipped into a pair of jeans.

"Usband," she snapped.

"All right, husband, then."

She shot me a dirty look.

"Where is he?" I prodded.

"G'way, mon," she cried as she pulled on a jacket over her T-shirt.

"I'm not going away until you calm down and answer my questions. Where's Kordell?"

She shrugged her small shoulders in defiance. "Dun know."

"I don't believe that."

"He catch you here, you done, mon."

"That I believe. And that's why we're going to do this quickly. Tell me where I can find Kordell and I'll leave."

"Dat's a lie."

"No; it's the truth."

"You aks and I tell. Den you kill me dead."

"No, that's not how this is going to go down," I said. "I give you my word."

"Wutless," she spat.

I shook my head, took a step forward, looked deep into her dark brown eyes. "My word is one of the few things I have left that isn't worthless."

She said nothing.

I said, "Now, let's try a different approach. Tell me your name."

She hesitated but finally said, "Imogen."

"A beautiful name," I said. "All right, Imogen. Now we're getting somewhere."

Her eyes kept darting to an ashtray sitting on the makeshift night-stand next to her bed. A large cone-shaped joint lay in the middle of it.

"You want that spliff?" I said. "You can have it if it'll help calm you down."

I took her silence as acquiescence. Reached for the joint, handed it to her.

She placed it between her lips while I searched for a light. Once I'd given up she pointed at the small armoire across the room. On top of it I found several cheap lighters, a few pipes, and a package of rolling papers. I grabbed one of the lighters, turned to her, and thumbed the flint wheel. Held the flame to her joint as she took one large pull then another.

"All right," I said as she blew a stream of smoke into my face. "Now that our heart rates have returned to normal, how about you and I go have a brief chat in the living room?"

* * *

D is is some major fuckery, mon," she said as she dropped onto the sofa. "Why don't you jus' step?"

"Listen, Imogen. I'm not out to get your husband in any trouble. I just need to speak with one of his associates."

"He dun have any associates, my usband. He dun work, mon."

"All right, one of his friends, then."

"He dun have any frens either, ya undastan? He got me. Dat all he need."

"Look," I said, "you're making this a lot tougher than it needs to be. Let me put this simply. I need to speak with Lennox Sterling."

Immediately, Imogen's expression changed. She shifted in her seat, crossed then uncrossed her legs. Tugged at the collar of her oversized T-shirt. Her eyes went to the door but she kept her head completely still. Finally she drew her legs up onto the sofa, pulled her knees to her chin, and held them there with her arms.

"I'm no informa," she said.

"And I'm no cop."

"Then what you want with dat rude bwoy?"

I'd hit a crossroads. How much do I tell her? Go with the truth or dish out a lie?

"Does he have a girlfriend?" I asked.

"Lennox? Why do you care? You fancy him, is dat it? Dat's what all dis is about, Johnny?"

I shook my head. "Please, Imogen, just answer the question. Does Lennox Sterling have a girlfriend or not?"

" 'Course he does. Have you evah see him? He be a general, mon."

"A general?"

"One smooth operator, undastan? A genuine Mr. Mention. Hose like a—"

"All right, stop there," I said, a palm in the air. "I don't need anatomical details. I'm only interested in the girl. Tell me about her."

"His ooman be a cave bitch. White as man juice, mon. When Lennox linked up with her, I tell him she's salt, bad luck. He get vexed, tell me I'm jealous. Dat I just want him to eat unda the sheet like he used to."

I held up my palm again. "What's her name?"

"Her name Shauna. Cave-bitch name."

"Relax," I said.

Her tone grew angry. "Dun tell me ease up when you come to my crib with a gun and your questions, undastan?"

"How old is Shauna?" I said.

"How do I know, mon? You think I split her open and count da rings?"

"Could she be eighteen, nineteen?"

"Mos def, mon. Lennox, he likes dem young."

"Where can I find her?"

"Dun know where da skettle is. She left this slump few days ago. But Lennox, he know. He always know where his oomen are."

"Where can I find Lennox?"

"Today be Satday. So tonight you find him dropping legs at a bashy in Kenny."

"Kenny?"

She rolled her eyes. "Kensington, mon."

"You have an address?"

"Sure I give you da address, Johnny. But you go dere, you gonna need a whole shitload of tacks."

"Tacks?"

"Bullets, mon. For dat beeg gun of yours."

Chapter 38

Seated across from Ashdown and Zoey in the rear of a small, dark Kensington pub called the Brown Bear, I relayed my conversation with Imogen Rickets back in Toxteth.

"So where's this club we're looking for?" Ashdown said.

"Not so much a club as a party," I told him. "More like a rave. In the basement of some old, abandoned church."

"Lovely."

While I waited for them, I'd done a bit of research on Kensington. Five years ago the area had earned the distinction of becoming Liverpool's guns-and-murder capital. And it had successfully defended its title against contenders like Anfield, Toxteth, and Birkenhead ever since.

Our waitress came by and bussed some of our plates. I ordered another espresso.

"Have you slept at all, Simon?" Ashdown asked.

I thought about it. Since receiving Kati's e-mail, I'd spent one night on an Aer Lingus flight to Dublin, one night on the sofa at the Radisson, one night sleeping somewhat fitfully at Gilchrist's house in Glasgow, and one night traveling to Liverpool on the Dodge Tomahawk.

Ashdown said, "Gilchrist lent us another Grand Cherokee. After our meal, you can stretch out in the back and catch some shut-eye."

I nodded. I liked the idea of catching a few hours before the party kicked off.

Zoey reached across the table. "You look as though you've something on your mind, little brother."

I sighed, lifted my eyes to look at her. "Something Angus Quigg mentioned. About Shauna's so-called father."

"What about him?"

"Well, whoever this 'father' is, he may well be the son of a bitch who took her twelve years ago."

Ashdown frowned. "Quigg described him a bit, didn't he?"

"Quigg said he was a businessman. An *older* businessman. More like a grandfather, he told me. That's what keeps clawing at me. In my head, I'm trying to dig something up, but I'm not sure what exactly."

"Start with the most obvious," Ashdown said, "Hailey's biological grandfathers. Your father-in-law, what's his story?"

"Crotchety old bastard from Richmond, Virginia. Filthy rich, not a cent of it earned. All old money. Most of it from Big Tobacco."

"He was cleared?"

"Yeah. He was home with my mother-in-law when Hailey was taken. In fact, Tasha was on the phone with her mom when it happened. He was outside arguing with one of his neighbors about landscaping."

"And *your* father was cleared."

I nodded. "Anyway, my father hasn't been back to the United Kingdom in thirty-five years."

"How was your dad fit for money at the time?"

I shrugged. "He's a doctor. He's always had plenty."

"Plenty? As much as your in-laws?"

I shook my head. "Nowhere near what my in-laws have. They live in a different stratosphere." I glanced at him. "What are you thinking?"

"Just wondering if the FBI truly covered every angle."

"For instance?"

"For instance, they cleared your dad. But what if he'd hired someone? Professionals, I mean."

"My father didn't even want his own children," I said, staring down at the table.

I winced as I remembered Zoey was sitting right across from me.

Ashdown said, "Your father had a mistress, right? Isn't that what you told me on the drive from Dublin to Glasgow? That he was seeing a married woman down in Raleigh, North Carolina?"

"So?"

"So, you'd mentioned that *her* husband was filthy rich. What if your father was trying to pry her away? But she couldn't leave behind the lifestyle she'd become accustomed to. What if there was a prenuptial agreement in place? If she left her husband for Alden Fisk, she wouldn't get a dime. What if your father knew that? What if he needed a way to tap into your in-laws' money?"

"There was never any ransom demand."

"What if things went awry before a phone call could be made?"

"If they were professionals," I said, "they'd still have made the call."

"Not necessarily. Your father knew you were a U.S. Marshal, didn't he? If he hired professionals, they knew you'd demand proof of life before you paid any bloody ransom. What if they couldn't provide it?"

"We would have found a body," I argued. "If not right away, eventually. We combed the woods, dredged the lakes. Volunteers spent days and days digging through landfills in ninety-degree temperatures looking for some *sign* of her. Nothing was ever found. Not so much as a shoe."

Ashdown shook his head. "What I'm saying is, what if she got away? What if she simply escaped?"

"She was six, Detective. And if she did somehow manage to evade her captors, why didn't she run to the nearest cop? Her pictures were all over the D.C. area. Someone would have recognized her. And she was smart. She knew her name. She knew her address and telephone number. She knew to dial nine-one-one in the case of an emergency. She could even read and write at a second-grade level, for Christ's sake."

"What if they'd threatened her, Simon? What if they'd told her they'd kill her parents if she ever tried to escape? What if she kept running in order to keep you and Tasha safe?"

"Are we still talking about my father?" I shook my head. "He'd have to be pure evil, wouldn't he?" I looked at Zoey. "He's rotten but he isn't that, is he?"

"You'd know better than I would."

"He has a conscience," I said. "He isn't a pure sociopath. He couldn't have lived with that kind of secret. He would have had to tell me. Especially if she had escaped and there was a chance I could find her and bring her home."

Ashdown leaned forward. "You said that he *begged* to meet with you in person right after Hailey went missing."

"So?"

"So maybe he *did* need to tell you what happened. But he couldn't do it over the phone. He'd have known the feds were listening in."

I thought about it, said, "I suppose he wouldn't have admitted it to me in person either."

"Why not? He'd have suspected you'd turn him in?"

"No," I said. "Because he'd have known I would have murdered him."

Chapter 39

Inside the confessional, I could feel the music thumping beneath my sturdy, wooden chair. I took a deep breath and checked my watch under the light of the flame from the platinum Zippo that Zoey somehow filched from Kinny Gilchrist back in Glasgow. I'd been waiting fifteen minutes. Ten more and I'd have to devise another strategy.

But then my BlackBerry vibrated. A text from Ashdown read:

Three men, unarmed. Two entering rear of church. One remaining at door.

I set my BlackBerry down and placed my right hand inside my jacket. Wrapped my fingers around the grip of the .45.

Moments later a dim light switched on, revealing a dark wooden lattice directly in front of me. On the opposite side of the lattice was a small sliding window, which opened seconds after the door to the adjoining compartment opened and closed.

Through the lattice I could see only a large shadowy form. A pungent blend of smoke and sweat instantly filled the entire space.

The male voice on the other side of the lattice intoned, "In da name of da Father, and of da Son, and of da Holy Spirit." He possessed an accent more British than Jamaican. "What can I do for you, son?"

I tipped my head forward. "I'm in need of salvation, Father."

"Aren't we all?" he said softly. "Imogen tells me you are also in search of peace. Or shall we say *a* piece?"

"That's right, Father."

"Well, you have come to da right place."

Slowly, he enumerated my firearms options. A Walther P99. A SIG Sauer P226. A Heckler & Koch MP5SF. A Browning 9 mm.

My BlackBerry lit up without sound.

Immediately the voice on the other side of the lattice turned angry. "You were told *no* electronic devices."

I quickly scanned Ashdown's text:

Both men neutralized. Outside: Jomo Newell. Inside: Kordell Rickets.

A second text immediately followed:

Confessional: Lennox Sterling confirmed.

"Sorry, Father," I said. "It was just a text."

"Turn it *off*," he insisted.

"I'd prefer not to, Father."

He stood, turned toward the door.

I said, "I wouldn't do that if I were you."

Although I couldn't see him clearly, I estimated he stood at least six four, maybe six five. A virtual giant.

I said, "I have an HK .45 pointed at you. You open that door, I'm going to fire. Maybe I hit you. Maybe I miss. But from what I can make out, you're a fairly large target. And I'm a damn good shot." I paused. "So have a seat, Father. Please."

After some consideration, he sat. Said, "You will be gunned down da second you pull dat trigger, mon."

"No, I won't, Lennox. See, your mate Kordell Rickets is no longer standing outside this confessional. And your other friend Jomo Newell is no longer outside guarding the rear entrance to this church."

Several seconds passed in silence. Then: "What have you done, mon?"

"Don't worry," I said. "They're fine. I have no intention of hurting you *or* them unless I have to. So how things go from here is pretty much up to you."

"What do you want?"

"Just information."

"Who are you?"

"My name doesn't matter," I said. "All you need to know is that I'm not a cop. I'm a private investigator from the States. I accept only one kind of case. I search for missing and abducted children."

Sterling had calmed. "I have no children, mon. Abducted or otherwise. So what do you want with me?"

"Tell me about Shauna Adair."

"Shauna?" he said testily. "She is *my* girl, mon. Why are you asking me about Shauna?"

"What was she doing in Dublin?"

"I dun know. She wouldn't tell me. But it was something to do with her father, I think. He is one son of a bitch, he is."

"What's his name?"

"She never told me his name. She calls him Daddy, I call him da son of a bitch."

"Why is he a son of a bitch?"

"Why do you think? He's a racist, mon. A coward."

"Why do you think he's a racist? Because he doesn't like you?"

"Because he didn't like me before he met me. He told her, 'You go out with one of dem neggas, we done.'"

I processed this, said, "So she chose you over him. But if Shauna's relationship with her father is done, why would she have gone to Dublin for him?"

"Like I said before, I dun know, mon. But my guess is, he got himself into some kind of trouble again. It's all he's good for, her old man. And no matter what, every time he calls, Shauna goes running."

"What kind of trouble does he get himself into?"

"Trouble with the filth. Trouble with his competition. Trouble with his own mates, even."

"What kind of competition?"

"Drugs, innit? He sells drugs. And not just ganja. All kinds. Even da hard stuff."

"Where does he sell these drugs?"

"He's based out of London, mon. But Shauna says he has legit businesses all over da UK and Ireland."

"In Liverpool?"

"Not Liverpool, but Manchester."

"What kind of legit businesses does he run?"

"Shauna never told me. She doesn't like talking about her old man, and I can't blame her."

"But you've met him?"

"Once. And, believe me, once was enough."

"Where is Shauna now?" I asked.

"I dun know, mon. She hasn't called me since she left six or seven days ago."

I cursed inwardly. "You live together, right?"

"That's right, mon. I love her. I love her like the sun."

"Poetic," I said. "So when she returns to Liverpool, she'll return to your place."

"I hope so."

"You hope so? Where else would she go?"

"A drugs den, maybe. She's hooked, thanks to her old man."

"Hooked on what?"

"Skag, mon. Brown. Gear. Horse. Smack. Whatever you want to call it."

"And she can't get heroin at home?"

"I don't allow that shite in my house, mon. I am clean. I only smoke ganja, have an occasional drink to celebrate."

I changed course. "How old is she, Lennox?"

"She says she's twenty-three."

"What do you mean, 'She *says* she's twenty-three?'"

"I mean, I asked her once da year of her birth, and it took her counting on her fingers to answer me."

I thought about what Quigg said when I asked him if Shauna could possibly be eighteen. *"She'd have to be an auld soul, I think."*

"What else do you know about her past?"

"Nothing, mon. Only what she tells me. She says she grew up in London, says that's all I need to know."

"She returns there? To London, I mean."

"Only once in a while."

"Where in London?"

"I have no idea, mon. She tells me nothing about London. But when she comes back to Liverpool, she's sometimes carrying matches for a pub in da East End."

"What's the name of this pub?"

"Da name of da pub is Night's End, innit?"

"Do you know if she has any contacts in London?"

"Besides her old man? None dat I know of."

"How about here? Does she have any friends in Liverpool?"

"She's got only me, mon. My mates are her mates."

I rose from my chair. "I want you to take your ID and slide it under the door. Nice and slowly."

He did as he was told.

"One more question," I said. "Why would a private investigator have followed Shauna up to Dublin?"

He chuckled benignly. "You said before you're a private investigator, right? So why don't you tell me?"

Chapter 40

At midnight, I labor down the stairs and find Tasha seated alone at the kitchen table, staring down at the phone.

"Another prank?" I ask.

She nods but says nothing.

I go to the fridge, sit across from her with a cold bottle of Dasani in my hand. I'm not even thirsty. These past few weeks I've found myself walking around with bottles of water and soda, mugs of coffee, cups of tea without ever putting my lips to them. They're just props, there to occupy my hands so that I don't find myself biting my nails or picking at the skin around my thumbs.

"It's difficult to get used to the quiet," I say.

Tasha's expression doesn't change. She's been worse these past couple of days as more and more feds are taken off the case, sent out on other assignments. There's a political scandal in Washington and it's been filling the front pages, replacing Hailey's story inch by inch by precious inch.

"It was bound to happen," I say.

I fix on her eyes, red-rimmed and empty, her entire body sagging beneath an unfathomable weight. I want to take her in my arms, lift her from her chair, put my lips to hers, and carry her upstairs. But it's too late for any of that. She hates me. And she has every right to.

Regardless of what happened, I've been a bastard to her, and I deserve it if she decides tonight to pack her bags and take a limo to her parents and never come back. All our blaming each other, the endless back and forth, it didn't help one bit in finding Hailey. All it did was wreck what little we had left in the world.

Tears stream down her face. I say nothing, just watch them fall as I've done all along.

She dips into her pocket, removes a pill bottle. Unscrews the childproof cap and drops two tablets into her palm. I've given up trying to identify which pills she's taking and how many and how often. I've given up on just about everything at this point.

She reaches across the table. For an instant, I think she's reaching for my hand. But no. She's reaching for my bottle of Dasani.

I slide it across the table to her. Say, "We've done everything we can, Tash."

She swallows her pills but doesn't reply, doesn't so much as glance in my direction.

"We've put up thousands of flyers, we've combed the wooded areas, we've made countless pleas on local and national television. There's nothing else we can do at this point."

"*Isn't there though?*" she suddenly shouts at me.

The fact that she's spoken at all, let alone at such volume, startles me.

Calmly I say, "We've been at this for weeks, Tash. We followed the FBI's instructions to the letter. It kills me but there's nothing else for us to do."

"*Isn't there though?*"

"We can drive around more if you'd like. We can hop in the SUV right now and take a ride through the District. Is that what you want to do?"

No answer.

"Rendell and West, they're continuing to do everything they can too. We can't fault them, Tash. They want to return our daughter home to us, and they're doing their damnedest. They're only taking agents off the case now because there's nothing those agents can do."

"Isn't there though?" she mutters softly through her tears.

She drops her face into her hands and I stand, move behind her to take her into my arms, but she pushes me away with what little strength she has left in her.

Her eyelids are drooping. Which means she's taken a muscle relaxer or several tranquilizers. Maybe both, I don't know. I've asked before and she assures me it's none of my business and I've since conceded she's right.

Where are you, Hailey?

The images that materialize in my head when I ask myself that question night after night are becoming too painful even to contemplate.

Locked rooms.

Underground bunkers.

Attics, basements.

Beds with badly soiled sheets. Handcuffs wrapped around rusted pipes. Bed sores and lacerated wrists and ankles.

Blood pooling on a cement floor.

Vomit rising.

Sitting in her own feces as she waits.

Thinking of me. Of Tasha.

Until she sees that face.

Her captor, his visage pixelated in my mind so that I can't make him out.

Him. Approaching. Slowly, as he always does. Replacing all her other thoughts with terror.

What does he want from her now?

I see him coming for her but I'm helpless to stop him.

With a closed fist, he delivers a strike to her battered face.

Rips off her tattered clothes.

She screams.

The screams of my six-year-old daughter echo in every chamber of my mind.

And there's nothing I can do to save her.

Isn't there though? Tasha cries. *Isn't there though?*

Aloud I say, "We'll die if we continue on like this, Tash."

She says nothing.

I say nothing more.

I lift my bottle of Dasani off the table and head back upstairs, alone.

Chapter 41

The apartment Lennox Sterling shared with Shauna Adair was located in Croxteth, an impoverished neighborhood that, according to Ostermann's contact at the Merseyside Police, had recently become synonymous with gang violence. Evidence of this assertion could be found on at least one of the four corners of virtually every block, including the intersection I just passed, where a group of hooded teenagers loitered with lit cigarettes and tall aluminum cans poorly disguised inside brown paper bags.

I parked the Grand Cherokee that Gilchrist had lent Ashdown across the street from Sterling's building. After killing the engine, I sat stock-still in the darkness, watching the rearview mirror. A pair of headlights turned left at the end of the last block and no others followed. So I opened the door, climbed out of the SUV, and moved slowly toward my destination.

Ashdown and Zoey had remained behind in Kensington with Kordell Rickets, Jomo Newell, and Lennox Sterling himself. Whether it was from the high levels of THC running through their bloodstreams or they were mellow by nature, I didn't know. But the three of them took their instructions rather well. Especially once Ashdown flashed his badge. From their demeanor it seemed they were accustomed to dealing with the police, not as adversaries but as grudging partners in a dirty business. Which should have come as no surprise.

Weapons dealers rarely operated successfully without the cooperation of law enforcement, not just in the UK but around the globe.

When I reached the building I slipped my good hand into my pocket and retrieved Sterling's keys. A feeling of déjà vu arrived—and just as quickly passed—as I turned the key in the outer door. For a moment I'd been transported back to the concrete steps leading to my building on Dumbarton Street in D.C., where only a few nights ago I'd curled up like a ball in the freezing cold after realizing I'd misplaced my keys.

This time I opened the door without incident and started up the rickety stairs toward the third floor. I located apartment 3-F and used a second key to unlock the dead bolt. A moment later I stepped inside and closed the door behind me.

A wave of emotion threatened to overwhelm me. Was it possible that after twelve years I was standing in the entryway of the Liverpool flat occupied by my daughter? The very thought of it seemed surreal. And yet, for the first time in those twelve years, it felt entirely possible.

I took another step forward into the apartment. The place was old and worn but clean. It smelled of smoke but also of incense and potpourri—an unmistakable female touch that stirred something inside me.

What struck me most, however, was the fact that the apartment felt happy. Unlike my studio on Dumbarton Street, this flat was a place where life was lived. In the kitchen, there were Post-it notes on the refrigerator. All the necessary appliances: a toaster, a microwave, a panini grill, a blender. Even an espresso machine.

In the living room hung photos of the happy couple. Lennox with his well-toned arms around Shauna in front of a pub. Shauna with her lips on Lennox's cheek in a park somewhere outside the city. The couple holding hands on a bridge in Wales. A young man and woman in love. Not just sharing an apartment but sharing a life. Making a home.

The more I saw the more I smiled, until it started to dawn on me that this young woman couldn't have spent most of the past twelve years locked away in a basement, crying for her mother and father. It couldn't possibly be Hailey.

Could it?

I began opening the drawers one by one, first in the kitchen then in the dining room. Only once I'd finished in the living room did I venture toward the bedroom. Opening the door to their bedroom felt like some sort of violation, but I did it. As I stepped inside, a pair of headlights flooded the street below, then moved on. I walked to the window and watched a dark SUV hook a left at the corner. Aside from that vehicle the street remained empty.

I turned away from the window.

Is this where Hailey sleeps?

The bedroom was compact and cluttered. Clothes strewn everywhere because there was only one small closet. I imagined they entertained in the other rooms and this one remained private. I opened the drawers to the ancient armoire. Lennox's T-shirts and shorts and bandanas and watches occupied the top, his underwear and socks the second drawer down. I moved some stuff around and discovered a thick wad of British pounds, another of euros, and a third of U.S. currency, all large bills. Fifties and hundreds. In the back of the drawer I found a pistol. A .22 Ruger SR22 Rimfire. A three-and-a-half-inch barrel. Loaded. I slipped it into the pocket of my biker jacket.

Next drawer down was Shauna's. Her unmentionables. Bras, panties, nighties. I reached toward the rear of the drawer and inadvertently (but unmistakably) touched a sex toy. Immediately pulled my hand free and shut the drawer, shaking off my discomfort.

A few moments later, once my queasiness had passed, I opened the bottom drawer. Shauna's jeans and sweaters and sweatshirts and belts. I closed the drawer and moved next to the closet.

I reached for the top shelf and pulled down a few shoe boxes. To my dismay, there was nothing in them except shoes. One pair of kicks for Lennox, two pairs of heels for Shauna. The remainder of the closet was loaded with clothes.

I wasn't sure what I was looking for, only that I'd know it when I found it. But I was fast running out of places to search. A diary, maybe. An address book. A day planner. A yearbook. The things a young woman accumulates over the course of a teenage life.

I went to my haunches and opened the third drawer down in the armoire again. As much as I hated to rummage through it, I thought if there was anything private to find, like maybe love letters or family photos, this was where she would keep them.

I pushed aside something silk then something leather. Sweating, I ran a hand across my forehead and dug past the sex toys.

I found a thick paperback, *Imajica* by Clive Barker. A fantasy novel from the looks of it.

Is this what Hailey reads?

I flipped through the pages and found no highlighted passages, no notes in the margins. I read a few paragraphs, foolishly thinking it would help me understand her mind-set. Maybe even remind me of something in her childhood that would serve as a clue that this was indeed Hailey's reading material. But when Hailey was six, her favorite book was still *The Grinch Who Stole Christmas*.

"Let's read it again, Daddy, one more time, just once more."

I replaced the book and dug deeper still.

And found a smartphone. A Google Nexus 5 made by LG.

I turned it over and found no battery. So I pulled the drawer farther out and continued searching. I finally located the battery but no charger.

Why is she hiding it?

I attached the battery and powered up the device. My mind raced back to a few nights ago at Terry's when I first received Kati's e-mail but couldn't open the attachments because the battery had croaked. This phone turned on and I quickly checked the screen for a lightning bolt or something else to signal low power. But a small vertical image of a battery appeared in the top right-hand corner, half full.

Once I was sure she had some life in her, I inspected the icons. Telephone, camera, messages, browser. Excitement, I realized, was swelling inside my chest. My thumb moved toward the camera icon. Soon as I touched it, the phone went black. I slid my finger up the screen and located the saved photos.

Christ. Dozens of thoughts flooded my head at once. The first image was of Shauna with Angus Quigg in front of a pub in Springburn. Not only had I seen the picture before, it was tattooed on my mind. I'd studied it for five and a half hours as Ashdown drove me and Zoey from Dublin to Glasgow a couple of days ago. I slid right. Another photo I instantly recognized. Now, there was no question; in my hands I held Eli Welker's phone.

Which meant that Shauna *had* taken it off Welker the night she'd killed him.

It also meant she'd returned to Liverpool sometime in the past few days. Which meant Lennox Sterling had lied to me. Or that Shauna hadn't told him she was back.

Both scenarios seemed plausible.

Overriding all of that was the fact that I now had possession of Welker's phone. In my hands, I held a record of his e-mails and text messages and phone calls from his last days on earth.

Which meant I probably held in my hand the answer to my most vital question—*Who was Welker's final client?*

I opened the folder marked CONTACTS.

As I did, a sound emanated from the hallway.

For a moment, I froze and listened.

Seconds later there was no mistaking it.

Someone was at Lennox Sterling's door.

Hailey?

I pocketed the phone and reached into my jacket for the Heckler & Koch.

I doused the bedroom lamp and crept into the hallway, perhaps only half believing I was about to see my daughter for the first time since she was taken.

Chapter 42

Nearly shooting Ashdown in the hallway of the Tucker Bed and Breakfast in Edinburgh remained fresh in my mind. Which was why I returned the Heckler & Koch .45 to my waistband. If Hailey Fisk was about to step through that door and see her true father for the first time in twelve years, she damn sure wasn't going to find him training a gun on her.

Only it wasn't Hailey.

When the door swung wide, a hooded figure stepped inside, wheeled around to his left, and I suddenly found myself staring into the barrel of a .45 for the second time this week.

The hood fell from his head and the acned face of Duncan Mac-Bride stared back at me.

My thoughts swirled like a twister. The only explanation was that MacBride had patiently followed the Grand Cherokee all the way from Glasgow. First to Kensington then to Croxteth.

I judged the distance. This time I stood no chance of reaching the gun by charging at him.

In another flash of déjà vu I raised my arms in the air.

"Well, if it ain't the fecking frog," Duncan said with a crooked smile. "The cheese-eating surrender monkey."

"I take it Tavis Maxwell sent you," I said as calmly as possible. "Whatever he's paying you, I'll double it if you turn around and head back to Glasgow right now and put a bullet through the back of his skull."

Duncan's brother, Todd MacBride, stepped in behind him, a great big grin on his face. "Show us the two million pounds then, Fisk."

Since I was a little short, I needed to devise a plan B. And fast.

I said, "How about instead, I lend each of you boys a thousand pounds. This way you can both go back to Glasgow and have that dermabrasion procedure performed. Clear up those ugly fucking faces of yours. It's torture just looking at the two of you."

The four corners of their lips fell in unison. No one was left smiling except me.

And I really had nothing to smile about.

Because Duncan immediately raised his .45 and leveled it at my heart.

He said something as he fired. But, whatever it was, I sure as hell didn't hear it.

D on't forget to snap the photos, mate," Duncan said to his brother. "Without them, we won't collect on the contract."

"No worries," Todd said. "That bastart ain't going nowhere. First I want to have a look round this flat, see if there's anything we can nick."

"A million pounds naw enough for you?"

"'Course not," Todd said. "First of all, it's half a million, innit? Because I gotta split it with your junkie ass. Half a million pounds ain't retirement money, brother."

Duncan took a few steps toward the body. "Should I put one in the frog's face for good measure?"

"He ain't no frog. He's a bloody Yank."

"All right. Should I put one in the Yank's face, then?"

"No. At least naw until I snap the photos, right? If the old man can't identify the body, we're going to wind up with fuck-all."

"Good point." Duncan pocketed the pistol and pulled out a blade. "How about I cut an ear off, then? Like that nutter Mr. Blonde from *Reservoir Dogs*? The King will fancy that, won't he?"

"Have at it, brother. I'm gonna have a look round the bedroom."

As Todd's footsteps faded, Duncan leaned over the corpse. Grabbed hold of its left ear.

That's when I opened my eyes.

With my bandaged left I snatched him by the throat so that he couldn't make a sound. With my right I swiftly guided his knife hand away from me.

With all my strength, manipulated it.

Redirected it.

And helped him plunge the blade deep into his own chest.

He struggled for a solid fifteen seconds, which was ten more than I'd expected.

"Hey, you should see this bird's knickers," Todd MacBride called out from the bedroom.

Slowly I turned his brother over.

I felt for a pulse, but he was gone.

Leaving his eyes open, I took the .45 from his pocket and started toward the bedroom.

"She's into dildos, she is," Todd said with an ugly cackle.

I stood in the door frame of the bedroom, watching him tear through Shauna's underwear drawer.

I raised the weapon, leveled it at the back of his head.

"Dunc, you've gotta see this, mate. Nearly as big as mine, innit?"

After a few seconds, I lowered the gun and walked back the way I'd come.

Because I'd decided the worst thing I could do to Todd MacBride was leave him alive to mourn for his brother.

Chapter 43

I stepped into the hallway, quietly closing Sterling's front door behind me. Todd MacBride was still in the bedroom rifling through the couple's closet and drawers. He hadn't yet discovered his brother's body. I tucked away Duncan MacBride's gun and started down the stairs.

As soon as I stepped outside, back into the darkness, I unzipped the jacket that had saved my life. Opening it allowed me to fully breathe again. As I inhaled the cold night air, I placed a finger on the bullet that would otherwise have ended my life and sighed deeply. Made a mental note that if I ever returned to Bogota, I'd thank Miguel Caballero personally.

Meanwhile, I removed Eli Welker's smartphone from my pocket. First I returned to the photos. Swiped through the pictures of Shauna and Angus Quigg in Glasgow. As far as Shauna went, the ones Ostermann had sent me were the only ones on the phone.

I tapped Welker's CONTACTS icon and scrolled quickly through the names and numbers. Kurt Ostermann's number was in his phone, as was my friend Wendy Isles's, another investigator based in London. There were dozens of phone numbers listed only by code, each a combination of two letters and five numbers. File numbers, I assumed. No doubt correlating with thick folders locked away in Welker's office. Clearly he went to extraordinary lengths to protect the privacy of his clients. As frustrating as it was for me, I admired his fastidiousness.

Next I opened his e-mail. Within a few seconds I'd found the e-mail Welker sent to himself the day before he died. The photos of Shauna and Angus Quigg in Glasgow. In the text of the e-mail, there was a file number. MP-61371.

MP, I assumed, stood for Missing Persons.

I returned to Welker's contact list. Searched for MP-61371.

There it was, halfway down the list. Attached to an exchange in the United States.

I swallowed hard. Steadied myself because I suddenly felt dizzy. Then I tapped on the number, initiating the call.

It rang once, then a recording:

"Welcome to Verizon Wireless. The number you have dialed has been changed, disconnected, or is no longer in service. If you feel you have reached this recording in error, please check the number and try your call again."

I cursed inwardly then placed Welker's phone into my pocket and pulled out my BlackBerry. I dialed Kurt Ostermann.

"I've received a few e-mails from Welker's clients," he said as soon as he answered. "I have arranged meetings here in London with three of them and I'm trying to convince a fourth that I'm legit."

"Where are these clients located?" I asked.

"Two of them—and the one I'm still trying to convince—are located right here in England. One in Manchester, the others in London. The third is coming in from the States. Which state, he wouldn't say. Nor would he give me his name. But he said he'd get on a flight as soon as he could and e-mail me again once he arrived at Heathrow."

From the building behind me I heard Todd MacBride howl in grief.

In the darkness, I started walking across the street toward the Grand Cherokee, the hard wind now at my back.

"First thing," I said, "I need you to phone the Merseyside Police." I gave him Lennox Sterling's address. "Tell them there's a body. Two brothers entered the apartment to burglarize the place. One killed the other."

Ostermann took down the information.

"And you, Simon? What's your next move?"

"I'm on my way to London," I told him. "I guess you could say, I'm coming home."

Part Four

THE SONS OF LONDON

Chapter 44

There are nearly six million CCTV cameras in Britain, more than a half million in London alone. One for every dozen people or so. Meaning once you enter the largest city in Europe—the capital of England and the United Kingdom—you *are* under surveillance regardless of age, gender, race, ethnicity, religion, or criminal history.

Advocates for mass surveillance argue it's necessary to fight terrorism, to protect national security, to prevent social unrest. Critics say such measures violate privacy, infringe on civil rights, limit political freedoms. But there's precious little public debate. Because on September 11, 2001, many of these legal and constitutional questions flew out the window. Now it seems unlikely that they'll ever flutter back in.

Regardless of where we stand on the issue, most of us concede that mass surveillance doesn't necessarily create a totalitarian state like those that existed in the former Soviet Union and East Germany. But it seems at least equally as clear to many historians that such intrusions on privacy sure as hell can pave the way for one.

"If you asked me a few days ago," I told Ostermann, "I'd have said the more cameras the better. But right now I'm biased. Because those half-million surveillance cameras put us at a distinct disadvantage. Facing those kinds of resources, how the hell can we expect to find

Shauna in a city of more than eight million before Scotland Yard does?"

We were seated in a pub called the Sherlock Holmes on Northumberland Street a few steps from the Charing Cross railway station. We'd walked over from Ostermann's hotel, the Corinthia, after he made a deal with the concierge to hide the illicit Dodge Tomahawk I'd driven down from Liverpool after returning Gilchrist's Grand Cherokee to Ashdown and Zoey in Kensington.

Ostermann folded his hands beneath his chin. Although he must have been approaching fifty, he appeared much as he had when I first met him over a decade ago. And he actually looked *younger* than he did the last time I saw him in Berlin while I was searching for Lindsay Sorkin, the six-year-old American girl abducted from her parents' hotel room in Paris.

"The question, Watson," he said, staring over my shoulder, "is how do we turn that disadvantage into an advantage?"

I sipped my espresso. "Is that a Sherlock Holmes quote?"

"I've no idea," he said, turning his ice-blue eyes on me. "I've never read Arthur Conan Doyle."

I leaned back in my chair, gazed out the window at three bright red double-decker buses belching out dense black smoke as they sat in traffic.

"Why are we here, then?" I said, motioning toward Holmes's study.

"I enjoy Moriarty's Beef Burger," he said. "Robert Downey, Jr.'s Baked Camembert isn't bad either. Want to split an order?"

I shook my head, said, "Back to our disadvantage. I can't exactly walk into the Met and ask for their help. I'm still wanted for questioning in the death of Ewan Maxwell in Scotland. To say nothing of the body I left at Lennox Sterling's apartment back in Liverpool."

"British police are none too fond of German private investigators either," Ostermann said. "But that does leave us with at least one friend I believe we can count on. If you don't mind calling her, that is. She's a tad peeved with me at the moment."

Before I could ask why, the answer came to me. "You slept with her?"

"I did. But that's not what she's peeved about. I'd told her I had separated from Magda, which wasn't entirely true."

"Or true at all, was it?"

"Technically true. Magda was in Berlin, I was in London. We were separated by over a thousand kilometers, geographically speaking. *Including* the English Channel."

"I'll make the call, then." I finished my espresso. "No word yet from Eli Welker's final client, I take it?"

"Not yet. But soon, I'd expect."

"In the meantime, any chance his widow will cave on giving us a look at his physical files?"

"None. And now the NCA has locked off all access to his offices. Maybe your brother-in-law can get us in, but I certainly can't."

It suddenly occurred to me why Ostermann had been so eager to deliver the news to Welker's widow personally.

"Becky," I said. "Please tell me you didn't."

"Of course not. I gave her a shoulder to cry on, nothing more." He scoffed. "Is that really what you think of me, Simon? That I'd sleep with my friend's widow before his body had gone cold?"

"I'd hope not," I said.

"Good." He lifted his pint with a smug grin. "Because with a woman like Becky Welker, one must take his time to lay a foundation."

I produced my BlackBerry and dialed Wendy Isles. The call went straight to voice mail so I left a message for her to call me back as soon as possible.

"So," Ostermann said, "we wait for Wendy to call you so that she can assist us in gaining access to surveillance footage here in London. We wait for Eli Welker's final client to e-mail me so that we can meet with him, learn his identity, and find out why he hired Welker to track Shauna Adair to Dublin. That seems to me a fair amount of waiting. What do we do in the meantime?"

"Try to find this so-called 'father' of Shauna's, I suppose."

"Do we have anything at all to go on?"

"Nothing but a book of matches, I'm afraid."

"Matches?"

"Lennox Sterling told me that when Shauna comes back from London after meeting with her father, she sometimes has a book of matches on her. From a pub in the East End. He doesn't know if there's any connection, but I figure it's worth a shot."

"You have an address?"

"No address. Sterling only remembered the name."

"What's the name of this pub, then?"

"The Night's End."

Ostermann shrugged. "You ask me, the End is always a good place to start."

Chapter 45

TWELVE YEARS AGO

It's three A.M. and I'm sitting on a barstool at Terry's, working on my fourth or fifth pint of Harp. I'm tired. No, more than that, defeated. I'm utterly lost.

"Hand them over," Terry says. Only in his stubborn cockney accent it sounds like *'and them ova.*

I don't need to ask what he's referring to. I dig into the front pocket of my jeans and pull out my keys, slide them across the bar. I had no intention of driving anyway.

I'd arrived at the pub only an hour ago after Terry cleared the place out following last call. I've no desire to interact with people. There are enough of them still camped out in front of my house, day and night. Enough of them still inside my home as well. Though that number has greatly dwindled. A sure sign that Rendell's hopes continue to dwindle as well.

Terry opens the register and places my keys in the drawer. "You have your house keys?" he asks.

My laugh sounds more like a grunt. "You think Tash and I are locking our doors these days, Terry? What the hell would we do that for? The only thing we had to protect is gone."

"Missing," he says. "They'll find her, Simon."

I know better than to respond, than to engage my only real friend in that senseless circular conversation yet again.

I lift the pint to my lips. These are my first drinks since Hailey was taken. That I'm drinking at all is a sure sign to everyone, Terry included, that I've all but given up hope myself. I never drink more than a pint or two. Never enough to get drunk. And if there any reason at all for me to wake up early tomorrow morning, sober and ready to take on the day, I wouldn't be here right now. I'd be home. In bed. With Tasha. Where I belong.

"Is she faring any better?" Terry says. Except that glottal stops replace the letter *t* so that *better* sounds a hell of a lot more like *be'er*.

"She gets worse every day. We both do. But Tash, I barely recognize her anymore."

In the past two weeks my wife has gone from being a vibrant young mother to a desolate shell of flesh and bone. She's lost at least ten pounds, and she didn't have even five to spare. She spends her days in a chemical funk, popping benzodiazepines like they were sunflower seeds. When she isn't eating tranquilizers she's snacking on muscle relaxers, hoping to fall asleep. She's been to the emergency room twice for extreme lower back pain and been prescribed powerful opioids, which she keeps in her pocket at all times. When this began, I tried to talk to her about it. But as with everything else, I've since thrown in the towel.

"I take it her parents haven't been helpful?"

"They've done what they can. For the first time since I met them, I can't complain about their behavior."

"Even your mother-in-law?" Only he replaces the *th* sound with a *v*, and the final *r* vanishes completely, making mother-in-law sound like *muvva-in-law*.

"Even my mother-in-law."

"How about your own dad?"

I smirk without meaning to. It's been ten days now since Alden Fisk was cleared and not twenty-four hours have gone by without his calling, asking whether he can come by to help out. I've assured him it isn't necessary, made clear his presence was something neither Tasha nor I wanted, but he refuses to relent.

"Two days ago, I stopped taking his calls," I say.

Everything we'd been told had checked out. My father had indeed left Providence for Virginia Beach then gone on to Raleigh to carry on with a married woman not much older than me.

"If he means well," Terry says, "maybe you should have him by."

"If that's the kind of advice you're going to give, I'm going to take my business elsewhere."

"Do you think there's any chance he'll just show up?"

"Enough," I say, louder and angrier than I mean to. "I don't want to discuss Alden Fisk. Not with you, not with anybody."

"I apologize," he says.

But I've known Terry long enough to know he's offended. Thing is, with all this beer in me, I'm having trouble caring.

"I'm just making conversation," he adds. "Trying to understand the situation."

"Well, don't." I immediately regret saying it but it's as though someone or some*thing* else is controlling my tongue. "There *is* no understanding it, Terry. It's the Ninth Circle of Hell. Unless you've lost a child, you can't comprehend the first thing about it. So just don't bother trying, all right?"

An uncomfortable silence hangs over the bar.

"I *have* lost a child," he says finally. "A daughter, in fact. Every bit as beautiful as Hailey."

I look up at him, study his pained expression, wondering how in all this time he could possibly have been harboring such a secret.

He says, "I've told you, I believe, of me boyhood mate, Avery."

I nod. "The one who became a solicitor."

"A solicitor, right. Avery York his name was."

I recall him telling me about Avery, the London lawyer who reminds me a lot of my father. Terry and he grew up together in London during the forties and fifties. They'd had everything in common, even having been born in the same month of the same year. Both boys came from working-class families. Both possessed an absent father and a mother who wasn't entirely stable, mentally. They lived in the same neighborhood, attended the same schools for both their primary and secondary education. Both were good students who maintained top marks. They were equally athletic, equally competitive. They had the same color eyes, same color hair. When they reached full size, Terry was slightly taller at six one, Avery slightly more muscular. In their mid to late teens they'd dated twin sisters for several years.

Only when they were in their twenties did their paths finally diverge.

Terry and Avery had both been attending the law school at Newcastle University. One night while at an on-campus party thrown by undergraduates, they'd gotten into a row with a pair of rugby players from Northumbria University. Avery, drunk as an Irishman as Terry puts it, started the row, but it was Terry who finished it. Terry broke one rugby player's cheekbone with a fist and fractured the other's jaw with a kick, the latter coming well after any potential threat had been thwarted.

Both Terry and Avery were arrested but only Terry was charged. Only Terry was convicted of causing grievous bodily harm. Only Terry was sentenced to two and a half years. Not terribly long considering what he faced; the judge had used his discretion to go below the guidelines. But long enough that it spelled the end of his law-school career.

They remained friends throughout the ordeal and well beyond. But Terry's life had taken a decidedly different turn from Avery's.

Avery continued on at Newcastle and graduated with honors. He took a job with a large full-service London law firm and received a healthy signing bonus and an even healthier annual salary.

Meanwhile, Terry, as he tells it, used the connections he'd made at HMP Isis, a Young Offenders Institution in southeast London, and became "a pharmaceuticals salesman." Primarily selling cocaine-based products.

Avery York, the big-time solicitor, went on to marry a young woman of some means.

Terrance Davies, the small-time gangster, impregnated a heroin-addled harlot.

He'd previously told me she'd lost the baby in her fifth month of pregnancy.

Confused, I say, "The fetus, you mean?"

Terry shakes his head and lets out an audible breath.

"No," he says. "I've never been entirely honest about this because it's something I've never really wanted to talk about, Simon. But the child was born healthy."

His chin sinks into his chest and tears cloud his eyes.

"Once upon a time," he says, "I had a little girl."

Chapter 46

A Google search for "Night's End" in London didn't turn up any relevant hits. But before I could become too frustrated, I received a call back from Wendy Isles, who agreed to meet with me in the main lobby of the Corinthia.

"Needle in a haystack doesn't even begin to describe the uselessness of London's surveillance cameras in finding missing persons," Wendy said. "Or in catching criminals, for that matter."

Wendy ran a hand through her lustrous blond hair. Seated on a plush yellow sofa in the Corinthia Hotel's opulent lobby and dressed in an impeccably tailored black Burberry suit, she could well have passed for a fashion model. In just the brief time we'd been sitting here, she'd turned more heads than Roger Federer and Novak Djokovic in the finals match on Centre Court at Wimbledon.

"Only the Borough of Newham even trialed facial recognition software," she continued, "and it was an unmitigated failure. They inputted photos of countless local criminals over a period of years and the software failed to recognize a single one. This despite the fact that a number of those same convicted individuals were known to be living and lurking in the borough during all that time."

"So it didn't reduce crime," I said.

"Oh, it reduced crime by more than a third. But only because everyone was scared out of their bloody wits that they were going to be captured live on camera. Little did they know, they had nothing to fear because the computer failed to lock on a solitary live target."

"On the bright side, I suppose what you're telling me negates the advantage Scotland Yard has in finding this young woman Shauna before I do."

"Well, not completely, of course. You *are* one man, Simon. Last I checked, the Met employed over thirty thousand officers. Human beings still do *some* things better than computers after all. Especially in those numbers."

"So the only way to find her on video is to know precisely where she was and at precisely what time beforehand."

"That about sums it up. The half-million cameras in London may prevent some crimes simply because people realize that if the Met knows where and when a crime took place, chances are they can look at a picture of the perpetrator. By the same logic, the system is good for solving some crimes. It was useful after 7/7, and of course, just a few days ago, the Guards in Dublin caught on camera that little bitch who murdered Eli."

I looked away, hoping Wendy missed any reaction that may have momentarily appeared on my face.

"But searching for a particular person who could be anywhere in all of London," she said, "you might as well stand atop Big Ben with a telescope for all the luck you'll have looking at surveillance videos."

"All right, then."

"So who's this young woman Shauna you're looking for?" she asked. "A runaway from the States?"

I debated how much to tell her. I wasn't sure as to the nature and extent of her relationship with Eli Welker. She'd never responded to the e-mail I'd sent her from Dublin. And she made no mention of it today. It was possible she simply didn't recognize Welker from the small passport photo I'd sent her. In which case, she probably didn't know him all that well. But then, maybe she'd never even received the e-mail. Maybe it was delivered to her spam folder, or maybe it was opened and discarded by an assistant or someone else who worked at her firm. Maybe she simply hadn't gotten to it yet. Or maybe she'd changed her e-mail address and I just wasn't aware. In the past, whenever one of us needed the other's assistance, we'd pick up the phone.

In any event, Wendy Isles clearly hoped Eli Welker's killer would be caught. Imprisoned for life, if her tone of voice was any indication.

But would her thirst for blood be so insatiable if she knew that the killer might be my missing daughter?

Ultimately, I decided it was too dangerous to attempt to find out.

Chapter 47

Despite our very different lots in life, I think I've told you before, Avery and I remained close mates."

"He came in handy, you said."

"Right you are. When me and the boys would get into scrapes, we'd just call on our favorite barrister and Avery would come running." He pours me a cup of coffee and pushes it across the bar. "There was never any jealousy, you understand. Things happen as they happen, and that's the way they are. He felt no different toward me, nor I toward him."

The coffee's warm and only once I take the first sip do I realize a chill had moved through my body.

"Then in the early seventies, I got me lady pregnant, and it was a difficult pregnancy, as you can imagine, with her being addicted to heroin and all. But we pushed through. And the baby was born. Healthy, to me pleasant surprise.

"Less than a year later, Avery and his wife gave birth to a son. I played uncle to the boy, and Avery played uncle to me daughter, and all was right with the world. At least as far as I was concerned.

"But then something happened. Avery's wife began to fancy me. And if I'm going to be entirely honest, I began to fancy her as well. Still, though, I never would have acted on it. Because Avery was like a brother to me. Hell, he *was* a brother in every way except blood.

"Unfortunately, Avery took notice. And it ate at him. Every time we were together, I could see it in his bloody eyes. A concern, but deeper than that. A fear, maybe. Envy too. And anger, plenty of anger. He was competitive, you see. As was I. But never for a bird's affections. I thought he understood that. I think he *did* understand that. In his mind, at least. But sexual jealousy can't be explained in logic. It's part of our reptilian brains, isn't it? Something ancient. Something primal. And it brought out the worst in him, it did.

"We never talked about it. That would have been unimaginable at the time. Because there was nothing tangible. It didn't exist in the material world. It was in our eyes, in our hearts, in our loins, if you'll permit me to be crude about it.

"But for Avery, it was ever present. Like a cancer. And cancers need to be removed, don't they?"

Terry leans forward on the bar, looks me in the eyes. "Remember now, Avery knew every aspect of me world, every minutia of me business. As me solicitor it was practically required of him. So when he finally did what he did it was with pure, unadulterated malice."

I wait for him to go on.

He takes a breath, says, "Lona, the girl's mother, with whom I lived after our daughter's birth, was in no way the perfect mother, mind you. Was I even in love with her? I can't say. We had more of an arrangement than anything else. And yes, she benefitted from what I did for a living. Financially, of course. But in other ways as well. I was handling large shipments of cocaine at the time. I thought, well, far better her being on coke than on heroin. She had a child to care for. A toddler, two going on three.

"The coke made Lona sharper. And there was never a shortage, so there was no coming down. When she needed to sleep I simply supplied her with some downers.

"Of course, Lona hadn't had an easy life. There was good reason she was a prostitute when I met her. She'd grown up in an awful home with an alcoholic mother and an abusive father. Clichéd as it sounds, it was true. And so it shouldn't surprise you that Lona herself had a temper.

"Not a terrible temper, mind you. I've seen far worse. But a temper all the same. And at times she was short with the child. I'd talk to her about it. I'd watch closely. But with me business, I couldn't be there for them at all times. And so once in a while I'd return home to find a bruise on me little girl.

"Make no mistake, Simon, it *infuriated* me. I confronted Lona, threatened her with the police, did everything I could short of dishing out some of what she gave our daughter. And for months at a time it stopped, and everything was fine. In me mind, I said, 'If it happens again, I'll take me daughter and walk away.'

"Then one day, I had to leave London for a meeting in the Netherlands. I asked Uncle Avery, as he was affectionately called, to keep an eye on things for me. Just check in with Lona and the child, make certain everything's going smoothly and there are no troubles.

"He readily agreed. The thing between me and his wife had by then—at least I assumed—become a nonissue for him. Like a noise in your automobile. Something you eventually come to accept because it would cost much more to fix it than to let it go.

"When I returned to London a week later, I had just about settled in, kissed me daughter and her mother, when a pounding came from me front door. I didn't even have time to get out of me chair to open it when the filth came charging in.

"Avery had evidently seen a fresh bruise on me daughter. And instead of contacting me, he'd gone straight to the filth. And he'd told them about everything, Simon. The shipments, the buyers, the money, the people I'd had to lean on. He'd told them about everything. Every bloody thing I'd ever done to earn a quid."

Chapter 48

There was a good reason my Google search of "Night's End" in London didn't turn up any relevant results: The pub was actually named Knight's End.

When I arrived at the pub that afternoon, Ashdown and Zoey were already there, having driven straight from Liverpool in the Chairman's Grand Cherokee. During the four hours I'd spent driving to London last night, they'd gotten some much-deserved sleep at Hotel Indigo on Chapel Street a few blocks east of the River Mersey.

Knight's End didn't offer espresso so I ordered coffee. "Black, no sugar, please."

When the waiter moved off, Zoey asked whether I'd gotten any sleep.

"A few good hours," I told her. "Ostermann lent me his suite at the Corinthia."

"Posh," Ashdown said.

"Since his corporate client was paying, Ostermann also insisted I take advantage of room service."

"Oh? What did you have?"

"What *didn't* I have is more like it. After that tremendous breakfast at Gilchrist's and the Corinthia's room service, I don't think I can ever settle for my regular breakfast of an English muffin and jam again."

As we talked, I kept my eye on the middle-aged female behind the bar. She appeared none too friendly, and from the looks of this place I couldn't say I blamed her. Still, I wanted to show her a picture of Shauna and ask whether she'd seen her before. Since our waiter was just a kid who said he'd only started this past week, I didn't bother asking him.

"So, little brother," Zoey said, "how does it feel to be back home?"

"I've been back before," I said. "Always feels the same. As though I've always lived in London, in every universe but this one."

I thought about the day I arrived in London from Saint Petersburg ten years ago. Finally back in the west following my most eventful case yet. Relief flowing through me even as I continued looking over my shoulder. Adrenaline still pumping through my veins, keeping me alert despite my exhaustion. Scared to death in that good way that helps keep us among the living.

I removed my phone from my pocket and rose from my chair. The bartender had just served fresh pints to the two silent old soaks sitting at the end of the bar. She'd since returned to wiping down bottles of vodka and gin.

"Now or never, I guess."

I walked up to the bar as though to order a drink. From my periphery, I could see our young waiter bussing his own table nearby. Watching me, probably a little nervous that he'd done something wrong. That he was too slow or that he'd forgotten to bring one of us a drink. He spied on Ashdown and Zoey for a clue, but they'd begun an argument before I'd made it halfway to the bar.

"Need a bevvy, love?"

Why not, I thought, *if it'll make this go down easier.*

"Bombay and tonic," I said, pushing the notes across the bar. "And one for yourself, Miss . . ."

"Lizzy," she said. "Thanks, love."

She set up two rocks glasses in front of me.

I scanned the bar to make sure we were out of earshot. After the

Sherlock Holmes, it was nice to be inside a pub with no theme whatsoever. A simple black-and-white bar, nothing fancy. With the usual mirrors and neon signs and posters touting the usual brand names of beer and liquor and colas and energy drinks.

Lizzy slid my glass toward me and scooped up hers. We lifted them at the same time. She said, "Cheers m'dears," and we drank.

And I instantly remembered how much I loathed the taste of gin. It had always been Terry's drink, not mine.

"What the hell kind of Englishman are you?" he'd asked me one night after I'd declined a Tanqueray and tonic.

"Apparently, one with taste buds," I'd told him.

I set my glass down and called up Shauna's picture on my phone. Held it out to her. "Recognize this girl?"

She frowned, tossed her own drink into the sink and started wiping down the bar.

"So you're a rozzer, are you?"

I said nothing.

"What did she do? Beat the piss out of one of your mates?" She looked up at me. "Or maybe she beat the piss out of you."

"I'm not with the law," I said. "I'm private. And I'm trying to help her."

"Help her?" she said. "Or help yourself *to* her?"

"You have no idea how off you are, Lizzy." I leaned forward, lowered my voice. "Listen, she got herself in some trouble up in Dublin. I've been hired to find her and get her out of it, not to turn her in."

Her face closed down in skepticism. "Hired by who?"

"That I'm not at liberty to say."

She thought about it, shrugged. "I don't know where she is, love, so I can't help you either way."

"But you do know her?"

"You know I do. Or else why would you be here?"

I took a swallow of my gin and tonic. "How do you know her?" I said.

She stopped wiping down the bar to study my face. Either realized the question was sincere or decided the answer didn't matter one way or another.

"She's the boss's daughter," she said.

I swallowed my next question.

She caught my reaction, said, "You all right, love? You're white as a sheet. You look as though you're going to tip over."

She looked past me toward Ashdown and Zoey and tried to wave them over, but they weren't looking.

"What's your boss's name?" I managed.

"Isn't that part of the public record?"

"Sure," I said quietly, leaning onto the bar for support. "But you can save me some time and effort."

My BlackBerry began buzzing along the bar.

"You answer that," she said. "I'll be right back. I've got to pour an order for Andrew over there."

It was Ostermann's number. I pressed the phone to my ear, all the while following Lizzy with my eyes.

He said, "I just received an e-mail from Eli Welker's final client. He's arrived at Heathrow. I set up a meeting with him. The Corinthia, in one hour. Best you meet me in the lobby beforehand."

I pocketed the phone as Lizzy warily moved back toward me.

She said, "So you need the owner's name, do you?"

I nodded and pushed another wad of notes across the bar.

"All right, love. But anyone asks, you bloody well didn't hear it from me."

Chapter 49

When we arrived at the Corinthia forty minutes later, we found Kurt Ostermann standing near the front desk, flirting with an alluring desk clerk who looked an awful lot like his wife Magda back in Berlin. After several seconds I managed to summon his attention and he marched over to us while working a wide grin off his face.

"Kurt Ostermann, my sister Zoey Carlyle and Detective Chief Inspector Damon Ashdown of the National Crime Agency."

During introductions, Ostermann's gaze lingered a bit too long on Zoey for Ashdown's liking, and Ashdown made it known by suggesting Ostermann return to the front desk to continue his seduction of the desk clerk.

"Perhaps it's you I'd like to seduce," Ostermann said, no longer attempting to wrestle the grin from his lips.

"There's no time for this," Zoey said, stepping between the German and her ex. "Damon, if you want to be a complete arse, please do so outside on the footpath."

Ostermann ignored Ashdown's persistent glare and handed me the key to his suite. "Wait upstairs," he said. "Make yourself at home. As soon as the client arrives, I'll escort him to the room and introduce you as my associate."

In the light flooding into the lobby through the two-story windows, I noticed Ostermann's blond hair was graying ever so slightly at the temples. He might have put on five or ten pounds since I last saw him in Berlin as well. Although, I had to admit, having lost as much weight as I had over the previous eleven months, that particular observation might have been the result of a highly skewed perspective.

"Zoey," I said, "why don't you join me upstairs? A female presence might put this client, whoever he is, more at ease."

"A good idea," Ostermann deadpanned.

I turned to Ashdown mid-seethe. "Detective, mind keeping an eye on the lobby in case Mr. Welker's client decides to run?"

As Ashdown moved off in silence, Zoey and I headed toward the elevator bank.

"So what's your mate's story?" she said as we walked.

"Married."

"Happily?"

"Loves her like the sun," I said.

"Poetic."

"I thought so too."

We stepped into the lift with a young family, a handsome Irish couple and their two preteenage boys whose eyes had been following Zoey's ass through the lobby as though it were magnetized.

"Your German mate did seem rather randy," my sister said at her usual pitch. "I imagine he fancies playing away on that wife in Berlin. If he's on the pull, I assume you won't mind if we have it off later? Shite, I could use a good, hard shag after that dreadful quickie with Damon in Liverpool last night. Might as well have given him a gobble for all that I got off."

I stifled a heavy sigh and the six of us, packed like sardines, waited for the elevator doors to close.

* * *

A s Zoey and I waited on either side of a small table in Ostermann's room, my phone went off. I lifted my BlackBerry and checked the caller.

Kati Sheffield, full-time mommy and part-time miracle worker.

I put the phone to my ear, said, "Rising with the sun these days, Breaker?"

"Actually I haven't slept yet, Finder. Miles decided to turn his bed into a trampoline at eleven o'clock last night, so he and I spent the night in the emergency room."

"Sorry," I said. "He's all right, then?"

"Fractured clavicle."

I grimaced. "Broken collarbone? Those hurt like hell and take forever to heal. Twelve weeks, if I remember correctly."

"About half that for a child. I take it you've suffered one yourself?"

"I ride motorcycles," I said. "Sometimes rather recklessly. Comes with the job, I'm sorry to say."

"Speaking of which, I finally heard back from Her Majesty's Passport Office."

"And?"

"And there was a reason we couldn't find anything on Shauna Adair. Her birth record at the General Register Office in Southport was apparently wiped clean. There are no adoption or marriage records for her either. Only while I was in the ER, watching the victims of a particularly nasty bus accident being carted in, did I realize there was one other record we hadn't searched for."

In my head I saw the emergency room she'd just described.

"A death certificate?" I said.

"Exactly. According to her death records, Shauna Adair was born twenty-three years ago in the private wing of the NHS hospital in Westminster."

"St. Thomas'?"

"Right-o, Finder. Cause of death is listed as cerebral hypoxia. Manner of death is classified as homicide."

"Mechanism?" I asked.

"The coroner determined it to be manual strangulation. No sexual assault involved. According to a note in the file, the case is still open, which means the girl's murder remains unsolved."

"When did this happen?" I said, unable to suppress the urgency in my voice. "When did she die?"

There was a brief pause as she checked the date.

"Twelve years ago, Simon. When the girl was just eleven years old."

Chapter 50

When I step out of the shower Tasha's still asleep. I tie the towel around my waist and grab the wastebasket from the bathroom. There are used tissues everywhere. Balled up, worn through, torn to pieces from worry. Shreds of tissue lie on our dresser, on the hardwood floor next to our bed, beneath Tasha's pillow. I begin collecting them, a gesture that would earn me an angry stare were Tasha awake.

I walk out of the bedroom, snatch a few off the railing then head downstairs, past the dining room into the kitchen, spotting them everywhere I look. On tables and countertops, littering the carpet and floor tiles. The wastebasket fills before I finish. I'm about to dump it when I hear a rap at our front door.

"Morning, Aubrey," I say, stepping aside to let her in. "Have a seat in the kitchen. Help yourself to some coffee. Tash isn't up yet, but she should be any minute."

Aubrey wraps her arms around me. I pull her in tightly, do my best to keep tears from falling. It's been so long since I held Tasha, or anyone, that I don't want to let her go.

"I'm going to run upstairs and get dressed," I tell her.

"Pour you a cup, Simon?"

"Please."

She places her hands on her bare arms, closing herself off from the chill of the air conditioner.

"You keep your house like an icebox," she remarks.

Upstairs, Tasha is still sleeping. On her side, facing the middle of the bed, wrapped up in the white duvet. She spends more and more hours under these covers every day, rising only to relieve herself and to call downstairs to ask me to bring her bottled waters. She needs to hydrate. She loses an absurd amount of her body's fluids through tears.

I set the wastebasket down in the bathroom, drop the wet towel in the hamper. In the bedroom I slip into a clean pair of boxers, the jeans I wore yesterday. I grab a fresh T-shirt from the closet. Try to navigate through the fog in my head to remember whether I've put on deodorant. I think so, but just in case, I roll some on again.

I wait for it to dry before putting on my T-shirt. Staring at our bed, I lock on the Kleenex box positioned dead center on our king-size mattress. Erected like a wall. During the few random hours Tasha and I actually sleep in the same room at the same time, it stands between us like a barrier neither dares penetrate. Whether it's intentional on Tasha's part, I don't know. But its presence has distanced us even further.

Outside, the birds are twittering. Odd, since I don't remember hearing them since that first morning after Hailey went missing. When neither Tasha nor I could fall asleep. Since then I've woken every morning to . . .

What?

To Tasha's snoring. She'd never snored before but since Hailey was taken, it has become a constant sound, like the ticking of an analog clock. Not surprising when she spends all her days weeping and blowing her nose.

But this morning the birds are back. Except that it's nearing the end of summer so they'd never gone. Their singing was simply drowned out by Tasha's incessant snoring. But Tasha's not snoring this morning.

She hasn't made a sound.

"Tash," I say tentatively.

Louder. "Tash."

A hideous thought gnaws at some distant part of my brain but refuses to come forward. My feet carry me toward the bed. But I'm not sure whether I'm even moving of my own volition.

"Tasha," I say.

As I nudge her, my eyes drift to her nightstand and the four pill bottles standing there, lined up in a neat row like toy soldiers. For a moment, I fear all the bottles are empty. But clearly they're not.

I lift each bottle in turn.

Painkiller.

Muscle relaxer.

Tranquilizer.

Antidepressant.

Each bottle still contains a number of pills.

I place my hand on her arm to nudge her again. Her skin is icy to the touch.

The AC's on. "You keep your house like an icebox," *Aubrey just said.*

I grab Tasha by the shoulder and roll her over.

Her lips are blue.

"Aubrey!" I yell.

I call her name again even though I can already hear her hustling up the stairs.

There's a bottle of Dasani on the nightstand. Only a few ounces left in it, but I twist the cap and toss the water in Tasha's face in an effort to wake her.

"What's happening, Simon?"

The panic in Aubrey's voice mimics my own.

My fingers are on Tasha's neck. I don't feel a pulse.

I wheel around to see Aubrey, her eyes wide as she processes what's going on. But seconds later, there's a transformation. From terrified friend to the calm, cool nurse that she is in Costa Rica. She steps forward and takes control.

"Call nine-one-one," she says to me.

For a moment I'm frozen and she has to say it again, louder but just as calmly.

I dash around to the other side of the bed and grab the cordless. As I dial I watch Aubrey place her lips on Tasha's, creating a seal.

"Nine-one-one, what's the location of your emergency?"

Frantic, I rattle off our address.

"Police, fire, or medic?"

"An ambulance, please. Please, hurry."

"An ambulance is on its way. What's the emergency?"

"An overdose, I think. Prescription medication."

I hear the sound of my own voice but it doesn't feel as though I'm speaking. I can barely make out the words as I say them and I'm hoping the operator understands me. I hope I'm not speaking gibberish.

"Do you know which type of medication?"

Aubrey is performing chest compressions, counting to herself as she works.

"Sir, do you know which type of medication?"

"Hydrocodone," I say. "Benzodiazepines. SSRIs. Muscle relaxants."

"What's your name, sir?"

"Fisk. Simon Fisk."

Aubrey's back to Tasha's lips. I try to read her eyes but see nothing except determination.

"All right, Simon," the operator says. "Who ingested these pills?"

"Tasha," I say, my voice cracking beneath the weight of the call. "My wife, Tasha."

"Do you know how many pills she took?"

"I don't. There are still some left in each bottle."

"Simon," the operator says, "do you know whether this was an accidental overdose or a suicide attempt?"

Suicide. "I don't know. I've no idea."

"When did she take these pills?"

"Last night?" My voice doesn't sound like my own. "I don't know exactly what time."

"Has Tasha been depressed lately?"

Aubrey pauses and looks up at me. There are fresh tears in her eyes. That look of determination is gone, replaced by complete and total despair.

"Simon," the operator prods, "has your wife been depressed lately?"

"Of course she has," I say, crying. "Our little girl was taken a few weeks ago. And I gave her all the blame."

"It will be all right, Simon," the operator says. "An ambulance should be arriving at your house at any moment."

I stare at Aubrey. Her eyes are telling me it's hopeless.

Still, I look down at Tasha; I need to see for myself.

Oh, god.

A thick red-brown liquid is oozing from her nose and mouth onto the sheets. I don't know exactly what it is, but I know too well what it means.

Into the phone, I whimper, "It doesn't matter. It's too late. It's over. Now both my wife and daughter are gone."

Chapter 51

After disconnecting with Kati Sheffield, it slowly began to settle on me. Now there was no question, was there?

As I set the phone down on the table, Zoey asked if I was all right.

"It's her," I said. "There is no Shauna Adair, at least not anymore. She died here in London twelve years ago. The same summer Hailey went missing."

"What does this mean, Simon? That your daughter assumed this dead girl's name right after she was taken?"

I thought about it. "She couldn't have. Not right away. Not publicly anyway. Hailey was six that summer. Shauna was eleven."

"So it would've had to have been much more recent, right?"

I flashed on my last hour at Gilchrist's house in Glasgow. "Quigg told me he only met her a couple years ago. At a nightclub, here in London."

"Hailey would have been only sixteen," Zoey said.

What were Quigg's words when I asked him how old Shauna was?

"I don't ken. I have a 'naw ask, naw tell' policy, see."

"Quigg knew she was young," I said. "So did Lennox Sterling. When he asked her what year she was born in, she had to count it out on her fingers."

While I attempted to fit this piece of the puzzle with the one

I received earlier at Knight's End, the door to the hotel room received an abrupt rap. Then I heard the electronic click as Ostermann inserted his key card into the lock.

"If you won't tell me your name," Ostermann was saying as the door swung open, "I'll call you John. How does John suit you?"

"Like I'm soliciting a bloody prostitute," said a voice from behind him.

A *familiar* voice.

"John," Ostermann said, "I'd like you to meet my two associates. . . ."

He trailed off as his eyes fixed on me and Zoey, both of us out of our seats, each of our mouths hanging open. He turned to Welker's client, whose face had contorted much like ours had, whose eyes had nearly bulged out of his skull.

"Am I missing something?" Ostermann said. "Do you three know each other?"

"Simon?" my father said as his entire body stiffened. "Tuesday?" He looked hard at Ostermann. "I demand to know what the devil is going on here."

I blanked. This third piece of the puzzle, after Shauna's death certificate and the name of the Knight's End pub's owner, seemed not to fit with the others.

The door closed behind Ostermann and a befuddled Alden Fisk.

I took a step forward. My father appeared older, frailer, *smaller* than he ever had before. I'd seen him just over two years ago when I returned to the States from Minsk to ask for his help financing a network of clinics devoted to the children of northern Ukraine and Belarus.

He had looked old then but nothing like the man who stood before us now.

"*You* hired Elijah Welker?" I said to him.

I didn't attempt to mask the inherent anger and hatred in my voice. I figured it didn't matter. My father knew damn well just how I felt about him. He'd known since I was about twelve years old.

"I hired Eli, yes," he said with an air of defiance.

Already he was on the defensive and I wanted to know why.

"For what *reason*?" I said.

"To find my only grandchild, of course. But I suspect you already knew that or you wouldn't be sitting here, would you?"

"Why did you think you'd find her here in the UK?" I said.

He took a step backward, the contours of his face shifting as he came to realize that Zoey and I were as shocked to see him as he was to see us.

He said, "I think we're getting a little ahead of ourselves, Simon. Why don't you first tell me what led *you* here?"

My initial instinct was to toss up an impenetrable wall, to tell him nothing. But after twelve years I was too close to finding my daughter. Though I could be sure of very little at that point, of one thing I was entirely certain: I loved Hailey more than I hated my father.

"The photo of the girl wanted for Welker's murder in Dublin," I said. "A former FBI analyst I work with suggested it might be Hailey."

"And?" he practically hollered.

"And *what*?"

"Is it? Is the girl Welker was following my granddaughter?"

"We don't know," I said. "We haven't found her yet."

"Well, we'd better hurry, hadn't we? Before the police beat us to her. It would be a hell of a thing, after twelve years, to find her only to have her locked away in that godforsaken country for the rest of her life, wouldn't it?"

His belligerence shouldn't have taken me by surprise but it caused me some confusion.

"You still haven't answered *my* question," I said, moving toward him. "How did you know to look for her here in London? Why did you hire Eli Welker—a *British* investigator—in the first place?"

Alden Fisk looked from me to Zoey then to Ostermann.

A rare look of resignation fell over his visage. "I spoke to someone recently," he said in a tired voice. "An old mate from medical school here in London. He was vacationing with his wife in Newport, and he looked me up. He told me he'd encountered a boyhood mate of mine recently. A publican in the East End. And that this former friend of mine had mentioned living in the District of Columbia up until about ten years ago. Which would have included the time Hailey went missing."

There it was, the piece of the puzzle that linked all the others. Including the name the bartender at Knight's End had given me—the name of the current owner of Terry's Pub back in Washington, D.C.

"Nigel Cummings," I said.

My father's eyes narrowed. "Nigel Cummings? No. No, I know no one by that name."

"Then who the hell are you talking about?" I said.

He motioned with his chin at my sister and said three words that startled us all: "Tuesday's biological father."

Chapter 52

The story sounded familiar though there were some differences in the telling. Like the solicitor, for instance, he was gone, replaced by a man of medicine. A doctor.

"Until just now," my father said from his seat on the bed, "I couldn't know for sure."

"So what finally convinced you?" I said.

"The name of the pub, of course. The Knight's End. That's the name of the pub my medical school mate told me about. Before I heard those words come out of your mouth, I couldn't be a hundred-percent certain, you understand? Or else I would have phoned you, Simon."

"Get on with it," I told him.

"Turns out," he said in his measured cadence, "this is all about two boyhood mates. Born in the same city in the same month of the same year." He rose as though to emphasize the importance of what he was about to relate. "London. November, 1943. FDR and Winston Churchill were meeting with Chiang Kai-shek in Cairo and would then meet with Joseph Stalin in Tehran."

"Spare us the World War Two history lesson," Ostermann interjected, "if you don't mind."

"Pardon, *Herr* Ostermann." My father shifted his body so that his back was to Ostermann. "So, back to the two boyhood mates. They hailed from the same social class, you see. Both boys were well-built, sharp as swords, and competitive, to boot. In academics *and* athletics. They were both handsome devils, who attracted the same type of young lady. Smart, sophisticated women every bit as ravishing as Grace Kelly, Jayne Mansfield, or Marilyn Monroe."

I said, "Let's fast-forward a bit, shall we?"

His iron-gray brows bent inwardly, nearly meeting above his nose. "You never did demonstrate much patience, Simon. It's why I knew you'd never fit into medicine. Cop was more your speed, then *and* now, apparently."

"Two boyhood mates," I said as calmly as I could manage.

"Two boyhood mates," he repeated, trying to recapture his rhythm. "One of whom would grow up to be a doctor, the other a gangster. The doctor would go on to marry a wealthy woman. The gangster would have a child with a drug-addicted harlot." He paused, looked sympathetically at Zoey. "The gangster's daughter, as you may have guessed, was born less than a year before the doctor's son."

"Christ," I muttered.

The gangster, he went on to say, named his daughter Tuesday.

The doctor named his son Simon.

"Despite their different lots in life—all of which resulted from the boys' respective decisions, good *and* bad, and don't let anyone dare tell you otherwise—the doctor and the gangster remained mates. *Good* mates, I'd add. The doctor going so far as to risk his medical license in order to treat the gangster and his goons. Gunshots, stab wounds. Venereal disease, even. Oh, the venereal disease in the late sixties, early seventies. It shocked the conscience. You'd be amazed, Simon—"

"Let's move on, shall we?"

He huffed then finally pursed his lips and continued. "Their children, being roughly the same age, played together, of course. They were toddlers, they became close; as close as toddlers can be, anyway, given their degree of emotional maturity. But close enough that their fathers often joked about how the boy and girl would inevitably marry and have children of their own someday."

Zoey scoffed. "Since we've spent our entire lives believing we're brother and sister, I think we can skip this part as well."

Alden Fisk lowered himself onto the bed, folded his hands neatly in his lap, as he was apt to do. He'd always hated being interrupted. Some things, I suppose, never change.

He turned to her. "Although I wasn't your father, Tuesday, I *was* your doctor. And I cared for you very much. So when you were a toddler, and I began noticing unusual bruises on you—bruises that didn't completely jibe with the stories your parents provided as explanations—I became incensed." He lowered his head. "I gave it some time, however. Longer than I would have any other patient. In hindsight, longer than I *should* have."

After a brief pause he gathered his strength and looked at us. "See, I was torn about what to do. It *ate* at me for weeks. Ultimately, I decided to approach my mate. He told me times were tough, that things at home weren't going so well and, by the way, Alden, mind your own bloody business." His eyes moved to my sister. "But you, Tuesday, were my patient. And, as my patient, you *were* my business."

To speed things along I said, "So you reported your best mate to social services."

"That's right, Simon. As was my duty as a physician. The process, however, wasn't one I was entirely familiar with. I wasn't a pediatrician, after all. I didn't treat children. Only Tuesday as a favor to my friend.

"Anyway, I assumed Tuesday's parents would receive a phone call, be invited to the government offices for a conference. Maybe receive some counseling or be asked to attend a parenting course. But these were unusual circumstances, as I was later told. Because Scotland Yard, by that point, had been aware of the gangster's illicit activities. And this incident gave them the probable cause they needed to enter his premises unannounced."

"And they found your friend's stash," I said.

"That they did. And quite a stash it was. They arrested the gangster and the prostitute and took the child. Later, a hefty sentence was handed down to both of them. I spoke with my wife, Tatum, and we agreed we would take the child." He looked at me. "You were only three at the time, Simon. Tuesday, an immature four. So on the day we brought her home, Tuesday became your sister."

I glanced over at my sister. But she wasn't my sister. Not even a half sister. Not a sister at all. Four days after finding the only family I thought I had left, I was losing her all over again. And it stung like all hell. Because, although I hadn't said it in thirty-plus years, I loved her. Loved the little girl she'd been, and loved even more the warm, tenderhearted, fearless woman she'd become.

He turned to Zoey. "As time went on, Tatum began to take you to see your father at the prison. I wasn't fond of the idea; I thought it better you didn't know him at all. I wanted us to legally adopt you. You were still young enough that we could even hide the fact that you weren't our biological daughter.

"But Tatum insisted you see him, and I eventually dropped my objections. Choose your battles, and so on and so forth."

"What about my mother?" Zoey said.

"A lost cause, I'm sorry to say. Her drug use became even worse in prison and last I saw her, she was wasting away to nothing."

"Ah, there's Dr. Alden Fisk's famous bedside manner," I said.

"You want me to *sugarcoat* this, Simon?" he snapped. "What's the bloody point?"

Zoey turned to me. "Believe me, little brother, I can handle whatever your father can dish out."

I stared at my father, hoping he wouldn't be callous enough to point out the discrepancies in Zoey's statement. He glared at her in that condescending way of his but didn't challenge what she'd said.

"What happened to her?" Zoey asked. "My mum, what became of her?"

"Ultimately, she hung herself by her bedsheets and was buried in the prison cemetery."

Silence.

"Let me guess," I said. "Leaving the doctor's wife to fall in love with the gangster."

"If you could call it love," he said with disgust. "He didn't seduce Tatum out of love, he seduced her out of revenge. 'You destroyed me family,' he said the last time I ever saw him in prison. 'So I am going to *take* yours, Alden.'

"From that day forward, Tatum became cold to me. Slowly, she poisoned Tuesday against me as well. Then the gangster's mates started coming round my office all hours of the day. Harassing me, telling my patients I was a quack, trying to intimidate me into writing prescriptions for them. This lasted for nearly three years. Then Tatum—your mother, Simon—started to go to work on you. Tried to poison you against me. That's when I knew I had no choice but to take you and leave for the States."

My expression didn't change.

"Do I wish I did things somewhat differently?" he said, leaning forward. "You bet I do. But at the time, I was frightened of losing the only person I had left. I was afraid of losing *you*, Simon. I was afraid of losing my only son."

"Just how does all this fit in with Hailey's abduction?" I said.

"I only know bits and pieces," he conceded. "And even those, I only came to learn recently. But I'll tell you what I do know. A couple years after you and I left London, the gangster was released from prison. For good, this time. He'd been paroled on previous occasions, but each time he violated the conditions of that parole and was placed back behind bars. This time he was out. Officially, with no conditions. He'd served his time, you see." His head dropped and he stared at the floor. "And once he was out he went to live with Tatum and Tuesday."

Zoey and I exchanged looks. So this was the "clingy" guy, the man more fatherly than Alden Fisk. Mum's man, the one Zoey had mentioned back at the library at Gerry Gilchrist's house.

"After prison, the gangster became more violent than ever, I'm told. He struck your mother viciously for loving me in the first place. For ever marrying the man whom he insisted destroyed his life. He struck Tuesday whenever she dared mention your name, Simon. Finally, Tatum could take no more of it. She ran from him and changed her name." He looked at Zoey. "Yours as well, from what I've heard."

"My name is Zoey," she said without expression.

"Apparently, the monster blamed me for this as well. I'd somehow destroyed his family yet again, this time from abroad. He went into a rage. Started doing more and more blow. Taking greater risks, looking for bigger scores."

"Still in London, though," I said.

"Then. But not for long. According to a source Eli Welker never disclosed to me, the gangster was watching me all that time. He hired some lowlife private detective in Providence to keep an eye on me and my son. He wanted to *hurt* me the way I'd hurt him, if not worse. In a coke-induced psychosis, his life became all about vengeance." He paused. "Then, roughly ten years after we left for the States, he picked up a score so great, he could retire if he so desired. Not long after that, he supposedly started feeling the heat coming round the corner. The police were wise to him again, and he was determined not to return to prison. So he left for the States."

I stared at Ostermann, who remained speechless.

"He wanted a normal life," my father said. "A normal family. He wanted what I'd supposedly stolen. Only now he simply called it the American dream. As far as he was concerned, he'd timed things perfectly. You, Simon, had just left Rhode Island for American University in D.C. So that was where he decided to set up shop. A bar. An Irish pub, to be more specific."

"Terry's," I said, still grappling with my disbelief.

Chapter 53

Tasha's funeral in Richmond, Virginia, is brief. Marked by a hard rain. Tasha's parents are holding a mercy dinner at their country club after this but I've declined the invitation. Standing under an oversize umbrella in my only black suit, I watch the mourners head for their vehicles and try to decide how I feel about what Mr. Dunne told me earlier at the church.

"My daughter's death is being ruled accidental," he said.

I didn't think I'd heard him correctly. "I'm sorry?"

"The coroner's report will be released on Monday. I just thought you should know so that there aren't any surprises."

Stunned, I looked away.

He grabbed me firmly by the arm, insisted, "This is as much for you, Simon, as it is for Tasha. So don't make any trouble. Tasha's mother has already been through quite enough as it is."

Now, as the rain pelts my umbrella, I realize how carefully he chose his words. Tasha's suicide is going to be ruled an accident to aid Mr. and Mrs. Dunne in avoiding any further embarrassment. But he wants me to know that he knows what's been rattling around in my head in the days since Tasha's death. That I blame myself for her committing suicide.

He was suggesting that others would too.

Well, to hell with others.

Still, I've decided I'm not going to interfere. What appears on Tasha's death certificate is meaningless to me. I know the truth. That she took her own life. And I know I'm largely to blame for it. Rather than playing the role of loving husband and supporting my wife through our most trying times, I'd decided to hate her. To accuse her.

In the end, I unwittingly condemned her to die.

Special Agents John Rendell and Candace West look my way and bow their heads to offer their condolences. At first I think they're going to approach and I'm grateful. Because I never really thanked them for how hard they searched for Hailey. As a federal cop myself, I sympathize with their plight. Despite the books and movies and television shows, despite the legal pundits and bloggers and sensationalist reporters, results are not always the most precise indicator of whether you performed your job as well as you could have. Whether, like Rendell and West, you've gone above and beyond in your investigation and lost.

Aubrey Lang moves beneath my umbrella, stands on her toes, and wraps me in a warm embrace. Kisses my cheek before settling back on her feet.

"I'm so, so terribly sorry, Simon."

What she means is: *I was there with Tasha the entire time. And I don't blame you for her death.*

"I should've paid closer attention," Aubrey says. "I'm a goddamn nurse. How could I have missed the signs?"

"Her death was accidental," I mumble.

"What?"

But then she follows my eyes to a black limousine as it swallows Mrs. Dunne, then her husband.

"I'm skipping the mercy dinner," I tell her.

"Then I won't go either."

Behind us, Terry says, "Why don't you both come back to the pub, then? I've closed it for the day out of respect." He rests a hand on my shoulder. "But I trust the three of us could all use a bloody drink or six now, am I right?"

What he means is: *Best you not be alone just yet.*

I bow my head.

Terry removes his hand and places his long, thin arm around Aubrey's shoulder then leads the way to his car.

I follow them.

I don't pause, don't glance back at Tasha's grave.

The most pressing thought running through my head now is: *Will we ever find Hailey's remains so that we can give her a proper burial, so that she can finally and forever rest in peace next to the mother who so loved her?*

Chapter 54

Minutes before eleven o'clock at night Ostermann and I neared Knight's End, sitting in the rear of one of London's ubiquitous black cabs. Zoey remained behind at the Corinthia to mind my father. Ashdown, meanwhile, was paying a visit to his flat to collect items I told him we might well be needing later. The real reason I didn't want Ashdown with us, however, was because Ashdown had a career to protect, and things, if they went as I expected, were going to start getting ugly.

Two blocks away we hit a bit of traffic and Ostermann suggested we go the rest of the way on foot. I paid the cab driver and stepped into another bitter night. A single line of thought had been racing through my mind the entire ride. If only I'd accepted my father's request to pay us a visit twelve years ago when Hailey went missing. If only I'd welcomed him at Tasha's funeral. Hell, if only I'd invited him to our wedding seven years before that. He'd have come face-to-face with his old mate Terrance Davies, and none of this nightmare would have happened. If only I'd known their history, Hailey would have never been taken. Because the abductor wouldn't have been part of our lives.

By locking out my father, I'd doomed my wife and daughter. And I'll never forgive myself for that.

Trying to escape these thoughts as we ran through the East End,

I pulled out my BlackBerry. Slowed enough to go through my contacts and dialed a number that had remained in my phone for twelve years.

An eager voice answered. "This is Rendell."

"John, it's Fisk. I hope I'm not calling at a bad time."

"No worries, Simon. Where are you? What can I do for you?"

"I'm in London. You remember Terry Davies, right?"

"Your English friend, sure."

"Head over to his bar."

"All right. And do what exactly?"

"You'll need to search the entire premises; turn it inside and out."

"Simon, I'll need a search warrant. And in order to get that, I'll need evidence. And time."

"The bartender's name is Casey O'Connell. He's a nice guy but a bit of a mouth-breather. Say whatever you have to in order to get him to consent to the search."

"And if he doesn't consent?"

"Search the place anyway."

"Simon, if I do that, any evidence I find will be inadmissible in court. And anything *linked* to what I find will be thrown out as well. You know that. If you have something, I have to do this right in order to preserve the integrity of the prosecution."

"John," I said as I slowed to a halt, "there's not going to be any prosecution."

With that, I clicked off the line.

Ostermann and I pushed our way through the outgoing tide of merrymakers and stepped inside the Knight's End.

The young waiter, Andrew, from earlier in the day was the first one to spot us. "Sorry, mates, but it's chucking-out time."

"We're not here to drink," I said without stopping.

"Kitchen's closed too," he called after me.

I walked straight up to the bar where Lizzy stood with her back to us, wiping down bottles again.

"Where's your boss?" I said.

Turning, she seemed startled to see me. "We're closing, love."

"Where's your boss?" I said again.

"I told you this afternoon, I haven't seen him in days."

"How about his daughter?"

"His daughter hasn't been—" Her eyes darted past me and she shouted, "What in bloody hell are you *doing*, you prat? Put that lad down *now* before I call the bill."

I wheeled around, spotted Ostermann holding the kid waiter up against the wall by the throat. Christ, I thought. But before I could utter a word, he set the boy down on his feet, gave him a light tap on the face, and said, "There's a good chap."

It wasn't the first time I'd had to remind myself that Kurt Ostermann did things differently. I flashed on the evening two years earlier in Berlin when, in a dark alley behind the infamous SO36 nightclub, Ostermann knocked out cold the two kidnappers I'd chased from Paris. As a result of what happened in that alley in Kreuzberg, the kidnappers, Dietrich Braun and Karl Finster, ended up dead. Not by Ostermann's hand but by the Turks who'd hired them.

He started toward the rear of the pub.

Palms sweating, hands trembling in anticipation, I took one purposeful step in his direction before he stopped me cold with a look of pure fortitude chiseled into his face.

"I know where she is," he said. "Follow me."

Chapter 55

At Terry's pub, Aubrey and I sit across from each other at a tall but intimate bar table, both of us watching the rain slice through the night under the light of the streetlamp on the corner. In front of Aubrey sits a piping cup of black coffee, in front of me a pint of Harp. Terry is behind the bar, mixing his second gin and tonic of the past ten minutes.

For me, the beer is going down like drain cleaner. I want to numb myself but I know I'll never get more than one or two pints into my stomach before I toss them back up. It occurs to me there have long been rumors that Terry still sells illicit drugs. Right out of the bar, supposedly. I'd known nothing about it while I worked here and I wouldn't have wanted to know. What Terry did back in London to earn a living after being tossed out of law school and sent to prison for two and a half years, all for a single drunken fistfight, was his business. But in college I'd had my eye on becoming a federal cop and I hadn't wanted to do anything to risk screwing that up.

Since becoming a federal marshal I'd ignored the rumors. See no evil, hear no evil. But I admit, I've always been curious. Particularly since I know the bar inside and out and in four years I'd never come across anything so much as suspicious. All he has is the one large storeroom in back and at one time or another, I'd seen every inch of it.

Still, I wonder.

For a few minutes I consider asking Terry if he has anything stronger than beer. Like weed. Like coke. Like smack. Then I think better of it. I've never done an unlawful drug in my life and now's no time to start. Even though my career is no longer a consideration.

"I've decided to resign from the Marshals," I tell Aubrey.

My words catch her by surprise. "Really? Do you know what you'll do?"

I shake my head. "There's no rush though. I'll sell the house in Georgetown, take a little of the money to pay a one-year lease on a studio somewhere here in the District, and return the rest of the proceeds to Tasha's parents."

"The Dunnes won't take the money back, will they?"

"I'm not going to leave them much choice. They can take the money or I'll write a check to the National Center for Missing and Exploited Children. They can't object to that, can they? Maybe I'll even present that as their first option."

Aubrey lifts her brows. "I wouldn't be so sure about that. Tasha used to tell me that her dad's favorite saying was, 'Charity begins at home.'"

I can't help but smirk. "It doesn't mean what he thinks it means. When the phrase was first coined, the word *charity* didn't mean aiding the poor or helpless. Charity was more a state of mind, a mentality of warmness and kindheartedness. Like just about everything in this world, the phrase was eventually corrupted. Some attribute the quote to the English churchman Thomas Fuller, but all he did was add to the phrase. And what he added is now gleefully omitted by those who've shanghaied the words."

"What did this Thomas Fuller say?"

"He said, 'Charity begins at home, but should not end there.'"

"Jeez," Aubrey says, shaking her head, "the way it's used today, it sounds like it came straight from Ayn Rand."

"More's the pity, isn't it?" Terry says as he sets his gin and tonic on the table and takes a seat between us. He motions to Aubrey's coffee. "Sure I can't get you anything a bit stronger, love? I make a hell of a bone-dry martini, don't I, Simon?"

"He does," I say, though I'm fairly certain I've never had one. I detest the taste of gin.

Aubrey, never one to bow to peer pressure, switches topics by asking, "How did the two of you meet?"

"He used to work for me," Terry says, extracting a pack of cigarettes and a lighter from his suit jacket. "Here at the pub."

"I remember Simon working here all four years of college," she says. "But I also remember thinking it was odd he went to work at a bar since he didn't seem to like them very much. When we were at school, Tasha and I literally had to drag him out for a few drinks on Thursday and Friday nights or he'd have spent those evenings in the gym or alone in his room reading crime fiction."

Terry purses his lips. "I met him on your campus actually."

"At American?"

"Right, love. If I recall, I was putting up flyers for me Grand Opening. I stopped him to ask for directions to some building or another. And eventually talked him into escorting me personally. I caught his accent, of course, and once he confessed to being born in London, I told him he had to come work for me. He argued he wasn't much of a bartender. I said, 'Bullocks. You can start as me barback and work your way up from there. It took some convincing. *And* a substantial hourly wage. But I eventually got him to come round. Next thing you know we're best mates." He winks at Aubrey. "Or at least that's what I told the young lasses who came into the pub just to get an eyeful of him."

"Important thing is, we remained friends," I tell Aubrey. "So I had someone to spend time with once you started stealing Tasha away more and more frequently."

Aubrey smiles. To say it's the saddest smile I've ever seen is an understatement. I realize now that I love Aubrey like a sister. Love her like I'd love Tuesday if she were still in my life. If our father hadn't broken our family into pieces and spread us out on opposite sides of the Atlantic Ocean.

Terry lights his cigarette. "You won't believe what I read in the rags his morning. Those geezers in the mick parliament are proposing to ban smoking in pubs. In *pubs*." He takes a pull and blows a stream of smoke up toward the ceiling. "And the daft journo that wrote the story says the Yanks are likely to follow suit sometime in the next few years. Can you believe it? Ban smoking in *pubs*. Might as well ban *drinking* in pubs while they're at it." He takes another drag. "Arseholes they are, every last one of them. Couldn't organize a piss-up in a brewery. Never mind what banning fags will do for business. Imagine the aggro, will you? There may come a bloody day when I can't light up in me own boozer."

I throw back a sizeable portion of my pint. I love Terry too. Love him like a father. Like the father I've always wished I had.

Tears well and threaten to fall. So I lift the rest of my pint and carry it across the room. All the while wishing the rain would end without really having a sound reason why.

Why the hell should I care?

What concern is it of mine?

Let the skies open. Shouldn't matter to me. Might as well rain forever now for all the good the sun will do me.

Chapter 56

Ostermann ran his hand down the far wall, feeling for a seam. He looked back at the kid waiter, who motioned for him to look lower.

"Brilliant," Ostermann said as he kneeled before the hardwood paneling. "Here it is."

He reached into his jacket and pulled out a switchblade. "Eleven-inch Italian stiletto," he said as he flicked it open. "An anniversary present from Magda."

Sliding the knife between two innocuous-looking wooden panels, he used the blade like a crowbar and slowly pried open a heavy, hidden door, which stood only three and a half feet in height.

And opened onto complete darkness.

Still on his knees, Ostermann removed his phone from his pocket. He tapped an app titled Flashlight and a beam as strong as a miniature Maglite appeared. Directing it into the hole, the beam illuminated a steep set of concrete stairs.

"Simon," he said softly as he rose to his feet, "I think it's best you remain up here while I go down."

Wordlessly, I stepped past him, ducked my head, and cautiously started down the stairs.

The air was stale. Like an attic you haven't entered for years. It was cold at the top, and the temperature dropped relentlessly the closer

I came to the bottom. By the time I reached the last step, my breath was forming a fog so dense I could barely see past it.

With Ostermann right behind me shining the light from his phone, I stopped directly in front of a sealed metal door.

I felt my fingers curl into fists. Since Liverpool my left had been regaining strength and range of motion. Now it, like the rest of my body, was operating of its own accord.

I consciously opened my right hand and pressed my palm against the cold steel.

My breathing quickened.

My pulse raced.

Despite the temperature, beads of sweat began to form at my hairline.

"There," Ostermann said, aiming his light at a small panel door to my right.

Opening it revealed a digital keypad.

My anticipation instantly sunk.

"Type in Shauna Adair's birthday," Ostermann said. "Day, month, last two digits of the year."

In the darkness, I looked a question back at him.

Matter-of-factly, he said, "The waiter has spent some time with her down here. He asked that we not let his boss find out."

I pressed the keys slowly, deliberately, my frozen fingers slightly sticking to each one.

As soon as I entered the last number I heard the click of an electronic lock. Like the one on Ostermann's hotel room door only louder, heavier. This lock was far more secure.

It had been made not only to keep intruders out but to keep captives in.

I felt the sound in my stomach like the percussion of a bass drum.

I searched for a door handle.

"Push inward," Ostermann said.

I did; I pushed hard on the heavy metal door and slowly it came open.

And I froze.

Behind the door was a room that looked like a poorly finished basement. Cheap furniture, including a couch with cat-clawed upholstery, a pair of wooden chairs with uneven legs, a double bed consisting of only a mattress and box spring dressed in yellowing sheets. A single set of plastic see-through drawers against the left wall. The walls masked with hideous wallpaper, no doubt in order to conceal soundproofing materials and whatever other horrors lurked behind them.

And in the far corner, a pale form. Small, emaciated, curled up like a ball.

Next to her, on the floor, a syringe. A burnt spoon. Several black and gray Bic lighters. A pair of opened translucent vials, one empty, one half-filled with brown powder.

Alternative rock played quietly from hidden speakers.

I swallowed hard as I tried to process the scene revealing itself before me.

"Hailey?" I breathed.

Her name dissipated in a pathetic puff the moment it left my lips. Likely because it was much warmer inside the room than out.

Finally, I steeled myself and went to her. Each step like trudging through three feet of snow, my legs as heavy and leaden as they'd ever been. All that I'd faced in the past twelve years—as an investigator and the father of a missing girl—suddenly seemed trifling. Like waking from a vaguely negative dream set in the distant past.

Once I was within just a few feet of her I nearly lost my balance, my knees threatening to collapse beneath my weight as they had in our kitchen the day Hailey first went missing.

I lowered myself to my haunches and held my hands out to her, though I felt strangely certain that she wasn't remotely aware of my presence. Of *any* presence.

"Hailey."

I went to war with the dread building in the back of my throat and finally touched her head. Like being struck with a jolt of electricity an intense tingling shot up my arm, into my shoulder blades. I shuddered then set my jaw and boldly used both hands to take hold of her, to pull her toward me.

The term "skin and bones" could barely describe how she felt in my quivering hands. I was reminded of a feral cat I'd once fed as a child, of lifting him in my own matchstick arms just a few days before I discovered his feline corpse hidden deep within my father's azaleas.

I breathed in the scent of her, her short dyed hair so thick with smoke I nearly gagged.

A soft moan escaped her lips and I immediately lifted her into my arms and rose to my feet. Set her gently back down on the bed.

She weighed no more than ninety or a hundred pounds.

Sitting beside her, I took her face into my hands and searched it for some sign of life other than the feeble breaths emanating from her nostrils. As I held her, the lids of her eyes slowly began to lift like the curtains on a show. And in those moments I saw myself. I saw my wife, Tasha. I saw my daughter.

Looking at her now I didn't know how I ever could have doubted her identity. The grainy image caught on closed-circuit television outside the Stalemate should have been more than enough to convince me.

I whispered her name as though to say it aloud would cause her to vanish again. As it had once in my dreams.

Her lids fluttered and finally closed. But I'd already seen enough in those eyes to know.

This was the infant girl I'd gently taken from Dr. Bruce Chen's arms eighteen years ago at Georgetown University Hospital while a wholly depleted Tasha looked on from her spot on the operating room table with tears of joy in her eyes.

This was the one-year-old who first rose to her feet in a portable playpen on a freezing Thanksgiving night in the living room of her grandparents' colossal house in Richmond, Virginia, while everyone else watched the Ravens kick hell out of the Cowboys.

This was the shy and awkward toddler I'd sat and watched from my miniature plastic chair as she reluctantly joined a half-dozen other unwieldy children for circle time on her first morning of preschool.

This was the little girl who drew suns on every piece of construction paper she ever set crayon to, even scenes set indoors, simply because she treasured days when the sky was sky-blue and the sun was unobstructed by clouds.

This was the little girl Tasha and I watched dance through the sprinklers in our yard as we sipped sweet tea on our lounge chairs on the back porch.

This was the little girl I took sailing on Chesapeake Bay.

This was the little girl who, instead of shells, insisted on collecting the white sand from Maryland's Downtown North Beach.

This was my little girl.

The little girl who, for the past twelve years, had peered out at me from the photograph on my refrigerator. The little girl with whom I'd last known true happiness as we stood together with her mother in front of Cinderella Castle at the Magic Kingdom.

The little girl whom I'd last held in my arms the morning I left for Bucharest to track down a United States fugitive.

I placed my lips on her pallid face. Ran a hand through her matted black hair. Kissed her and gently set her head back down on her sickly motel pillow.

Only once I rose to my feet did I remember Kurt Ostermann was still in the small basement room with us.

"Simon, look," he said, pointing to a spot just under the bed.

Money, I saw. Loads of it.

Immediately I thought: *The reason she went up north.*

Her father had gotten himself into some kind of trouble. With his competition, Lennox Sterling had suggested. Maybe even with his mates.

She'd been in a rush, Quigg had told me. She'd moved with a definite urgency. She had to do something of grave consequence for her father.

For Terrance Davies.

Also known as Nigel Cummings.

I went to one knee and sifted through the bills. Tens of thousands of pounds if not a couple hundred thousand.

And secreted within those notes was a small, unsealed off-white envelope.

I opened it, withdrew its contents: a single page of typewritten instructions.

Silently, I read them.

To Ostermann, I said, "This money is a ransom."

A ransom, I thought. But also a ticket to see my daughter's abductor. Live and up close. In all likelihood, my one and only opportunity to make Terrance Davies answer for all he'd done.

Chapter 57

Ostermann remained behind at Knight's End to keep watch over Hailey, while I headed off to the East London district of Wapping, where Shauna Adair had been instructed to take the ransom to free Terrance Davies from an East End gangster known as John "Gentleman Jack" Noonan.

Lizzy, the bartender back at Knight's End, had provided what little information she could on Terry's captor.

"Dapper fellow," she said. "Looks a lot like the film star Michael Caine, he does. And a real charmer, from what I've heard. At least to the fairer sex. But to blokes? Goss is that he once ripped his own solicitor's throat out with his teeth like a rabid bulldog."

Unlike Terry, Jack Noonan had his hands in much more than drug trafficking. Based out of South London, Jack's firm was known to be active in gambling, extortion, money laundering, arms dealing, protection rackets, sex trafficking, and contract killing.

"What's his beef with your boss?" I asked.

"They had a row over territories, far as I know. Nigel—"

"His real name's Terry," I said. "Terrance Davies."

"All right, then. *Terry* started muscling in on Jack's action."

Unfortunately for Terry, Jack's action included much of London and its surrounding areas, including Essex and Kent. Over the past decade, working closely with the Colombian cartels as well as local

Yardies, Jack's syndicate had largely consolidated the organized crime industry. With politicians, Metropolitan Police officials, even some higher-ups in the newly formed NCA, Jack had become all but untouchable. As a result, most small-timers had been bought out or scared off. But not Terry. Terry remained intent on keeping his humble slice of London's East End.

"So after several warnings, Jack finally moved on one of Terry's mates—took the poor bastard's toes, all ten of them."

A rotten shame, she said, but it did bring Terry to the table. After a few days of talks, they came to an agreement wherein Terry would give Jack a percentage of his earnings from the disputed territory.

"Only Nigel being Nigel—or Terry being Terry, I suppose—he eventually welched. When Jack's boys came round to collect, Terry disappeared. Only Terry ain't no magician, right? He'd apparently only gone so far as Leeds in the North Country, when Gentleman Jack tracked him down."

Using his firm's Afro-Caribbean muscle, Jack got ahold of Terry and brought him back to London. In bad shape, Lizzy had heard—though his poor physical condition, she admitted, was nothing more than a rumor.

"According to the note, Jack's holding Terry in a warehouse in Wapping," I said.

"That's in the Borough of Tower Hamlets," she said. "Not far, right? Somewhere between the north bank of the River Thames and the Highway."

I asked her how Shauna became involved.

"Terry's got no one else he can trust, see. He knew someone sold him out in Leeds. Someone close to him. Had to be. Because hardly any of Terry's mates knew where he was going. So Terry told Gentleman Jack, 'If you want your dosh, ring my daughter. She's the only one can get it for you.'"

"And that's why she went to Dublin?"

"Actually, she would have made a few stops. Terry owns public houses all over the UK and Ireland. Only a few act as his true bases of operations, however. Shauna would have gone to the Doubled Pawn in Manchester, Bishop's in Glasgow, and the Stalemate in Dublin in order to collect the kind of money Jack Noonan was asking for."

"According to the instructions, the drop is supposed to happen tonight."

"Is the girl in any shape to make it?"

I shook my head. "I'm going to make the drop," I said.

"You? Why would you do that for Terry?"

"Let's just say I owe him. And tonight I'm going to even the score."

Lizzy lent me Terry's brand-new black Mercedes for the drive to the river. I parked near a former landmark known as Execution Dock, which was utilized by the Brits for hundreds of years to hang pirates who'd been convicted and sentenced to death in the Admiralty court.

I stepped out of the Mercedes and into the fierce wind blowing in from the Thames. Wapping somehow maintained its historic character as a maritime district even though most of the warehouses that remained standing had been converted into luxury flats.

Not the one I was looking for, however. The warehouse I was looking for was now owned by a Kuwaiti investment company. It wasn't in regular use, though it did from time to time host large events like major film premiere after parties.

I walked quickly up Wapping Lane, past Watts and Chandler Streets on my left, Raine Street on my right. Because of the time, the area was quiet. But had I arrived a couple of hours earlier, Wapping probably would have looked more like Temple Bar than an ancient warehouse district.

A large pirate ship fronted my destination. Directly behind it, the building itself was a grand mix of brown brick and iron. At its highest point, I could just make out a giant wild boar squashed beneath three massive barrels in the darkness. I checked my watch. As far as the instructions were concerned I was early, but not by much.

They're waiting for the girl, I told myself. That explained why there were no watchmen on the roof, no guards patrolling the surrounding streets.

They were waiting for a young woman roughly five five in height and weighing no more than a hundred pounds. They were waiting for a dispirited junkie who could barely lift her head to look someone in the eyes.

They were in for a surprise.

As I approached a side entrance I debated whether to keep my handgun concealed or to hold it out in the open, ready to fire.

In the end, I opened the zipper of my black biker armor. Reached inside and withdrew my .45.

Chapter 58

So much for the element of surprise. The moment I stepped inside the warehouse known as Tobacco Dock, I was greeted by a semicircle of seven well-dressed men, six of whom were armed with automatic weapons.

Christ.

The seventh man was a Michael Caine look-alike in his early- to mid-fifties. Dressed in a custom-tailored charcoal suit that all but screamed Harrods of London, he stepped forward and folded his arms across his chest.

"Please, put down that weapon, guv, or the boys here are going to be swabbing this floor till dawn."

For most of a millisecond I dwelled on the biker armor. Then I realized that with six automatic weapons aimed at me, chances were one or more shots would strike me in the head. So I lowered the HK, slowly went to my haunches, and set it on the cement warehouse floor as instructed.

As I rose, I said, "It's none of my business, but do you and your boys always gather around in a half circle with weapons drawn like you're posing for a poster for the next Guy Ritchie film? Or did I just arrive at a good time?"

He chuckled. "We watched your arrival, mate. Cameras, you know.

London is full of them these days. Government *and* private enterprise."

"So I've heard."

"I don't believe we've ever had the pleasure," he said, placing his hands in his pockets.

My own hands remained at my sides, fingers unclenched.

"The name's Bateman," I said in case Terry was within earshot.

The warehouse was, for the most part, empty. But there were doors on three of four walls that appeared to lead to additional rooms.

"Well, Mr. Bateman, do you have a first name? Or would you prefer to keep things formal?"

"Patrick," I said.

"All right, Patrick—may I call you Patrick?—this warehouse is private property. From the manner of your entrance, I suspect that you believe you have business to conduct here. From the manner of your dress, I assume it is business of a, let's be polite and say, *casual* nature."

"As a matter of fact, I do," I said, "Mr. . . . ."

"Oh, my apologies, Patrick. My name's John. John Noonan. But you can call me Jack."

"I'm here to conduct a transaction, Jack."

"A transaction?"

I couldn't help but mimic his formality. "To make an exchange," I said. "A purchase. A payoff, if you prefer."

He glanced at his watch, a high-end Tag Heuer. Though I didn't own much in the way of jewelry, I happened to have one just like it back at my studio apartment on Dumbarton in D.C. Given to me two years ago by the French police lieutenant Davignon. Coincidentally, it was a seizure from some Parisian drug baron not unlike Jack Noonan here.

"I see," he said. "Thing is, I have only one appointment scheduled for this evening. And it's with a young woman."

"I'm her surrogate," I said.

"I'm afraid *surrogates* aren't permitted under the terms of our agreement, Patrick. I made that quite clear in my instructions."

"She sends her apologies, Jack. She's fallen ill."

"Oh, I am sorry to hear that. Nothing too serious, I hope."

I said nothing.

"Well then, I presume you have brought my money," he said.

"I have it, Jack. And may I presume our friend Terry is on the premises?"

"Yes. Terry or Nigel or whatever he's calling himself these days, he most certainly is."

I smiled. "Good."

"Right then, Patrick. Let's proceed, shall we?"

"I'm game if you are."

His tone turned dead serious. "Well then, where is my money?"

"Half of it is on me," I said.

"Half? Patrick, I have to be honest. I don't like the sound of that."

"It's probably just the acoustics," I offered.

"Well, how about this, then? You give me half of my money, and I'll give you half of Mr. Davies."

Suits me, I thought. "The other half's nearby."

"And this half?"

"In my jacket."

"Open it, then. Slowly, please."

As I did, two of Jack's boys started toward me.

I lifted my arms as one of the two patted me down. After removing the sizeable envelope, he reached into another pocket and discovered Ostermann's switchblade.

He switched open the eleven-inch Italian stiletto and held it in the air for his boss to have a look.

"I'm a collector," I said.

Gentleman Jack shrugged. "Just be sure to keep it tucked away, Patrick. We wouldn't want one of us to have an accident, now, would we?"

The goon handed the switchblade back to me. I stuffed it into my inside pocket while he bent over and picked my gun up off the floor.

Jack's two boys then walked back to their semicircle, opened the envelope, and counted its contents.

"Exactly half, boss," one of them said.

"And the rest?" Jack asked me.

"In my car. I'm parked by the river."

"Well, let's go retrieve it then, shall we?"

"First, I want proof of life," I told him.

He let fly a long, theatrical sigh. "This isn't part of the agreement, Patrick."

I said, "I'd consider it a professional courtesy."

He glanced again at his watch and thought about it.

"Very well," he said finally. "Hand over your phone, Patrick."

I dug it out of my pocket and tossed it underhand to one of his boys.

Jack said to him, "Now go snap a picture of Mr. Davies and bring it back to us, will you?"

"Right, boss."

As he ran off, Jack added, "Be sure to get Terry's good side, Carl. And by that I mean his scrawny white arse."

In the meantime, the seven of us stood silently, gazing at each other across the bare warehouse floor.

The designated photographer was back a few minutes later.

He showed Jack the photo then walked it over to me.

I looked at the picture. Stared at it for more seconds than I could count as a tumultuous roar rose in my ears, and rational thoughts gave way to savage reverie.

"Satisfied, Patrick?" Jack asked.

"Not yet," I said. "But I will be."

Chapter 59

Two of Jack's boys accompanied me to the Mercedes. I opened the trunk and handed them the rest of the money. Half expecting them to shoot me straightaway. Dump my body in the River Thames. That, I thought, might be as elegant a punctuation mark as any to close out these past twelve years. I'd found Hailey, I'd saved my daughter. Ashdown would see that she was taken care of, wouldn't he? Or maybe Zoey. Hell, maybe even my father, though I wouldn't wish him on anyone, not even my worst enemy, let alone my only child.

She could return to Liverpool, to Lennox Sterling, I thought. She was happy there, as far as I could tell. And Sterling, despite his less-than-desirable occupation, seemed to genuinely love her. Only she'd still have her habit, which could kill her at any time. And then, there was Terrance Davies; he'd still be alive.

Instead of killing me and dumping my body into the water, Jack's boys counted out the cash and we all walked back to the warehouse in silence.

On the way, I wondered why the hell I'd felt so content to take a bullet to the back of the head. Was it simply because I'd found Hailey? Because I'd completed my life's work?

No, it was something far more selfish than that. I didn't care if they killed me because I was scared to face whatever came next. My work was far from finished. Sure, I'd found Hailey. But I sure as hell hadn't saved her. She remained a captive to the heroin. She was still chained to whatever psychological damage her abduction had caused her over the past twelve years. Not only was I far from finished, I hadn't even reached the hard part yet.

Once we were back in the warehouse and the entire sum was in Jack's possession, he said, "Well, Patrick, I must say it was a pleasure doing business with you."

"And Mr. Davies?"

"All yours." He turned to his boys. "Run along and get Patrick his prize goose."

Five minutes later, with one of Jack's boys on either side of him, Terrance Davies came walking out under the power of his own two feet. He hadn't been worked over, as Lizzy had heard. Hell, he looked fitter than he had the last time I saw him in the States. A little older. But he wore it well. Better than my father did, at least.

He was dressed in a black suit, similar to the one he wore to Tasha's funeral. As he walked, he kept his head down, dusting off his arms and shoulders and torso. Then he slowed to dust off his knees.

Finally he lifted his head, a satisfied grin on his face.

He came to a full halt when he saw me. And the grin instantly melted into a dire frown.

"What's this, Jack?" Terry said, his voice somewhat hoarse.

Jack looked at me. "Your girl's . . . surrogate, I believe."

I nodded.

"This wasn't the deal, Jack."

"Whatever do you mean, guv? I have my money. You're completely free to go."

"The hell I am," he said, pointing in my general direction. "This man's here to kill me."

Jack chuckled, bewildered. "I highly doubt that, Terry. He just paid a *very* substantial sum for you."

"Yeah, Terry," I said. "Why in the world would I want to kill you?"

I watched his Adam's apple travel up and down his throat.

Terry said, "Kill him, Jack. Kill him now."

That got Jack's attention. He stepped into the empty space between us.

"What in bloody hell is going on here?"

I said, "Tell him, Terry."

I made a decision right then that if Jack Noonan sided with Terrance Davies, I'd immediately make a move. I'd snatch Ostermann's switchblade from my pocket and charge at my old mentor and friend. I'd get to Terry. They could put a dozen bullets in me and I'd still keep going. I'd get to him.

Slice his goddamn throat.

Even if it cost me my life.

Because Hailey wasn't safe as long as that bastard was alive.

"His name's Simon Fisk," Terry said, gathering his courage. "We had a falling out, years ago, in the States."

"A falling out," I said. "Is that what you'd call it?"

Jack turned to me. "Are you here to kill this man?"

I said nothing.

"Tell me now," he pressed. "Or my boys here are going to be swabbing the floor until dawn after all."

"Whatever he tells you will be *lies*," Terry shouted.

Jack looked at him calmly. "I'll be the judge of that, now, won't I?" Then he turned to me. "This is important, *Mr. Fisk*. I had a deal with this man's daughter, Shauna. She gives me the money and I return her father to her in one piece. This was a ransom, not a bloody auction where the best offer wins."

"*Kill* him," Terry said again.

"*Shut up*, Terry." Jack took a step toward me. "You're here under false pretenses, Mr. Fisk. If you are at all familiar with my reputation, you know that I'm a fair man. But I don't like to be misled. And I sure as hell don't abide men lying to my face. Which is precisely what you did tonight." He motioned for two of his boys to come forward. "Well? What have you to say for yourself, Fisk? You're in *my* bloody manor now, aren't you? Plead your case."

I drew several quick breaths, knowing damn well any one of them could be my last.

"The girl who was supposed to bring you the money," I said, never taking my eyes off Terry, "she's not Mr. Davies's daughter. She's mine."

"A goddamn *lie!*" Terry shouted. "Shauna is me daughter, you know that, Jack. You've met her, for Christ's sake."

"Her name's not Shauna," I said calmly. "Her name is Hailey Fisk. And Terrance Davies stole her from my home twelve years ago. Snatched her out of my backyard when she was six years old."

Jack Noonan looked from Terry to me and back. "This is a pretty serious allegation, isn't it?" He placed his hands behind his back and began pacing between us. "No time for a DNA test, I'm afraid." He turned to me. "Let us assume for a moment that you are telling the truth, Mr. Fisk. That your daughter was indeed abducted twelve years ago. We could verify that on the Internet easily enough, can't we? But that Shauna Adair is actually your daughter—Hailey?—that's something else entirely. So, how do you intend on proving that to me?"

I thought on it, resisted the urge to tell Jack this was none of his business. That this was between me and Terry. Because Jack had made it his business. As he'd made clear just a few moments ago, this was his manor. And he had all the firepower. All I had was an eleven-inch blade and a headful of fury.

How could I prove Shauna was Hailey?

I had the e-mail images from Kati Sheffield. But if they weren't enough to convince me, they sure as hell wouldn't be sufficient to persuade Jack Noonan.

Jack held out his palm and one of his boys brought him a large handgun. He glanced at his Tag Heuer again. "I hate to be a stickler for time, but I don't have all night, you understand." He leveled the gun at my head. "So get talking or get dying, Fisk. Either way, I'm out of this bloody warehouse within five minutes."

Now or never.

"Mind if I make a call?" I said.

It was a shot in the dark, but it was the only shot I had.

Jack lifted a shoulder, said, "If you believe it will help. Be my guest."

I dug out my BlackBerry, turned on the speakerphone, and dialed Rendell. Hoping that he'd followed my instructions, that he'd found what I expected him to find, and most important, that he'd cooperate in this, well, unconventional paternity hearing.

"This is Special Agent John Rendell." His voice, tinny through the phone's speaker, echoed throughout the empty warehouse.

"It's Simon Fisk," I said. "You're on speakerphone, John. I'm going ask you a few questions for the benefit of a third party. I'd like you to answer as though you were on a witness stand. The truth, the whole truth, nothing but the truth. Understand?"

After a brief hesitation, he said, "All right. Shoot."

I watched Jack's boys instinctively place their index fingers on their respective triggers.

"Might want to refrain from using that word for the duration of this conversation," I said. "John, would you kindly define our relationship as succinctly as you can?"

"Twelve years ago, my partner Candace West and I were the Bureau agents assigned to lead the investigation into the apparent abduction of your six-year-old daughter, Hailey."

"Were you successful?"

"No, Hailey was never found."

"Where are you now?"

"Inside a bar in the District of Columbia, a few miles from where Hailey was abducted."

"The name of the establishment?"

"Terry's Pub."

"Owner?"

"Presently, the liquor license is in the name of Nigel Cummings."

"Previously?"

"Previously, it was owned by its founder, Terrance Davies."

"Have you searched the place just now?"

"With the consent of the full-time bartender, Casey O'Connell, I have."

"Why not the owner?"

"Mr. O'Connell advises that the owner lives abroad. In London. Before I identified myself as an FBI agent, Mr. O'Connell *very enthusiastically* assured me that he had full authority in all matters relating to the bar and the property."

"Find anything noteworthy during your search, John?"

He hesitated then said softly, "I ultimately found a secret room beneath the pub."

"And in the room?"

"In the room I discovered large amounts of illicit drugs, including ecstasy, cocaine, and heroin."

"Anything else?"

"The room is fully soundproofed and furnished with a worn love seat, a plastic table and chairs, and a mattress and box spring. Buried deep inside the mattress, I discovered a number of photographs, as well as several pieces of construction paper of various sizes and colors. All of which contain messages in what appears to be a child's handwriting."

I swallowed hard. "What do these messages say?"

Rendell hesitated again. "Are you sure, Simon?"

"I'm sure, John."

"They're messages asking for help. The author says she was stolen by a man she calls 'Uncle Terry.' She's signed each message, 'Hailey Fisk.'"

"And the photos?"

"They're of Hailey, Simon. They appear to have been taken over the course of about two or three years—all in the hidden room below the bar."

Trembling inside, I managed to hold my gaze on Terry. During the course of my conversation with Rendell, Terry's skin had become progressively waxen. Now he resembled a porcelain statue about to splinter into a million little pieces.

I held out the phone to him. Said, "Care to cross-examine the witness, Mr. Davies?"

Chapter 60

Jack said, "Well, it appears we have quite a predicament here, don't we, Terry?"

I'd just clicked off a much briefer call with Kati Sheffield, who had proudly asserted her credentials as a former computer analyst for the Federal Bureau of Investigation, then described her search for records relating to a London resident named Shauna Adair—and her ultimate discovery of Shauna's death certificate.

"Kati," I'd asked, "did you have a chance to compare the recent photos I sent you? The photos of the girl we found in the locked basement of Knight's End?"

"I did, Simon," she said anxiously. "It's her. With one-hundred percent certainty. The girl you found at Knight's End is your daughter. Shauna Adair *is* Hailey Fisk."

I offered the photos into evidence, so to speak. Jack studied them for less than a minute before motioning to one of his boys.

"Return Mr. Fisk's firearm to him," he said.

"For *fuck's sake, Jack!*" Terry bellowed.

"Shut up, Terry. Another word from you, and I'll offer Mr. Fisk my *personal* assistance. And believe me. You do *not* want that."

I took back the HK but tucked it into my jacket. Said, "Thanks, but I won't be needing this, Jack."

Another of his boys handed me my phone.

Jack said, "I don't have gift wrap, Simon. But I do have zip ties if you'd like. And I could have a couple of my boys help you carry your package to the car. I believe you said you're parked by the river, right? That could be of some convenience, I'd imagine."

"I'll pass, Jack. But I do have one favor to ask."

"All right, then."

"I'd like to borrow these premises."

Jack seemed to think on it. "I've only let them, Simon. So they are my responsibility."

"I understand. Nothing will be damaged."

"And you'll clean up after yourself?"

"You have my word."

"Then by all means, have at it, Simon." He nodded to me, said, "I too have a little girl. Two of them, in fact."

I said nothing.

He added, "I'd just ask that you wait ten minutes before you begin so that the boys and I are well off."

"Thanks, Jack."

He bowed his head. "A good night to you, Simon."

Then he and his crew took their leave without looking back.

Running's only going to make it worse," I warned Terry after he took a half step backward.

We were alone in the large warehouse. There were plenty of exits but Terrance Davies had no hope of making it to any of them. And he damn well knew it.

"Listen, Simon. Before you do anything, let's have a chat, you and me."

"I don't think we have anything to talk about, Terry."

His voice rose in pitch and took on the distinct tone of desperation. "Don't you at least want to know *why*?"

"I already know why."

He spread out his arms, palms wide. "I took great care of her, Simon. You have to believe me. I loved her like I loved me own daughter."

"Equivocate all you want. Doesn't change what you've done."

He puffed up and tried indignation on for size. "If I'm guilty of anything, Simon," he shouted, pointing a finger at me, "it's punishing you for the iniquities of your father."

"I'd already paid for the iniquities of my father," I said calmly. "You knew that when you took her from me."

His shoulders slumped. "It was twelve bloody years ago, Simon. I was a different man. I was lonely, wasn't I? You knew that. You remember."

I still hadn't moved from my spot. Roughly ten feet stood between us.

He dropped to his knees in front of me. "I beg of you. I'm an old man, aren't I?"

I thought of Gerry Gilchrist and his story about Arthur Thompson and the Ponderosa. Then about Edie and her son, shot dead at a Baltimore Burger King over a couple hundred bucks.

"I regretted it the moment I got her back to the pub, Simon. I regretted it right then. But I saw no turning back. I'd passed the bloody Rubicon, you see?"

I thought of the first time I'd killed a man. Ten years ago. In Saint Petersburg, Russia. The incident that put me on the Kremlin's radar. The killing that brought me here to London—for the first time in twenty-five years—in order to lie low.

The child I'd been tracking was named Natalya. She was eleven years old. The child of a State Department employee and an SVR operative who'd been posing as a Russian diplomat at Washington Station on Wisconsin Avenue in the District.

The morning I'd received the call, I conferred with the mother's lawyers and obtained confirmation that she'd been granted full custody by a D.C. family court. By noon I was on a plane to Moscow.

When I arrived in Moscow, I took a bullet train to Saint Petersburg. At an operating speed of roughly 155 miles per hour, the trip took just under four hours.

From the station I took a taxi to Petrogradskaya, a largely residential area on the banks of the Neva River. In a sushi restaurant named Yakitoriya, I met with a CIA case officer who was in Russia as a banker under nonofficial cover, meaning he wasn't under the protection of the American embassy. If his spying activities were discovered, the United States would deny any ties and he'd be subject to Russia's draconian laws relating to espionage and treason, after, of course, he was tortured. The banker provided me the address of the former diplomat/spy, along with a report on his daily movements and his daughter Natalya's routine.

Late that night I disabled the alarm system and entered the Russian's two-story home. The banker had given me the blueprints. In and out, I thought; the job would be a piece of cake. Only the intelligence I received didn't take into account that the unattached former spy might get lonely and invite a prostitute into his home.

The prostitute was in the kitchen, slicing an apple, when she caught me with the child, who'd been cooperative once I told her I was returning her to her mother in the States.

The prostitute screamed.

I removed my Glock and commanded her to be silent, but by then it was too late. The Russian spy was already barreling out of his room with a shotgun on his shoulder, and it was kill or be killed, so I shoved Natalya behind me, raised my Glock, aimed it at his center mass, and fired twice.

Natalya watched her father tumble down a full flight of stairs before rolling to a stop, drenched in blood. Then she watched him die in front of her.

That night I'd passed a Rubicon of my own.

There was no turning back.

"Your daughter's *alive*," Terry cried from his spot on the floor.

"Taking *my* life tonight won't amount to no justice. That's not 'an eye for an eye,' is it?"

I said nothing.

Once he finally realized that my heart held nothing but rage, he closed his eyes and sank deeper into the cold concrete floor.

Feebly, he said, "Can I have one last fag, Simon? Can you at least grant me that? Me hands are trembling. It's all I ask. Please."

When he opened his eyes, I bowed my head and he fished a crumpled package of cigarettes out of his suit jacket. The first three cigarettes he pulled out of the package with his quivering fingers were broken. The fourth was damaged but likely to hold. He placed it between his lips.

Feeling around in his suit, he said, "They took me bloody matches." He looked up at me, the ruined unlit cigarette dangling from his lips. "I don't suppose you'd happen to have a light?"

I pulled Kinny Gilchrist's platinum Zippo from my pocket and tossed it to him.

After several tries, the flint wheel finally sparked.

He lit up.

Inhaled.

Exhaled.

Tossed the lighter back to me.

"When Tasha died," he said with a shaky voice, "it was like losing me Lona all over again. She killed herself too Simon. Hung herself with her bedsheets while still behind bars. On account of what your father done."

I took a single step forward. "I heard the story, Terry. Twice. I don't need to hear it again."

He blew a column of smoke up at the ceiling. "You need to hear the *truth*, don't you? You bloody well need to hear *that*."

"The truth is right in front of me," I said. "On its knees."

Shaking his head, he cried, "It's not the *whole* truth though, is it?

You blame me for taking Hailey, all right. But if you blame me for Tasha's suicide, you're burying your bloody head in the sand, aren't you, Simon?"

I said nothing.

Terry said, "It was your behavior what killed your wife. At least be man enough to accept your share of the fault."

"My wife died of a broken heart," I said. "You and you alone had the hatchet in your hand."

"Bullshit, Simon. *Bullshit*. I've read the stories about you. I've read the interviews. I've read Will Collins's true crime book. 'Me beloved Tasha this, me beloved Tasha that.' Only that's not how it was in those final days, was it? You *blamed* her for what happened, didn't you? Your blame is what done her in, isn't it?"

"None of it would have happened were it not for what you did."

"But Tasha was blameless," he said. "You can admit that, can't you? You bloody killed her, Simon. You bloody killed your own wife. With resentment, you did. And you know what? It wasn't her fault in the least. I had it all planned out, didn't I? For me, it was just another job of work. Just another score. I'd planned on taking Hailey from her school. Would have been cake too. Had it all planned, I tell you. But no, you put it all on Tasha, poor Tasha, she wasn't looking at what she was doing. At least admit, Simon, you're as responsible for her death as I am. Every bit. You killed that beautiful young bird, sure as I did."

I stepped forward so that I was hovering over him.

He said, "I was going to off you, Simon. I was going to top you in order to hurt your father. Back then in '92. Then I learned you had a falling out with him, and I changed me tune. Instead of topping you, I recruited you. I became like a bloody father to you. Like a grandfather to your daughter. Hailey, even two years after I took her, still referred to me as Uncle Terry. After that, she called me *Dad*. Still does, doesn't she? Kill me, Simon, all right, but know you're killing someone your daughter *loves*. Again."

"Almost done with that cigarette?" I said.

"I became a father to you. Even after I discovered you'd become just like Alden. Married a woman not for love, but for her money."

"The hell I did."

"You took that big house though, didn't you? You let Tasha's parents pay for that posh private school for Hailey."

"You don't know anything about me, Terry."

"Oh, but I do, mate. I do. I do, and it's bloody killing you. That's why you're gonna top me, innit? Because you can't live with yourself. With the things that you've done."

I said nothing.

"Look at you, Simon. Indignant just like your old man. Know why I took her, mate? Because I fell in love with that child. And no, don't you dare fucking look at me like that. Not in a sexual way. I never laid a bloody hand on me Shauna except in love. Never touched her but in any way that a father should touch a daughter."

I wanted to shut him up but a dam had suddenly collapsed and countless questions came flooding into my mind.

Did it matter that he hadn't sexually abused her? Of course, it mattered. But did it matter enough to spare his life?

Did it matter that he'd lost Zoey all those years ago and blamed that loss on my father, who'd turned him in, possibly out of nothing more than sexual jealousy?

Did it matter that he believed I played a role in my own wife's suicide?

Did it matter that he may have been right?

All of a sudden I felt dizzy, confused, a white blaze framing my vision.

My mind went to the call I'd made on my way to Wapping.

When I'd first gotten into the Mercedes, I'd plucked my wallet from my back pocket and dialed the number I'd been handed when we'd first landed in Ireland.

Edie had answered.

"You may not remember me," I'd said. "My name's Simon. We met on the Aer Lingus flight from D.C. to Dublin."

"Of course I remember you," she said in her slight British accent. "I may be on in years, but I haven't lost the plot, have I? At least not yet anyway."

I smiled. It felt good to hear her voice.

"What can I do for you, love?"

"You can convince me," I said.

There was silence on her end of the line as she no doubt reflected on our conversation of five nights ago and filled in all the pages I'd purposefully left blank.

"You've found him," she said, "the man who stole your daughter all those years ago."

It wasn't a question.

"Is she . . ." She paused. "I was about to ask whether she was alive. But it doesn't matter, does it? Not for the purposes of this conversation. Doesn't matter at all."

Again, she was merely stating fact.

"Simon, I can't tell you what to do, love. You know that. This is your burden, I'm afraid. You're the one who will have to live with the consequences, not me."

I told her I understood and she continued.

"All I can say is, murdering that man will only add another link to the chain of violence. I *know* the desire for revenge. I know how bloody strong it is. But do you need to add to that chain? Or are you better than that?"

"What happened to your son's killer?" I asked her.

She sighed deeply. "He finally died in prison. A natural death. And I was relieved that it was over, my dealings with the Maryland penal system at least. But I wasn't happy. Nothing could have brought my son back."

"Did you forgive him?"

She hesitated again. "Forgiveness is something else entirely, love. It's something that happened, and I've moved on with it as part of my life. I still hate what that man did all those years ago. But I no longer hate *him*."

She was right, of course. In every way she was right.

Edie was a good person.

Better than me.

She always had been, I'd bet.

And she always would be.

I thought of Rob Roy Moffett back at HMP Shotts in Scotland.

"Guess you and I are just different, then," he'd said.

"I guess we are."

I looked down at Terry. And I pitied him some. He'd a hard life. He'd screwed up one night at a party by letting his temper get the best of him and for that he was tossed out of medical school, his future disintegrated by a single drunken fistfight.

And maybe my father *had* wronged him.

And maybe he really *did* love Hailey like a daughter.

And maybe he *was* truly sorry for everything that had happened these past twelve years.

I thought about all of it.

Then I thought about what he'd done.

I thought about coming home to D.C. to learn from his own mouth that Hailey had been taken.

I thought about that first night and all nights after that, wondering where my little girl was.

And I thought about Tasha. About that first morning. About all those weeks of tissues and snoring.

I thought about the birds.

About her funeral.

About what I'd done.

I lowered myself to my haunches. Looked Terry in the eyes and said, "You're right. I'm as much to blame for Tasha's suicide as anyone."

A half hour later I was back in Terry's Mercedes, heading east toward Knight's End. At a red light on Cable Street I braked behind a red double-decker and studied my hand. After a few seconds, I unwrapped part of the bandage and flexed my fingers. Full range of motion had returned and, aside from the lacerated palm itself, the injury no longer hurt.

Half a minute later the light turned.

After another half mile, I passed the double-decker bus and thought back to the scene at the warehouse. What would I tell Ostermann? What would I tell Ashdown and Zoey? What would I eventually tell Hailey?

I drew a deep breath and decided that for the time being I wouldn't tell anyone anything. Because what could I say?

In the end, the violence I'd done to that man couldn't be put into words.

Chapter 61

Back at Knight's End the lights were out. Black curtains were drawn so that no passersby could see in. I stepped up to the front window and inspected my reflection in the glow of the streetlamp.

A few minutes later, Lizzy opened the door. Inside I found Kurt Ostermann seated with Damon Ashdown, each of them holding a pint.

"Is it done?" Ostermann said.

"That part," I told him.

I walked past them and went to the hidden door. It was slightly ajar. Carefully, I opened it the rest of the way and descended the cold concrete stairs.

In the room below, I found Hailey lying on the bed, her head resting on Zoey's lap. Zoey held a wet cloth to Hailey's forehead. In the corner stood the kid waiter, Andrew.

"Gonna be a long road for this one," Zoey said softly.

"Does she need a hospital?" I asked, knowing full well I couldn't take her to one. At least not here in London. Not in the UK. Not in the EU. Whatever name she now went by, she was still wanted for the murder of Eli Welker in Dublin.

Zoey shook her head. "When she fully comes to she'll want a hit. Best to wean her, but given your situ . . ."

She didn't need to say the rest. I too was wanted in connection with the murder of Ewan Maxwell in Glasgow. By now, maybe Duncan MacBride in Liverpool as well. We needed to get the hell out of London, and fast. Hailey and I, wherever we went, would be starting our new lives as fugitives from justice.

Cruelly ironic, I thought. When all this started I'd been hunting fugitives. Now I'd become one.

And once that happened, there was no turning back.

"Are you taking her?" the kid asked.

I'd forgotten he was there.

"What's it to you?" I said, not unkindly.

"I . . . I just love her, don't I?"

"You and me both." I went to the bed and sat next to Zoey. Turned to the kid and asked for some privacy.

Once he was gone, I said, "I feel as though I regained a daughter but lost a sister."

"Bullocks," she said. "You and I will always be brother and sister, won't we? Doesn't matter that we had different biological mums and dads. Blood doesn't mean shite, does it?" She paused, looked into my eyes. "Please say no, because if it does I'm right fucked, aren't I? Being the daughter of that monster and all."

I held her to me.

Said, "I don't know what anything means anymore, Zoey. We just do our best and hope for some luck."

I stared into Hailey's ghostly white face. "Any way to bring her around?"

Zoey nodded. "Let me run upstairs and fetch my handbag."

Ten minutes later Zoey held a syringe in her right hand.

"Naloxone," she'd said when she first came down the stairs with her handbag. "It's a pure opioid antagonist."

"Why do you have it?" I asked.

"All heroin users should carry it round. It counters the effects of an overdose."

"How does it work?"

"Tricks the brain into thinking there are no more opiates in the body."

"Is it safe?"

"Safer than heroin. Certainly safer than a heroin overdose."

"Did she overdose?" I asked with some alarm.

Zoey shrugged. "Technically, yes, I suppose. Her life's not in danger. But she has all the symptoms of an OD. Excessive sleepiness, shallow breathing." She lifted the lids of Hailey's eyes. "Dilated pupils. And she didn't wake when I spoke to her loudly while you were gone. I tried rubbing her chest firmly. That didn't bring her round either."

Now she twisted Hailey's arm, asked me to hold it in place. She removed a rubber tube from her handbag and tied it around Hailey's upper arm just below her meager bicep. She tapped the inside of Hailey's forearm, searching for a vein.

"Found it," she said.

She started the injection.

"How long does it take?"

"She'll come round pretty much straightaway."

Before she finished the sentence Hailey opened her eyes. Immediately they filled with tears and she tried to push herself up on the bed.

"Hold her down," Zoey said.

Hailey was sweating, twitching, crying, pleading for another hit.

I took her by the shoulders and held her down, tears welling in my own eyes, threatening to fall.

"Sadly," Zoey said, "Naloxone sends you into immediate withdrawal. It's an awful feeling but it will pass."

I looked toward Hailey's gear on the floor, specifically at the half-empty vial.

"Shouldn't we give her some," I said, "to make her feel better?"

Zoey looked me in the eyes. "Are you mad? More heroin will send her straight back into overdose." She leaned over Hailey and said, "It's all right, love. You'll start to feel the dope again in about forty minutes and the sick feeling will go away, I promise."

It was pure agony watching her like that. But I trusted Zoey and I told her that.

"Kind of funny," Zoey said, "when you really think about it. I used to believe I had a mind for medicine because my father was a doctor. But all along, it was because my father was a bloody career drug dealer and my mum was an addict."

I leaned over and kissed my sister on the cheek.

She smiled, tears forming in her own eyes. In that moment I saw her clear as day as she'd appeared thirtysome years ago on the opposite side of a loose circle on our primary school playground, singing "The Farmer Wants a Wife."

With the back of my index finger I wiped a tear away from her cheek.

"Run upstairs now," she said. "Say good-bye to Damon. He's a right bastard most of the time. But his heart's in a good place, innit?"

Ashdown's heart *was* in a good place, I decided. Upstairs, shortly after Ostermann excused himself and went outside for a smoke, Detective Chief Inspector Damon Ashdown conceded that he had been able to intercept my call from D.C. because he'd issued an alert for the name Simon Fisk the very day he was assigned to Interpol Manchester.

"I never imagined we'd meet under these particular circumstances," he said as he set down his empty pint glass. "But when I first discovered your name linked to the young American girl who went missing in Paris, I figured I might one day be of assistance. Possibly in getting your arse out of hot water with UK authorities."

"You put yourself at considerable risk these past few days," I told him. "Your career, your safety. Your very *life* a time or two. Why, Detective? Why take those chances for someone you'd never even seen before?"

He grinned. "You were family, weren't you? At least once upon a time you were, even if we'd never had the opportunity to meet in person."

"You did all this for Zoey," I said. "You want her back, don't you?"

His grin faded as he shook his head. "Want her back? No. No, Simon, that ship has sailed. I know we can never be a couple again. But I *do* love her. Love her more than I've ever loved anyone. And I'd go to war with the devil himself if I thought it would do Zoey a lick of good."

I nodded but said nothing.

He said, "She's had a rough go of things, hasn't she? Time and again she's walked through the fire. And each and every time she's come out the other side that much stronger. I love her, sure. But more important, I admire her. And after four decades on this earth, half of them spent rummaging through the wreckage of unfinished lives, there aren't many people I can still say that about."

Chapter 62

An hour later Hailey and I were in Ostermann's suite at the Corinthia. Hailey was resting in the bedroom while Ostermann and I stood across from each other, reluctant to say good-bye this time, because both of us knew, it was probably our last.

"Where will you go?" he said.

"Better if you don't know," I told him.

He motioned with his strong chin to the bedroom. "Does she know what's going on?"

"Not really. When she finally came around and started feeling better, she kept asking for Terry."

"What did you tell her?"

"I tried telling her who I was."

"And?"

"And there was no recognition in her eyes. None at all. She asked me where Terry was again, and I told her I didn't know. She went ballistic, so Zoey told her Terry was all right. That someone else brought Jack Noonan the ransom."

"Probably for the best for the time being." Ostermann turned and paced the length of the room. "Stockholm syndrome, I'd suspect."

I shrugged. "I don't know. Maybe something more than that."

"It'll take time, Simon. Time and patience."

"It'll take that, all right."

"And your father? Where is he now?"

"He headed back to Heathrow as soon as Zoey told him we'd found Hailey. That's the last we'll ever see of him."

Now that I knew the truth, now that I knew *why* he'd taken me from my mother and Tuesday in London, I could probably forgive him that. But I could never forgive him for all the secrets and lies, for all the bullying and emotional blackmail. I could never forgive him for the way in which he raised me in the States over the next decade. I could never forgive him that.

My BlackBerry buzzed in my pocket. Ashdown's number appeared on the screen. With a sudden feeling of foreboding, I pressed the phone to my ear.

"You need to get the hell out of there, Simon," he said urgently. "They're on their way."

"Who?"

"The NCA. They have your location. Which I can only assume means you still have Eli Welker's bloody phone."

Christ, how could I have made such a stupid mistake?

I dug Welker's phone from my pocket and ripped the battery from it.

"They're after Shauna Adair, specifically, Simon. But chuck your phone out as well. Just in case."

I nodded. "Right. Soon as I hang up."

"Which needs to be now, Simon. Good luck."

Before I could thank him Ashdown was off the line, and hints of red-and-blue lights entered the room through the open curtain.

I tore the battery off my BlackBerry and tossed both phones onto the bed.

Ostermann grinned. "You have no manner of luck, Simon, do you? No manner of luck at all."

"Help me with Hailey," I said.

Together we ran into the bedroom.

'm experiencing a bit of déjà vu," Ostermann said in the stairwell minutes later.

"That's been going around a lot these days."

Only this time Ostermann and I were heading downstairs rather than up as we had in Berlin two years earlier. And thankfully, we wouldn't be jumping off the roof onto another building this time.

Once we hit bottom, we bound through a red metal door into the parking garage.

"This way," Ostermann said. "The concierge hid your bike near the service entrance. So you may have caught a bit of luck after all."

A few seconds later a big blue tarp came into view.

We ran toward it and Ostermann pulled the cover free as I held on to Hailey.

I set her on the bike.

"You've only one helmet," Ostermann said.

"Put it on Hailey."

"I'd argue, but Magda always said you were pretty thick in the head, so you should be fine."

I peeled off my jacket and helped Hailey slip into it. Then I got onto the bike.

Ostermann stared at my black T-shirt, which had a tiny hole just over my heart from Duncan MacBride's bullet in Liverpool.

"It's fairly cold out there," he said.

"I'll think warm thoughts."

I lit the ignition.

"Speaking of warm thoughts," he said, "mind if I call your sister?"

The machine roared to life, all five hundred horsepower.

I turned and looked at Ostermann, expecting to find a smile. But he'd been dead serious.

"All right, then," I said.

I grinned and showed Ostermann my middle finger.

In my mirror I saw him smile as Hailey and I sped off.

Chapter 63

I've read about a man named Gustavo Zapata. He lives in Tampa and works out of his home. Some papers call him a vigilante. And at first glance, I suppose, that's what he is. He commits wrongs, in order to put things right.

This past week I resigned from the United States Marshals Service.

Sold the Georgetown home and returned most of the money to Tasha's parents. They fought me at first. But when I mentioned donating the money to the National Center for Missing and Exploited Children, they had a sudden change of heart. Somewhat surprisingly, they agreed that it was a brilliant idea. "Just let us do it," Tasha's father said to me. "You know, for tax purposes."

Of course.

I park my Ford Explorer and step into a motor vehicle dealership in Arlington, Virginia.

A salesman immediately approaches. "How can I help you today, sir?"

"I want to trade in my SUV. Get something smaller."

"What kind of vehicle are you looking for?" he asks.

My eye catches on a sexy black sportbike.

"Ah," the salesman says, "the Kawasaki Ninja 500R. Great middleweight bike. Perfect for starters. A regular thoroughbred when it comes to handling."

"I'll take it."

Yesterday I signed a lease on a studio apartment on Dumbarton Street in the District. It's a tight fit, even for one person. But the lease is only for six months. By then I'm sure I'll be more in the mood to find myself something else. Something a little bigger. A little nicer. Right now, though, I'm just too grief-stricken to do any serious looking.

The transaction for the motorcycle takes the better part of two hours.

When the deal's finally done, the salesman offers to have the bike washed and waxed.

"Not necessary," I tell him. "I'll drive it off the lot as is."

"Sure thing, Mr. Fisk. Will you at least let me fill her with gas?"

"Have at it."

Twenty minutes later I make a right turn out of the dealership.

The bike rides smoothly. It's nice and light, comfortable. Yet packed with plenty of power. It handles even better than I'd expected.

Only once I'm on the road do I realize why I decided on a bike. On a bike you have to concentrate on the road. *Really* concentrate, or else it's all over. End of story. Take your mind off the road for a second and you're done. A car, on the other hand, leaves you plenty of time to think.

Too much time, especially during a fourteen-hour ride from Arlington to Tampa.

After the summer I've had, I could use a little time off from thinking. Just now I'd prefer to concentrate on the endless stretch of blacktop in front of me.

According to the articles I've read, Gustavo Zapata is a former Army Ranger. His referrals usually come from government types. Overall, his business is very hush-hush. But I figure I can find him.

If I can find fugitives in every corner of the world, I'm pretty sure I can locate one good guy residing in the center of the Sunshine State. And if I can't, well, then I have no business considering doing what he does anyway.

Which is retrieve children who have been abducted by noncustodial parents and taken overseas to a country that doesn't recognize U.S. custody decisions.

Apparently, thousands of American parents are placed in this distressing situation every year.

As a formal U.S. Marshal, this is something I think I'd excel at. And more important, I'd be doing some good. I'm under no illusion; I won't be able to handle stranger abductions because they'd hit too close to home. But parental abductions are a different animal entirely. And if it's at all possible for me to save a few mothers and fathers from going through what Tasha and I went through this summer, I at least have to give it a try.

I know my way around foreign countries.

I know how to lie low.

I know how to fight and how to fire a gun.

And perhaps best of all, as I search the globe for other parents' missing children, perhaps one day I can find my own. Or at least locate the man who took her.

I want to know who he is.

I want to know why.

And I want to make him answer for what he's done.

But for the next fourteen hours I'll remove all this from my mind and concentrate on the highway.

After a couple of hours stopping and starting on several different roads, I finally reach exit 84A toward Rocky Mount, North Carolina.

With the Beltway and Virginia behind me and the Carolinas,

Georgia, and Florida in front of me, I check my mirrors and steer my bike toward the exit to the interstate.

When I reach the ramp, I take a deep breath.

Lean into the turn.

Hit I-95 and accelerate.

Epilogue

A couple of years ago, at the suggestion of a sex peddler in Odessa, I read a book that described Moldova as the unhappiest place on earth.

Yet it is in a small village in this impoverished, landlocked country, where for the first time in twelve years, I truly feel happiness.

The drive from London to Moldova was an exhausting 1,600 miles and took roughly thirty hours on A4. In Belgium, I ditched the Dodge Tomahawk in favor of a somewhat more modest bike—an Italian MV Agusta F4.

We've been here in the former Soviet Republic four months and the weather's finally begun to break. The villagers tell us to expect heavy showers and thunderstorms in the early summer but milder temperatures into July and August.

The best of it is that Hailey's finally coming around. The physical symptoms of her withdrawal peaked just before we arrived, complicating things at the border—heftily raising the price of our bribes—and causing us some added difficulty as I searched for our new living arrangements.

Those first few days after we arrived were downright frightening.

Despite the frigid temperatures, Hailey was constantly sweating. Her stomach cramped so badly she was sure she was dying. Severe muscle spasms in her back and neck consistently led to horrific migraines.

The migraines made Hailey sensitive to light, so we spent much of that first week in total darkness, with her writhing in pain on a worn mattress and me running outdoors to empty alternating buckets of vomit and diarrhea.

She couldn't (or wouldn't) eat, and I had to beg—and sometimes even force her—to drink enough water to keep her from getting dehydrated.

One evening she was in such obvious distress that I finally broke down and risked our delicate new freedom by phoning one of the few people on the globe whom authorities might actually expect me to call.

"I will come there," she said the moment I finished explaining the situation to her. "I will come to Moldova and help you."

"Don't be ridiculous, Ana," I told her. "You can't leave your home and career in Warsaw to help someone you barely know and haven't seen in nearly two years."

"Do not be an idiot, Simon. I *do* know you; it is you who obviously does not know me. Because if you knew me at all, you would know that I cannot *not* come to Moldova to help you now that you have called."

I knew her better than she thought. Though I could never tell her (and had trouble even admitting it to myself), it was precisely why I had called her. I needed Ana as much as anyone could need someone else. Truth is, I'd needed her ever since I last left Warsaw almost two years ago. I'd just been too goddamn stubborn—too much of a bloody *Fisk*—to concede the fact to myself. Because I hadn't wanted to pull her away from everything she knew to join me in my desperate and melancholy world.

But now things were different, weren't they? Hailey was once again in my arms. And my head, if not my life, was full of anticipation and promise. I finally felt as though I had something to offer the beautiful and brilliant Polish lawyer Anastazja Staszak—even as a fugitive living with a fugitive teenage daughter in a ramshackle cottage in one of the poorest countries in Eastern Europe.

Ana arrived in Moldova twenty-eight hours later.

Following a few days under Ana's care, Hailey's physical symptoms started to subside. But if I'd thought we were through the worst of the withdrawal, I was wrong.

Because even then Hailey could hardly sleep. And on the rare occasions she finally dozed off, she woke minutes later in fits and starts. Howling for more gear.

"Glass, flake, some *jellies*," she'd cry.

Something, anything to ease the anxiety and irritability and sleeplessness. A number of times, in hysterical rants, she offered sexual favors in return for a hit, and I'd have to step outside and have myself a cry. Only Ana could ever calm her and only at times when she was willing to be calmed.

But things are much better now.

In the meantime I've been studying Romanian, the primary language spoken in Moldova. Thus far, Ana's gotten us by with her Russian. But I suspect that at some point, we may have to move to another part of the country, likely on short notice. And we may well end up in a village with no Russian speakers.

With her flare for languages Ana's picking things up much more quickly than I am. And more and more frequently, she's insisting I speak to her exclusively in Romanian. Frustrating as hell at times, but I'm trying.

Meanwhile, Ana's English over the past couple of years has improved exponentially. Her command of the language is absolutely superb. Yet her Eastern European accent remains fully intact—and as sexy as ever.

"You may compliment my English all you want," she tells me as I sit down at our cottage's lone table, "but only if you do so in Romanian."

She clearly hasn't gotten any softer in the past two years either.

But it's one of the many things I love about her.

Hailey hasn't been very forthcoming about her experiences over the past twelve years. But I've read enough about the psychology of kidnap victims to know not to push her. As difficult as that may be at times.

Clearly she developed a strong emotional bond with Terry over the past decade. Whether it's Stockholm syndrome or something else entirely, I can't say. I *can* say that if it weren't for Ana, I'd be having a much tougher time dealing with all this.

Ana has also gotten far more information out of Hailey than I ever would have been able to.

"There was no sexual relationship between them," Ana has assured me. "Of that I am certain she is not lying. As awful as it may be to hear right now, she still thinks of him as her father. And it is going to take time for her to come to accept what truly happened to her."

"Has she been to school?" I asked.

"She claims to have been home-schooled. To what extent I am not sure, but she is a very smart girl so maybe she did not need such a rigorous program in order to reach the educational level she has reached."

"And what level is that, do you think?"

Ana shrugged but not diffidently; she was genuinely struggling with the answer.

"It is difficult to separate the emotional from the intellectual, Simon. Emotionally, she is still very much a child. Intellectually, I would say she is approaching adulthood. If she wants to go to university in a few years, she will eventually catch up, I am sure."

I sighed. "And here I had her matriculating at Edinburgh University in the fall."

Ana smiled warmly. "Her dreams—and yours for her—will not be out of reach for long, Simon. You just need to give her time. And space. And love. Love, most of all."

"What happened in Dublin?" I asked. "Did she tell you?"

"At the pub, you mean?" She looked away. "Hailey thought Elijah Welker was one of Jack Noonan's men. He had been following her since Glasgow. She thought he meant to take the money so that Noonan could kill her father. She thought that was what Noonan had wanted all along."

I nodded. "Has she mentioned Tasha at all?"

Ana shook her head.

"I don't know what I'll tell her about her mother," I said. "Over the past twelve years I'd convinced myself I was innocent in Tasha's death. But I wasn't. I didn't fully realize it—or maybe *admit it to myself* is a more accurate phrase—until I was in that warehouse with Terry."

She placed her hands on top of mine. "You cannot accept the blame, Simon. It will do no one any good. Not you and certainly not Hailey."

I lowered my eyes to the table. "She talks about him still. Doesn't she?"

"Terry? Yes. She talks about him more than anything else. For twelve years he lied to her, Simon. He manipulated her, kept her cut off from most of the world. In the beginning I believe he censored everything she read or watched on television. He brainwashed her. I do not think she spent most of the past twelve years in a basement. But in a way, it was like that for her. He kept her in a cage simply by keeping her in his heart, and making her believe that he was the only person alive who loved her."

"She asks to speak with him?"

"She often *demands* to speak with him. She has even threatened to kill herself if we do not allow her to contact him."

I buried my face in my hands.

"But we will watch her, Simon. We will keep her safe, not only from others but from herself."

I nodded sadly but said nothing.

After a minute, Ana asked, "What happened in that warehouse, Simon? You never told me."

"It's not important."

She leaned forward and placed her hand on the top of my head. "If I ask you something, it means it is *very* important."

I allowed a small smile and looked into her deep green eyes like I did the first time I saw her at her law firm in Warsaw. Like I did as we'd sat across from each other drinking coffee on the way to Krakow. Like I did as she'd persuaded me with physical force to eat pierogi for the first time in my life in Poland.

I thought back to that conversation.

"Well?" she said.

I step out of our cottage on a cold, drizzly morning to find a small crowd gathered in a circle nearby. Most of the crowd are women, many are crying, and one woman's sobs are louder and more desperate than all the others put together.

Behind me, Ana steps outside, sees the scene, and immediately starts toward the crowd. I follow her. Together we skirt a pair of wild hens then slip through to the center of the circle, where a middle-aged woman kneels, bawling, while a young girl—no more than sixteen or seventeen—tries futilely to comfort her.

In Romanian, Ana asks one of the women in the crowd to explain what's happening. Once she gets her answer, Ana turns to me and tells me the story, mercifully in English.

"The young girl," she says, "her name is Katya and she is from our village. She just returned from Ukraine. Months ago, she and her friend Svetlana—the older woman's daughter—were offered jobs as waitresses at a bar in Odessa."

I already know where this is going but I tell Ana to continue as I process the information.

"Once they arrived, the girls realized there was no bar, only a brothel. Before they could even think, their passports were taken and they were driven to a cramped and filthy apartment in the city. The man who had offered them the jobs showed up with his friends and they raped both girls and beat them when the girls tried to stop the men from raping them again."

I look at the older woman who is now clinging to Katya's knees.

"Within a week," Ana says, trying to keep the strength in her voice, "the girls were forced to service ten or fifteen men a day. Mostly businessmen and tourists, but locals too. Over those months one of these businessmen became Katya's regular client and he fell for her. He purchased her from the pimps and bought her a plane ticket back to Chisinau and she hitched a ride from the capital very early this morning."

"And Svetlana?" I ask.

"The man told Katya he did not have enough money to pay for both girls, only one. She did not want to leave Svetlana behind, but she had no choice. Svetlana's mother is so distraught because Katya said that Svetlana had once told her that if they were ever separated she would kill herself. She thinks Svetlana will do it first chance she gets, which will be in a few days when the girls are supposed to service wealthy American tourists on a boat in the Black Sea."

I take Ana's hand and guide her to the center of the circle and ask her to translate for me.

"Tell her I'm going to get her daughter back to her," I say.

Ana stares at me for a moment. A wall of water builds in front of her green eyes. But then she nods and turns to the woman and as she speaks, the large crowd finally quiets some.

When Ana's finished, the mother looks up at me and rattles off a number of hysterical questions in Romanian.

Ana says, "She asks, How is this possible? When are you going to do this? She is poor; how much money will you need?"

"Tell her I'll leave in an hour and I'll be in Odessa by nightfall."

"And the money?"

"I'll make sure I'm well compensated by the men who took her daughter."

Ana translates and the desperate expression on the woman's face slowly morphs into one of hope. She tries to get to her feet but stumbles and slips in the mud.

Finally, Ana helps her up and the woman brushes herself off as best she can and stands before me, her mud-caked hands clamped together in front of her chest.

Only now do I realize just how small and frail the woman is.

After a moment, she removes from around her neck a stainless-steel chain with a charm the size of an American silver dollar. She opens the charm and hands it to me.

Inside is a picture of her sixteen-year-old daughter, Svetlana.

As I look at the girl in the photo, a lump forms in my throat. A slow burn begins at the base of my neck and quickly travels upward until I am almost overwhelmed by a familiar roaring in my ears.

Ana says, "She needs you to know that Katya told her there are lots of men guarding the girls. Lots of men with lots of guns."

"Tell her it's all right," I say calmly. "Tell her I'm going to get her daughter home to her, whatever it takes."

Ana translates then turns back to me. "Why, she wants to know."

"Tell her this is what I do. What I *have* to do. Tell her I'm a professional."

Acknowledgments

To Kelley Ragland, Elizabeth Lacks, Andy Martin, Hector DeJean, Paul Hochman, and everyone else at St. Martin's Press and Minotaur Books, thank you for joining me in bringing Simon Fisk to life.

Thanks, too, to Robin Rue and Beth Miller and the entire team at Writers House for going above and beyond the call of duty.

Thanks also to Adrienne Sparks for assisting me with all things marketing.

To Joel Price, Dotty Morefield, Vincent Antoniello, Jason Quintero, Stuart Goldstein, and David Rosenfelt, thank you for your continued friendship and guidance.

And to my lovely wife, Jill, to whom this book is dedicated, my son, Jack Douglas, and my daughters Maya Kailani and Kyra Skye, thank you for your patience, understanding, and encouragement. As always, I couldn't have written this work without your cooperation.

Finally, to my readers—old and new—I am so grateful for your support. To those who post comments on my Facebook page, follow me on Twitter, or contact me through my Web site, thank you for keeping me company these past twelve months. I look forward to chatting with you again soon.